Small town Swoon

Small town Swoon

USA TODAY BESTSELLING AUTHOR

Melanie Harlow

Entangled Publishing, LLC
644 Shrewsbury Commons Ave., STE 181
Shrewsbury, PA 17361
rights@entangledpublishing.com

Amara is an imprint of Entangled Publishing, LLC.

Visit our website at www.entangledpublishing.com.

Edited by Nancy Smay, Julia Griffis
Cover illustration and design by Hang Le
Stock art by Anastasia Pechnikova/iStock and Marina Danchenko/iStock
Edge design by Bree Archer
Map illustration by Francesca Weber
Interior design by Britt Marczak

ISBN 978-1-64937-898-9

Manufactured in the China

First Edition May 2025

10 9 8 7 6 5 4 3 2 1

ALSO BY MELANIE HARLOW

1. Cherry Blossom Inn
2. Harbor Lights Salon & Spa
3. Bayview Service Station
4. The Pier Inn
5. Lush Wine Bar
6. Main Street Coffee
7. Larry's Barber Shop
8. George Buckley's House
9. Ari DeLuca's House
10. Moe's Diner
11. The Sweet Shoppe
12. Waterfront Park
13. The Lighthouse
14. Farmer's Market
15. Chapel by the Sea
16. Buckley's Pub
17. Austin Buckley's House

*For my first little firefly as she leaves home
to light up the world.*

A dream needs believing
To taste like the real thing...

When your breaking point's all that you have
A dream is a soft place to land

May we all be so lucky

SARA BAREILLES

Chapter 1

DASH

"I'm sorry, Dash," my agent said over the Bluetooth speaker in my car. "You didn't get the part."

"They said no?" I asked in disbelief as my SUV inched forward in L.A. traffic. I'd been so sure last week's audition would finally be a yes. "But it went so well. I thought they really liked me."

"They did, darling." Izzie's tone was soothing. "But they ended up going with a name."

"I have a name," I argued.

"Of course you do," Izzie assured me, because it was her job. "But so far, the only thing your name is associated with is playing Bulge on *Malibu Splash*. We need to change that."

I slumped in the driver's seat as traffic came to a stop again. My agent was right. For the last five years, I'd played the hot but one-dimensional lifeguard on a beach show mostly popular with teenagers. Now that the final season was over, I was eager to move on to meatier, more mature roles. But despite the fact that I was twenty-seven, I couldn't get a single casting director to see me as a leading man in a big-budget film.

Out the driver's side window, I saw a billboard for an upcoming spy thriller, the kind of movie I'd give my right arm to be in. "I told you my friend Mike got seen for the next Katherine Carroll project, didn't I? The wartime drama called *All We've Lost*?"

"Yes, Dashiel. You told me." Judging by my agent's tone, I might have mentioned it multiple times.

But I couldn't help it. Carroll was one of the top directors in the industry, famous for her breathtaking visuals and heart-stopping action sequences. And she often cast lesser-known actors in major roles because she felt the audience's lack of familiarity with them contributed to an overall sense of unpredictability and tension.

At the moment, I was feeling pretty lesser known.

"I saw the script. The role of Johnny is perfect for me," I told Izzie as traffic began moving again. "A small-town guy who goes off to fight the war, gets shot and captured, and falls in love with a nurse behind enemy lines. She risks her life to help him escape, and then he risks his to go back for her."

"Sounds romantic."

"I can *do* that kind of part, Izzie." I easily imagined myself huddled in a trench, nothing to my name but a rifle, a tattered love letter, and the will to survive. "Can you get me an audition?"

Izzie sighed. "You always get the same feedback after reading for those kinds of roles, Dash. They like you, but your work lacks emotional depth."

The familiar words stung. "I'm working on it, okay? I'm going to sign up for some coaching with that method acting guy."

"But method acting is about mining *your life experiences* for strong emotions. You need to connect more to your *own feelings.*"

"My own feelings are irrelevant," I insisted. "It's about the *character.*"

"You can't convey the full range of a character's emotional pain when you refuse to explore your own."

"I'm not refusing to explore it. I just don't have any," I lied. "I'm remarkably well-adjusted." My emotional pain was nobody's business. Not my agent's, not any casting director's, and certainly not the moviegoing public's.

"Everyone has emotional pain, Dash. It's just that some people keep it all buried, and good actors know how to mine it for gold." Another big sigh. "You know what? I'm not booking any more auditions for you until you agree to a psychic healing with Delphine."

I suppressed a groan. My agent was always threatening to drag me to her woo-woo friend who cleansed auras or something. She was convinced I had some sort of spiritual black cloud hanging over me. "I don't need a psychic healing, Izzie. I just need a lucky break."

"You want to play the sexy, romantic lead in a gritty wartime drama?" my agent pushed. "You want to make people believe you'd risk it all for love? You have to get out there and do it for real, Dash. Right now, you don't have a place to go to dig into those emotions. You don't let yourself *feel.*"

"I *feel*," I protested in defense. "I choke up every time I watch *Toy Story 3.*"

"That is not the same! Have you ever even been in love? Do

you know what it's like to fall for someone so hard you'd put everything on the line to be with her, like that character does?"

"It's called *acting*. I want to *play* the guy who falls in love, not *be* him."

"What do you have against love?"

"Nothing! It's just not for me." I turned into the gym parking lot. "Love is for older people, Izzie. Like wrinkles. Or gray hair."

"Are you listening to yourself? No wonder you can't go deeper with your characters. Your focus is entirely on the surface level."

I pulled into a parking spot and glanced in the rearview mirror. Ran a hand over my scruffy jaw. "Yeah, but my surface level is really nice. I'm growing a beard now that *Malibu Splash* is done. It looks good."

She laughed before scolding me again. "Stop it. You can't charm your way into an Oscar, Dash. It's not enough to be ridiculously handsome—in fact, that's often a detriment."

Tired of arguing, I opened the car door and stepped into the late spring California sunshine. "Fine. I'll talk to the spirit lady. It's not like I have anything to lose."

"I agree," Izzie said. "Let's not waste any time. I'll pick you up at ten tomorrow morning, and we'll go to her shop."

We hung up, and I headed into the gym.

It was usually a place nobody bothered me, probably because it was full of guys like me—cocky, good-looking dudes with athletic bodies who'd left their hometowns full of confidence, ambition, and maybe even some talent. Everyone was ripped, everyone was driven, and everyone was hoping for the *one big break* that would land them on the A list.

But I hadn't come out to Hollywood just hoping to get by on my face or my biceps. I worked hard. Ever since I was a kid, I've loved the idea that you could forget about yourself and just get lost inside someone else. Live in *their* minds, speak *their* words, experience *their* feelings instead of your own.

It wasn't like I didn't take it seriously. I'd enrolled in classes. I'd gone to every open audition I could and did commercials for everything from toothpaste to taco sauce. I'd spent plenty of nights parking cars, waiting tables, and bartending, and I knew what it was like to crash on friends' couches because you couldn't afford rent.

When I'd gotten the role on *Malibu Splash*, I'd fallen to my knees with gratitude, certain it would serve as a stepping stone to where I really wanted to be.

Now I was hoping it wasn't the best I'd ever get.

• • •

"This is it?" From the passenger seat of Izzie's car, I scanned the storefronts of a typical L.A. strip mall, a dubious expression on my face. Dollar store, wig boutique, nail salon, crystal shop, bubble tea parlor. In front of the crystal shop was a sandwich board with a metaphysical menu on it.

Tarot Cards $60

Aura Cleanse $75

Chakra Analysis & Alignment $85

Full Psychic Healing (includes Relief from Energy Blocks and Spiritual Attachment Removal) $220

"This is it." Izzie pulled into a spot in front of the bubble tea parlor.

"Spiritual attachment removal?" Skeptical, I folded my arms over my chest. "I don't need an exorcism, Izzie. I just want better acting jobs."

"That's why we're here." She put her car in park and pointed a red-tipped finger at me. "Now don't go in there with a bad attitude. You have to have an open mind."

Grumbling under my breath, I got out of the car and followed Izzie into the shop. As my eyes adjusted to the dim light, I saw crystals, books, and decks of cards displayed on tables of varying heights. In the air hung the scent of patchouli, and New Age music played softly. A barefoot young woman wearing jeans, a gauzy white blouse, and armfuls of bracelets greeted Izzie with a hug, and then turned to me. "Hello," she said, offering a hand. "I'm Delphine."

"Hey. I'm Dash." As I shook her hand, it struck me how much she looked like someone I knew from back home—my sister Mabel's best friend, Ari DeLuca. The resemblance was almost uncanny. She had the same shade of brown hair that fell in corkscrew curls over her shoulders, the same heart-shaped face, the same wide-set dark eyes. Ari had practically grown up at our house and had been like another little sister to me.

Until one day she wasn't.

"Oh." Delphine's eyebrows furrowed as she continued to clasp my hand. "Wow. You've got some dark, cloudy energy in your aura."

"Can you clear it?" Izzie asked nervously.

"I can try." Delphine squared her shoulders like she was preparing for battle and motioned for me to follow her. "Come on back."

"I'll wait out here," called Izzie. "Good luck."

Walking behind Delphine through a curtain of beads into a

small, dark room, I noticed she was built sort of like Ari too—medium height and curvy.

Ari's curves had seemed to come out of nowhere. One day, she was a skinny middle school kid whose baggy clothes hung on her gangly frame like sheets on old furniture. Then suddenly I turned around and she was a smoking hot bombshell showing off an hourglass figure in low-cut jeans and crop tops, not to mention that cute little uniform she wore when she worked at her parents' diner. I remembered sitting at the counter as she poured me a cup of coffee, some seriously unbrotherly thoughts in my head.

But I'd kept my hands to myself. Even that night when she'd snuck into my bedroom. Slipped into my bed. Offered me her V card.

Talk about a stellar performance—I had to pretend I didn't want her that way, hide my erection beneath a pillow, and feed her a bunch of lines about being older and wiser than she was and wanting to protect her from making a big mistake. After all, she was only sixteen, still a junior in high school. I was nineteen and about to leave for L.A. And as much as I wanted to take her up on that offer, I did the right thing and turned her down.

Needless to say, she did not appreciate my chivalry.

"Take a seat," Delphine said, gesturing to one of two folding chairs on either side of a rectangular table.

I sat down and looked around. The walls in the room were painted black, and the only source of light came from a stained-glass table lamp, its amber shade hanging with beaded fringe. Also on the table was a deck of cards, a collection of rocks, and a Purell hand sanitizer.

Delphine gave it a couple pumps and rubbed her hands together as she took the seat across from me. "So. What can I do for you?"

I shrugged. "Tell me the future?"

She smiled with Ari's plush lips. "I'm afraid I can't do that, Dash. I'm clairsentient, not clairvoyant."

"What's the difference?"

"People who are clairvoyant have the ability to perceive events in the future. People who are clairsentient have the ability to perceive emotional or psychic energy that is imperceptible to the five standard senses."

"So you can't tell me if something is going to happen for me or not?"

She shook her head. "The future is all in your control."

"If that were true, I'd be on the set of an action thriller right now."

"Why do you think you're not?"

"I was hoping *you'd* have that answer."

"I don't. Not yet, anyway."

"Okay, fine. I'm not on the set of a blockbuster movie because the universe won't give me a break. So I'd like it if you could put in a good word for me using whatever direct channels you have to…" I waved a hand in the air, imagining nebulous matter above our heads. "Higher powers."

"If you want the universe to give you the opportunity, Dash, you have to give the opportunity to the universe."

Was she saying I hadn't tried? Hadn't worked for it? Hadn't put myself out there, risking rejection over and over again? Irritated, I stood up. "Look, this is a waste of time. I should just go."

"Wait a minute," she said, scooting to the edge of her chair and laying her hands on the table, palms up. "Just wait a minute. Sit down. Let's try something."

I glanced at the beaded curtain, my rational brain telling me to leave the room, because this was complete bullshit. But then I looked back at her, and in the golden glow of the lamp, her familiar eyes beckoned me to stay. She tilted her head toward the empty chair, and I felt compelled to sit down again.

"Now," she said. "Give me your hands and close your eyes."

A little reluctantly, I placed my palms on top of hers and lowered my eyelids. She was silent for so long that I opened my eyes to peek at her. "Aren't you supposed to say something?"

"Shh," she scolded. "I was creating a psychic space for our energies to meet. But I can see you now."

"And?"

"Your energy is...heavy. Dense. Dark."

"You mentioned that," I said tersely.

"There's a lot of doubt here. Fear of failure." She paused. "You've experienced setbacks recently."

I thought of all the auditions that had led nowhere. The roles I couldn't even get seen for. The parts that went to bigger names. "Yes."

"You've given them too much energetic power. Your ego is taking up too much space."

I frowned. My ego probably was a little outsized, but so far, I wasn't terribly impressed with her psychic abilities. This was Hollywood—it wasn't that big a stretch for her to surmise that I was an actor. Izzie might have even told her. And all actors had big egos and experienced setbacks.

"You've been told you don't feel things deeply enough," she went on.

Okay, that was a little more personal, and definitely on the nose, but Izzie still could have mentioned that to her. "Maybe."

Delphine gripped my hands tighter. "But it's not true. You *can* feel things deeply—and from the heart—but you don't want to. You avoid intense emotions because you're scared of being vulnerable."

"I'm not scared of anything," I said quickly.

"You've been this way for a long time." Delphine was silent for a moment. "You experienced a loss early in your life that has stayed with you."

I neither confirmed nor denied her statement. That loss wasn't something I ever discussed, and no matter what Izzie said, I wasn't going to mine it for emotional gold.

"Yes," she said, as if it was obvious. "The blockage was started a long time ago and has only grown since then. You definitely need some clearing. I'm going to try." Her expression was one of utter concentration, her mouth tight, her brow pinched. "Shoot. I can't budge it. There are too many layers across too much time."

"Is this where you try to upsell me on the energy-clearing machine?"

She shook her head slightly. "You'll have to do it yourself. It will take a lot of introspection and hard work."

Impatient, I bounced my leg beneath the table. "Look, just tell me what to do and I'll do it."

"You must stop hiding your deepest emotions." Delphine spoke with increasing intensity. "You must shed the layers of protection you've put into place. You must eliminate the blockage in order to access the deepest reaches of your heart's reservoir."

"Could you be a little more specific, please?"

"You must strip down to your purest self."

I stopped bouncing my leg. "Strip down? Like…get naked?"

"If that helps you to get comfortable with vulnerability, then yes." She lifted her shoulders. "Sometimes our clothing is just a metaphor."

"A metaphor for what?"

"The protective walls we put around our hearts. They keep us safe, yes, but they also keep us hidden. You must stop hiding."

I thought for a moment. I *did* like being naked. Even if it wasn't *exactly* what she meant, it sounded a lot easier and way more enjoyable than going at my childhood trauma with a pickaxe. "And this will help me get better acting jobs?"

"I believe it will help you show the universe you are ready to receive what awaits you. That you are open to accepting its gifts." She leaned forward in her chair and pinned me with her dark brown eyes. "Tear them down, Dashiel Buckley. Let in the light. What you seek is within."

. . .

"Well? What did she say?" Izzie demanded as we got on the road back to my house in Los Feliz.

I stared out the passenger window, rubbing my index finger beneath my lower lip. "A lot of weird stuff."

"Did she clear up your dark, cloudy energy?"

"No. She said I have to do it."

"Did she say how?"

"She said I need to strip down to my purest self. Get more comfortable with being vulnerable." I shrugged. "Apparently, clothes are contributing to the walls around my heart, and I need to get rid of them."

"*Clothes* are your problem?" Izzie asked incredulously.

"That's what she said," I insisted, even though it wasn't *quite* what she'd said. "My homework is to get naked more often."

Izzie shook her head. "Far be it for me to doubt Delphine's wisdom, but I feel like there has to be more to it."

"Well, I don't know what."

"I do. You need to get out of Hollywood for a while."

"You think I should leave town?"

"Yes! You need to get away from the scene, Dash. Nothing is real here. It's all artifice—costumes and sets and props. You need to go someplace genuine and authentic, someplace where you feel safe. Like your hometown in Minnesota."

"Michigan."

"Wherever." She flipped a hand in the air, as if every town that wasn't L.A. was all the same to her. "What's it called again?"

"Cherry Tree Harbor." I thought about the small town on the coast of Lake Michigan where I'd grown up. "I'm headed there in a couple weeks for my brother's wedding. I guess I could go a little sooner."

"That's right! Which brother is getting married again? The single dad with the twins who fell in love with the nanny?"

I laughed. I had four siblings—three older brothers and one younger sister—and Izzie was forever trying to keep them straight. "No, that's Austin."

"The former Navy SEAL who opened the bar?" she guessed hopefully. "The one dating the country music star?"

"Nope, that's Xander," I told her. "*Devlin* is the brother getting married. He's the middle sibling, the one who lived in Boston who swore he would never tie the knot and then eloped out of the blue last fall."

"Oh, right!" Izzie thumped a hand on the steering wheel. "With the girl whose family owns the ski resort."

"Yes. They renovated the place over the winter and decided to renew their vows there, so the families could attend."

"And your younger sister is..."

"Mabel," I said. "She's in graduate school."

"Virginia, right?"

"Right." I glanced at her. "I'm impressed with your recall."

"You talk about your family a lot. You must miss them."

"I do," I admitted.

"So go *home*, Dash," she said. "Take a month off from this grind. Reconnect to your childhood self. Take long walks in the woods. Meditate. Strip away all the protective layers—and I don't mean just your clothes. Open up your heart, look to see what's buried there, and let yourself *feel* it. Better yet, let yourself *show* it."

That last part didn't sound like a ton of fun, but I hadn't been home in over a year, and I did miss my family. We'd always been close. My mom had died when I was only six, and my dad raised all five of us on his own. He'd never remarried, and he'd recently sold Two Buckleys Home Improvement, the business he inherited from his father and had run for decades, first with his brother and then with my brother Austin. Without work to distract him, I worried about him being lonely now that all his kids were grown and gone. Maybe I'd show up at the house and surprise him. He'd like that.

"Okay," I said, pulling out my phone to change my plane ticket. "But can you please see about getting me an audition for the Katherine Carroll film? I'll fly back if I have to. Or I can send a video. Whatever they want."

"I might have to call in a favor, but yes. I think I can do it."

"Thank you." I opened up the airline app and switched my flight so that I was leaving this Saturday morning—in two days— and flying home a month later. I figured that was long enough to walk around naked and get reacquainted with my childhood self or whatever. I wasn't convinced it would help, but on the off chance Delphine wasn't totally batty, I'd make the effort.

Sometimes those woo-woo people were right about stuff.

Funny how she resembled Ari DeLuca so closely.

I wondered what Ari was up to these days. I knew she'd gone to the Culinary Institute after high school and then moved to New York City, but recently Mabel had mentioned she was back in Cherry Tree Harbor working at her parents' diner. Maybe I'd go see her.

Surely enough time had gone by that she'd gotten over the rejection. After all, it had been eight years.

She couldn't still hold a grudge, could she?

Chapter 2

ARI

> *Moe's Morning Skillet*
> *Fried Chicken and Waffles*
> *Lemon Blueberry Buttermilk Pancakes*
> *Baked French Toast w/ Maple Coffee Syrup*

I yawned as I wrote the Saturday morning breakfast specials on the chalkboard behind the counter at Moe's Diner—two old favorites and two creations of mine, which was the deal I'd struck with my parents.

"Tired?" my mother asked as she began brewing the coffee.

"A little."

"What time did you get home last night?"

"Late," I said, frowning at the way my printing sloped downward. I erased everything and started again. "Xander was short-handed at the pub, so I offered to stay longer. Then I came in early this morning to bake."

"You're working too much and not getting enough rest," my mother admonished. "I'm worried about you."

"I'm fine." I yawned again.

"Why do you need a second job?"

"I just bought a house, remember? And I make good tips at the bar."

"But you don't have any time for your *personal* life."

I snorted. "What personal life?"

"That's my point! You're young and beautiful, you should be out dating and having fun. If you need help finding someone, I can—"

"*No*," I said, glaring at her over my shoulder. "No more fixing me up with anyone. I've either known them since kindergarten and watched them eat too many boogers or they live in their mom's basement and just want to talk about gaming. I'd rather be single."

Her heavy sigh told me how she felt about that.

"Hey, listen," I said, switching tracks before she started naming all my cousins who'd gotten married already. "I'd like to add some new things to the summer menu using in-season fruit. I've been testing out this galette that would be fantastic with Michigan strawberries and rhubarb. And I've got this idea for smashed cherry, basil, and goat cheese sliders on—"

"That sounds too fancy for Moe's," my mother interrupted. "People come here because it's familiar. They know what to expect."

"But it's boring."

"It's comforting," she countered.

"You let me add a few dishes last summer, remember? A

couple of them were really popular." I put the chalk away and hopped off the counter.

"And expensive," she reminded me. "You insisted on those pricey ingredients, and we had to charge more. Dad didn't like that."

"He never said that to me."

"He wouldn't—he adores you too much. But Moe's Diner has been in the DeLuca family for three-quarters of a century! He doesn't want to be the DeLuca to run it into the ground."

"I'm not going to run Moe's into the ground, Mom. I'm just trying to *elevate* it a little." I made a lifting gesture with my hands.

"But Moe's is down to earth, Ari. That's the appeal. It's not that Dad and I don't appreciate your skills, because we do," she said earnestly. "Nothing made us happier than when you came back home and said you wanted to work here." She turned and cradled my face in her hands. "After all, you're the only child we've got—our little miracle baby."

I rolled my eyes but tolerated the brush of her thumb across my cheek. My parents hadn't thought they could have children, and I'd been a late-in-life surprise gift. I appreciated being loved and wanted, I really did, but the whole *miracle baby* thing was getting old. "Can you please stop calling me that now? I'm twenty-four."

"I know, darling. We're getting older too. And there's no one we trust but you to take the reins, to keep Moe's alive for the next generation."

"I get it, Mom."

"We haven't wanted to burden you," she went on, "but the truth is, Ari, the last few years haven't been the greatest. Tourism is down, there's that new breakfast place up the street, we replaced all the kitchen equipment last year and we're still paying off the loan…" Her voice trailed off, and the lines in her forehead grew deeper. "It's not as easy as it looks to keep this place in the black."

Guilt slammed into me when I thought about the fact that they'd also paid for me to go to culinary school in the last few years *and* given me a big down payment for a house. "I understand," I said gently, taking my mother's wrists and pushing her hands down. "And I want to help. I just think taking a risk on a few new ideas here and there might be a good way to infuse new energy into the place."

"What energy?" Now she was studying my face with that critical look a mother somehow perfects during the teenage years. "You look exhausted. Can you get a nap in before your shift at the pub tonight?"

"Maybe. But I'm dog-sitting for Mr. Buckley this weekend, so I have to go feed Fritz and let him out at some point."

"But you've got bags under your eyes."

"I'll put some tea bags on them later."

"It's already six-thirty. We open in half an hour. Maybe you should go put the tea bags on now." My mother was always hopeful I'd meet the love of my life one Saturday morning at the breakfast counter. "You never know who might walk in."

"Yes, I do. First Gus, then grumpy old Larry, and maybe Fergus McGee. They're all seventy years old, and they don't give a shit about the bags under my eyes. They just care that the coffee's hot."

My mother pursed her lips and folded her arms.

"I promise to get a nap in later," I lied. "Now drag Dad out of the office, go home, and finish packing for your trip. I've got this."

She sighed, her arms falling to her sides. "I suppose I could use a little extra time to help your father. He's moving slower than ever these days."

Worry needled its way under my skin. As much as they drove me nuts, I loved my parents fiercely—they were kind and generous and beloved in the community for good reason. My mom had the biggest heart of anyone I knew, and the best memory. She never forgot anyone's name or what their favorite dish was, and she always remembered to ask about the elderly grandmother they'd mentioned or the pet who needed surgery or the sick friend who needed prayers. She was the reason everyone always felt so welcome at Moe's—she made everyone feel like family. She worked tirelessly to keep this place alive.

And my dad and I had a special bond. He taught me to cook my first dish—spaghetti and meatballs with the DeLuca family sauce—and shared with me his philosophy about why cooking mattered so much. *Food is love*, he always said. *Food is family and friends, tradition and celebration. Food puts the flavor in life!* When I'd decided to follow in his footsteps and become a chef, he'd cried tears of joy. I knew he saw me carrying on the DeLuca legacy, and I was proud to do it. I just wished I had a little more freedom to interpret the legacy for myself. Put my own spin on it.

But tradition was everything to my family. And my family was everything to me.

"He works too much," I said, glancing toward the office where my father sat at the desk in a chair that was now perfectly shaped to his backside. He'd retired from the kitchen five years ago because he couldn't be on his feet so much anymore. Lately, his back had been bothering him. Heart problems ran in his family, but the DeLuca men were notoriously terrible about seeing doctors.

My mother laughed. "If that isn't the pot with two jobs calling the kettle black."

"Dad is going on seventy, Mom. It's not the same. He should think about retiring completely."

"He will when he's confident you're ready to take over," my mother said. "But he doesn't want to overwhelm you. I barely got him to agree to this vacation."

"I'm going to kick him out of here right now," I said, heading into the kitchen. When I reached the office, I knocked on the open door. "Hey, Dad."

He turned in his swivel chair, a grin overtaking his face. "Hi, angel. I was just thinking about you."

"You were?" I leaned against the doorframe, noting the bags under his soft brown eyes and the salt-and-pepper combover he wore to hide his receding hairline.

"I was remembering when you'd come into the diner early with me—before dawn sometimes—and bake biscuits," he said. "You'd stand at my side on your little stool and fold the dough just so with your little hands."

I smiled at the memory. "But not too much, because you didn't want me to melt the chilled butter. I remember we'd put the butter in the freezer before we made the dough."

"That's the secret," he said, winking at me. "What can I do for you?"

"You can get out of here and take a vacation."

He chuckled. "Just like your mother, telling me what to do."

"Because we know what's good for you," I said, taking him by the arm and helping him to his feet. I didn't miss the way he winced as his back straightened up. Or the fact that he looked a little pale beneath his olive complexion. "Now go. Sun and fun await."

But instead of heading for the door, he caught me in his arms and began to slow dance, crooning "It Had To Be You" in my ear.

"Dad," I said, laughing, "what are you doing?"

"I'm dancing with my favorite girl."

Smiling, I eased him toward the door. "It's time to go. Exit stage left, please."

"Okay, okay." He released me from his arms. "You're sure you can handle things here?"

"Yes, Dad. Moe's Diner can survive ten days without Moe." I took him by the shoulders, turned him around and steered him out of the office. "Now get lost."

When my folks were gone, I went into the bathroom to wash the chalk off my hands. In the mirror, I studied the woman wearing the pink diner uniform and remembered when she'd worn a white chef's coat. How she'd bleached it relentlessly to keep it pristine. How she'd eventually shoved it in a dumpster the day she left New York, along with her crushed spirit, broken heart, and failed dreams.

After drying my hands, I checked to make sure that the ladies' room was stocked with toilet paper, soap, and paper towels. Then I knocked on the men's room door and checked that restroom as well. On my way back toward the counter, I made sure each table and booth had syrup, ketchup, mustard, relish, salt, pepper, and napkins in the dispenser. When I was finished, I glanced up at the framed photos on the wall—they were a mix of vintage black-and-white snapshots of famous people standing next to my grinning grandparents, who'd opened Moe's Diner back in the fifties, and autographed headshots of celebrities who'd eaten here in the following decades.

One headshot in particular caught my eye. It always did.

Dashiel Buckley, star of *Malibu Splash*.

Despite my melancholy mood just moments ago, I chuckled with satisfaction at the mustache, horns, and pointy little beard I'd drawn with a Sharpie on the glass over his handsome mug.

Served him right—*no one* should be that good-looking.

The photo was black and white, so you couldn't even appreciate the indigo blue of his eyes or the golden hue of his skin. Plus, it was just a headshot, so there was no way to admire his broad shoulders, his bronzed chest, his rippling abs. It was all on full display in every episode of *Malibu Splash*—and I'd secretly watched every season multiple times.

But I'd never admit to that. I was still mad at him for rejecting me the night I finally decided I'd crushed on him long enough, and *tonight was the night*.

The night I'd get him alone. The night I'd offer him my virginity and insist that he take it. The night he'd finally realize he was crazy about me too, and it didn't matter that he was moving to L.A. to be an actor and I was just a teenage diner waitress… what mattered was *our everlasting love*.

Of course, that's not how it went down.

I mean, parts one and two happened almost exactly as I imagined them. It was a Saturday night. I was sleeping over at the Buckleys' house, which I did all the time. I waited until the house was dark and silent. Until Mabel was asleep. Until I heard Dash come in from his job as a barback at the Pier Inn. Until the time on my phone screen said 2:22 a.m., which I thought would be lucky.

With a pounding heart, I carefully slipped out of Mabel's bedroom and tiptoed down the hall. Opened Dash's bedroom door—it didn't even creak—closed it behind me, and timidly approached his sleeping form on the bottom bunk. (The top one, which had been Devlin's growing up, was empty.)

"Dash," I whispered.

He didn't wake up right away. As my eyes adjusted to the dark, I saw that he was sleeping shirtless, and the covers were only at his waist. The sight of his bare chest thrilled me—in a few moments, I would feel it pressed against mine.

"Dash." I sat on the edge of his bed and placed a tentative hand on his bicep. His skin was smooth and warm.

"Huh?" His eyes opened, and he blinked a couple times. "Ari?"

"Yes." Summoning every ounce of courage I had, I leaned over and pressed my mouth to his.

At first, he kissed me back—I would swear on my life he did. Fueled by his open lips and the yearning of my lovesick heart, I pulled back the covers and slipped in beside him. Gingerly, I placed my hand on his hot, hard stomach and slid it down inside the elastic band of his—

"Jesus!" He scrambled backward, but since it was a twin bed, he didn't get very far before he tumbled off the other side. Popping to his feet, he grabbed a pillow and held it in front of his crotch. He spoke in a furious whisper. "What the hell are you doing?"

"I wanted to be alone with you."

"Why?"

I took a deep breath. This was my big line. "I want to give you something."

He paused. "What?"

"Me." Getting to my knees, I lifted the T-shirt I'd worn to bed over my head. My heart knocked crazily against my ribs—I'd never taken my shirt off in front of any boy. "I want you to be my first."

"Oh my God. This is not happening." Without looking at me, he reached for my shirt and tossed it onto the bed. "You need to put this back on and get out of here."

"But don't you want to—"

"No! Ari, listen to me." He turned away from me and spoke to the opposite wall, like he didn't want to see my breasts. Like I was a hideous monster he couldn't bear to look at. "I don't—want you that way."

"But you kissed me back."

"That was a mistake. I was…confused," he finished. "You're like a little sister to me."

Mortified, I tugged the shirt over my head.

"You don't really want this either. Trust me," he went on, his tone becoming a little cocky and condescending. "I'm older and wiser and I know you'd regret it."

"You don't know anything about me," I said as hot tears of humiliation splashed down my cheeks. There was no way he could know how many years I'd spent pining for him. Attending every one of his football games. Sitting rapt in the audience at every school play. Pouring coffee for him when he'd come into the diner and sit at the counter, my heart pounding with glorious agony every time he smiled at me and asked for a refill. I'd dreamed about this night forever—and he'd just ruined it by rejecting me.

I would *never* get over this.

"I hate you," I said impulsively, because I loved him so much I couldn't breathe.

Finally turning around, he watched me scoot off the bed. "Look, let's just forget this happened, okay? No one ever has to know. Can't we be friends?"

But I was already hurrying out of his bedroom and back

down the hall toward Mabel's, where I crawled back into the second twin bed in her room and sobbed silently into the pillow.

He didn't love me. He didn't want me. I wasn't pretty enough or old enough or sexy enough. He thought of me like a little sister and always would. Why had I ever thought it could be different? Why did my heart have to want *him*, of all people, so badly? Why did this have to hurt so much?

I hated him for real, I decided. And I'd hate him forever.

Okay, fine—the hate was a shield for my annihilated pride, but cut me some slack, okay? I was sixteen, I was highly emotional, and I'd been in love with Dashiel Buckley since I was twelve years old. I needed to hate him to get over him.

So I perfected the art of the eye roll when his name was mentioned, the dirty look if we were in the same room, and the dismissive sniff when he tried talking to me like nothing had happened. But when he left for California a couple months later, I cried myself to sleep.

Of course, eight years had gone by, and by now I realized that Dash had done the right thing. Didn't take the sting out of the rejection or make it any less awkward when he came home for a visit, but over time, I was able to see things from his point of view.

Not that I'd admit that to him.

After all, he'd gotten his big Hollywood break. He had tons of adoring fans. His picture splashed all over the internet. His name linked with gorgeous *it* girls. He didn't need *me* to like him.

So I didn't.

Much.

I glanced up at his perfect smile again, dismayed when my heart fluttered the way it always did. No other guy had ever compared, and I'd never had those feelings for anyone else.

Maybe I'd find that Sharpie and black out a few of his teeth.

· · ·

Around four-thirty that afternoon, I let myself into the Buckleys' house without knocking, same as I'd been doing for twenty years—as soon as my parents had let me walk around the block by myself.

I'd always loved being at their house, which seemed like so much more fun than mine, since I was an only child and Mabel had four rambunctious older brothers. Mrs. Buckley had died when Mabel and I were only three, so my mom had been like a second mother to Mabel, and Mr. Buckley had always been wonderful to me. He was even helping me with some of the painting and carpentry in my new house. So when he asked me to look after Fritz, his German Australian Shepherd mix, while he was away for a few days, I was more than happy to say yes. He'd given me a key to use, but even if he hadn't, I knew exactly where the fake rock containing the spare key was hidden—beneath Mrs. Buckley's rose bushes to the left of the patio.

Unlocking the door, I stepped into the kitchen, pushing the door shut behind me. It was quiet and dim, lit only by the light above the stove, and smelled faintly of ripe bananas. Fritz, who normally came hurrying over when he heard the door, was nowhere to be seen. I was taking my sneakers off when none other than Dashiel Buckley came sauntering around the corner.

Stark.

Naked.

His thick, wavy hair was wet, as if he'd just gotten out of the shower. For a moment I was paralyzed, one shoe on, one shoe off, my pervy eyes going straight for his crotch. I only caught the briefest glimpse before he saw me.

"Jesus!" he yelled, turning away from me. But that only presented me with his backside, which was just as mouth-watering as his front. "Ari?"

"Sorry!" I squeaked, trying to tug my high-top back on, hopping on the other foot. "I didn't know anyone was here! I just came to let the dog out!"

Fritz, who'd trotted in at Dash's side, looked back and forth between us, panting with his tongue hanging out.

I feel you, Fritz.

Dash grabbed a dish towel off the counter and faced me again, draping the cloth in front of his hips like a toreador's cape. "It's okay, I didn't tell anyone I was coming home. Let me just go put some clothes on, and—"

"Actually, I'm late for work. I'll just go." Finally managing to get my shoe on, I yanked the door open and dashed back to my car, my shoelaces flopping.

Sliding into the driver's seat of my crappy old Honda, I yanked the door shut and gripped the steering wheel with both hands before leaning forward and resting my forehead against it. My pulse refused to slow down.

What was he *doing* here?

Fuck, he looked good.

That face. Those shoulders. The abs. The long, thick, dangling—

No. Don't think about the dangle.

Turning on the engine, I reversed out of the driveway and peeled down the street, tires squealing. Then I called Mabel.

"Hello?"

"No one told me Dash was going to be home!" I shouted.

"What?"

"I just went over to take the dog out for your dad, and Dash was there!"

"He couldn't be. He's in L.A."

"I'm telling you. *He is home.*" I thumped the steering wheel three times. "I just saw him naked in the kitchen."

"What?" she squealed.

"I let myself in, same as always, and he came strolling around the corner in his *birthday suit*!"

"Why on earth was he naked in the kitchen?"

"I don't know, Mabel! I didn't stick around to ask him!" Beneath my work clothes—black pants and a fitted Buckley's Pub T-shirt—a sweat had broken out.

"Are you sure it was Dash?"

"Mabel. Please."

She started to laugh. "He probably didn't care. He was practically naked on *Malibu Splash* all the time."

"Well, *I* cared." My eyes were on the road, but I wasn't seeing stoplights and yellow lines. Just skin. Muscles. And the dangle.

I'd have turned on the A/C if it worked. Instead, I rolled down the window.

"Are you still mad at him?"

Eventually, I'd confessed my foiled attempt at seducing her brother to Mabel. I was no good at keeping secrets from her. "Yes. No. I don't know. I can't think right now."

"I'm Team Ari forever, of course, but I do hate that my best friend and my brother can't be in the same room together."

"We can be in the same room, Mabel. But not while he's naked!"

"That's fair."

"He didn't even have the decency to leave the room! He just

stood there covering himself with a small kitchen towel like it was a fucking fig leaf."

"Gross. I'm sorry you had to see that."

"I suppose I'll live." My pulse was starting to decelerate. "Your dad must not have known he was coming home either."

"Maybe he wanted it to be a surprise."

"Then he got what he wanted." My car made a whining noise as I turned onto Main Street. "He shocked the bejesus out of me."

She laughed. "I wonder if he'll go into Buckley's Pub tonight. Are you working?"

"Yes." Thinking about Dash walking into the bar tonight kicked my heart rate right back up again.

"Hopefully, he'll have clothes on if he does."

"He better," I said, still trying not to think about the dangle. "He darn well better."

Chapter 3

ARI

*H*e came into the bar just after eight, and I knew the minute he entered. The air took on an electrical charge that tickled the back of my neck and made my hair stand on end.

When I glanced toward the front door, I saw him throw his arms around Xander and give him several thumps on the back. They were both tall, fit, and handsome, but they didn't look much alike. Xander was dark-haired and bearded, with deep brown eyes. Dash had been light blond when he was a kid, but his hair color had deepened as he grew older. Tonight, it was mostly covered by a baseball cap, probably to decrease his chances of being recognized. His jaw, always clean-shaven on *Malibu Splash*, now had light brown scruff. It gave his good looks more of a rugged feel that punched me right in the lady bits.

Thankfully, he wore clothes—jeans that showed off his round, muscular ass and a fitted hunter-green Henley that hugged his chest and arms. I tried not to stare as Xander showed him around the place. When the tour ended by the bar, I busied myself slicing a few more limes.

"Have a seat," Xander said, gesturing toward an empty bar stool. "Ari will take care of you. I'll be back in a few."

Steadying myself with a breath, I placed the napkin down in front of Dash and forced myself to look him in the eye. My heart rattled worse than my car engine. "Hey, Dash."

"Good to see you, Sugar." The corners of his mouth twitched as he called me by my childhood nickname in the Buckley family—bestowed when I was eight years old, and Mabel and I had attempted chocolate chip cookies from scratch in their kitchen. Despite all the boasting I'd done about my baking skills, I accidentally mistook salt for sugar and never lived it down.

"You too."

"Of course, I'm not seeing as much of *you* as you saw of *me* earlier today."

I would be calm. I would be cool. I would ignore what his eyes were doing to me. "What can I get for you?"

"Do you always enter a house without knocking?"

"I'm sorry about that. I didn't know anyone was home, and your dad asked me to look after Fritz for the weekend. He gave me a key."

"I didn't realize he'd be gone. I wanted to surprise him." He gave me an easy grin and lifted one shoulder. "Sorry if I offended you."

"I wasn't *offended*," I said, wiping an invisible spill from the bar.

"No? I couldn't tell, the way you ran off."

"Well, you were *naked*!" I looked around to make sure no one could hear me. "Why were you *naked* in the kitchen?"

"I was doing an acting exercise."

"An acting exercise?" I repeated dubiously.

"Yes. Where I strip down to my purest self. It helps you to shed the layers of emotional protection." His eyes twinkled. "Sometimes our clothing is just a metaphor, Ari."

I refused to be flirty with him. "So can I get you a drink or not?"

"Sure. Xander says there's a local whiskey he likes. Brown-Eyed Girl?"

I nodded. "Rocks?"

"Please."

Turning my back on him, I tried to ignore the way my heart was merrily skipping over beats like a carefree child through a field of wildflowers. Did it not recall the way Dash had stomped on it? I wondered what he was thinking as he watched me pour his whiskey over ice. Was he remembering that night in his bedroom? Maybe he never gave it a second thought. Probably tons of girls had thrown themselves at him like that.

Maybe I needed to get over myself.

I brought him his drink, trying not to stare at his mouth on the rim of the glass as he took a sip.

"So, how are you?" he asked. "It's been a while."

"Busy." I started slicing limes again, but my hands felt jittery.

"I didn't know you were working here."

"Just Fridays and Saturdays."

"And you're still at the diner too?"

I nodded, working my knife faster, gripping it harder. "Yep."

"Living with your parents?"

"No," I said. "I bought a house."

"Oh yeah? Where is it?"

"On the—ouch!" I'd sliced my left index finger, and blood spilled from the gash. I grabbed it with my other hand, but I must have had lime juice on my fingers, because it stung like a motherfucker. "Dammit!"

Dash was off his stool and racing around the bar in a heartbeat. He ran the water in the sink, grabbed my wrist and held my hand beneath the cold flow. "Can someone get me a clean towel?"

A barback handed him one, and I stood there in a daze as Dash rinsed the cut, examined it, then pressed against it with the clean towel. I could feel my pulse in my finger.

"Ari?" Dash looked me in the eye. "Are you okay?"

I nodded, although I felt woozy.

"I think you need stitches." He turned to the barback. "Can you grab Xander for me?"

"On it."

"Ari, come here and sit down." With one of his hands still holding the towel around my injured finger, Dash put the other on my lower back and led me around the bar, where someone vacated a stool for me.

I perched on it and looked down at the blood seeping through the towel. "Oh, shit."

Xander appeared at my side, his expression concerned. He took one look at the bloodstained towel and said, "You need to go to the E.R."

"That's not necessary," I said. I *hated* needles—the thought of stitches was worse than the pain of the cut.

"Yeah. It is." Xander's tone told me not to argue. He put a hand on my shoulder. "Do you have insurance?"

I nodded. "Through the diner."

"Okay. I'll cover any costs that insurance doesn't." He looked at his brother. "Dash, do you have a car?"

"Yes. I rented one."

"Good. Take her now."

I gave up fighting—no way I'd win against them both. "Can someone please grab my purse? It's behind the bar."

"I've got it," Dash said.

Three minutes later, he pulled open the passenger door of a luxurious black SUV, and once I slid in, he set my purse on my lap and buckled my seatbelt. As he leaned over me, I caught a whiff of his cologne, or maybe it was a hair product or even just his skin. Whatever it was made me want to bury my face in his neck and inhale deeply.

He shut the door and hurried around to the driver's side, while I closed my eyes and squeezed the towel around my finger. Of all the nights I'd imagined us driving off somewhere together, never once was it the emergency room.

"How's the pain?" he asked, speeding away from Buckley's Pub.

"Not too bad," I lied.

"I'm sorry, Ari. It's my fault."

I stared at him. "Why would it be your fault?"

"I was making jokes and distracting you while you were trying to work." He actually sounded sincere.

"It was an accident, Dash. I wasn't being careful enough."

He pressed his lips together, saying nothing. His profile was chiseled perfection, making my heart throb as hard as my finger.

When we arrived at the closest hospital, Dash dropped me off at the emergency room doors and told me he'd meet me inside after parking the car.

"You don't have to stay," I told him.

"I'll be right in."

I was sitting in the waiting room, listening for my name to be called, when he appeared in the doorway. My heart skittered at the sight of him scanning the room, looking for me with that concerned expression on his face. He'd ditched the ball cap, and his hair was slightly disheveled, as if he'd just run his fingers through it.

When he spotted me, he came over and sat down in the chair next to mine.

"You don't have to stay," I told him again.

"Are you going to keep saying that, hoping I leave?"

"Maybe."

He leaned back, crossing an ankle over one knee, arms folded over his chest. "Well, I'm not leaving. How's the finger?"

"Hurts."

"Do you want me to call someone? Your parents?"

I shook my head. "They're out of town for ten days. Anniversary cruise."

"Boyfriend?"

"No boyfriend," I said, staring at my sneakers.

"Good."

I risked eye contact.

He shrugged, his mouth curving up on one side in a sexy crooked grin. "Might have been awkward to call him, since you saw me naked today."

I looked at my feet again.

"So have you recovered from the trauma of that experience?"

"I'm pretending it didn't happen."

"Oh. Cool. We're good at that."

"Good at what?"

"Pretending things didn't happen."

I sniffed. Raised my chin. "I'm sure I don't know what you mean."

He laughed softly. "Oh, is that the game we're playing?"

"You were the one who said we should forget it ever happened." I lifted my shoulders. "And I have."

"So the frosty treatment over the last eight years is because of something else?"

I finally looked at him. "I haven't been frosty to you. I've barely seen you."

"You've barely *looked* at me," he corrected. "We've been in the same room plenty of times since then, and I've never been able to get you to talk to me. The last words I heard out of your mouth were 'I hate you.'"

I dropped my eyes to my towel-wrapped hand. "I don't hate you. I was just embarrassed."

"Still? After eight years?"

"You rejected me, Dash. Maybe you don't remember what it's like to be sixteen, but I do. Feelings are big. I know it's not your fault that you didn't feel the same way, but I can't help it that I wasn't okay for a while after you turned me down."

His voice grew softer. "I'm sorry. I didn't want to hurt your feelings, but I didn't think it would be right to...do that." He nudged my foot with his. "So can we be friends now?"

"Friends?" I feigned shock. "A big Hollywood celebrity like you wants a nobody friend like me?"

"You're somebody to me, Sugar. You always will be."

A warm feeling engulfed me, flooding my limbs, pooling in my belly. Attention from him always did this to me. "Then I guess we can be friends. But you have to promise never to bring up that night again."

"Deal."

"Ariana DeLuca?" called a nurse.

I rose to my feet, and Dash stood too. "Do you want me to come back with you?" he asked.

It was on the tip of my tongue to say no, but then I thought about needles again. "Would you?"

"Of course." He put his hand on my lower back and walked me toward the nurse. "I was coming no matter what you said."

. . .

He stayed with me the entire time—through the intake process, in the triage area, and while the doctor examined my finger. When she decided I needed a few stitches, I immediately looked at him.

Getting up from the chair in the corner of the small room, he came over and put a hand on my back. "You're okay."

I looked up at him, dizzy with fear. "Don't leave."

"I won't. I promise." His voice was calm and reassuring. "You don't have to be scared."

"I'm not scared," I said, my voice cracking.

"I know you don't like needles." He rubbed my shoulder blade.

"How do you know that?"

"I heard you say it once. It stuck with me."

The doctor, a woman with dark skin and close-cropped hair, worked quickly. It was over in a few minutes, and when I was bandaged up, the nurse gave me discharge instructions.

"Keep the finger dry for forty-eight hours," she said. "After that, you can shower. No baths. Wash the area gently a couple times a day, and keep it elevated when you can. No strenuous activities that would cause it to reopen."

"When can I get the stitches out?"

"One week," the doctor replied, washing her hands at the sink. "You can take over-the-counter meds for pain, but if the pain gets a lot worse or you see signs of infection—the nurse will give you a list—come back right away."

"Got it." I nodded. "Thank you."

"No driving tonight." The doctor turned around, drying her hands on paper towels. "You might be drowsy from the pain meds."

"I've got her," Dash said. "I'll get her home safely."

His hand was still rubbing my back.

• • •

It was almost ten by the time we left the hospital. Dash wanted me to wait at the doors while he pulled the car around, but I insisted on walking through the parking lot with him. I needed the fresh air—my head was spinning.

At his SUV, he opened the passenger door for me and helped me in. "I'll run you home now and go back to get your car later," he said, buckling my seatbelt for me again. "Xander can follow me, and I'll drop it off to you."

Oh, God. My car.

It was an embarrassing piece of shit with like ten different problems I couldn't afford to get fixed. If you went seventy on the freeway, the steering wheel shook. It made a whining noise when I turned right. The check engine light had been on for months.

I did not want Dashiel Buckley to drive it. But what choice did I have?

"Okay. Thanks." I looked up at him. "I'm sorry if I ruined your first night home. I'm sure you didn't want to spend it watching me get stitched up in the E.R."

"I mean, it's not the *most* fun Saturday night I've ever had, but I was glad to do it." He smiled and shut the passenger door, giving the roof of the SUV two thumps.

Or maybe that was my heart.

He got behind the wheel and started the engine, and I gave him directions to my house. "Nice," he said as he pulled into the driveway. Putting the car in park, he leaned forward to peer out the windshield at the small, two-bedroom ranch.

He probably lived in a mansion in Beverly Hills with a swimming pool and gourmet kitchen. Marble countertops. Viking range. "It's getting there," I said. "I got a good deal because it needed work."

"Who's doing the work?"

"I'm doing as much as I can, but actually, your dad has been helping me too. My dad tries, but he has a bad back."

"I'm glad my dad is helping you. Gives him something to do." He leaned back again. "I'd like to see the inside sometime."

"It's a little late," I said, mostly because I'd left the house kind of messy. After my shift at Moe's, I'd intended to get some painting done, but instead I'd fallen asleep face-first on the couch, accidentally keeping the promise I made to my mom earlier. I'd woken up with just enough time to change my clothes and run over to the Buckleys' house to feed the dog. "And I have to be at the diner at six."

"I don't mean tonight," Dash said. "But maybe while I'm home. I'm in town for a month."

"Oh, wow." An entire month of having to deal with his close proximity. Seeing him around town. Maybe pouring him coffee at the diner while my poor heart ached, just like old times. "That's a long time."

"Yeah, I was already coming home for Devlin's wedding, and since I haven't been back in a while, I just decided to make it a more extended visit. Spend some time with my dad."

"Sounds nice." Unbuckling my seatbelt, I opened the car door and got out. Dash hopped out too and quickly came around to my side, guiding me with an arm around my shoulders up the front walk. "Dash, it's just a cut finger," I said. "My legs aren't broken."

"I know, but I promised the doctor I'd get you home safely."

We climbed the two wooden steps onto the porch—which needed a fresh coat of paint—and he handed over my keys. "Do you have an extra key for your car?"

"Yes. Give me a minute." I let myself into the house, grabbed my extra key from a drawer in the kitchen, and brought it outside. "If it's too much trouble to get my car back here tonight, I can just walk to the diner in the morning. It's not far."

"It's no trouble." He took the key from me, and our fingers brushed briefly. "I'll leave it in the driveway and put your key in the mailbox."

"Thank you." I hesitated, shifting my weight from one foot to the other. "Um, my car is...not nice."

He shrugged. "Don't worry about it."

"No, I mean, really, it's a shit show. As soon as I can afford something better, I'm going to get rid of it."

"You should have seen the piece of crap I drove around in L.A. before I got *Malibu Splash*." He grinned. "I guarantee your car is nicer."

"I doubt it. But anyway, thanks for everything tonight."

"You're welcome. I'm glad I was there to help." He glanced toward his SUV. "Guess I'll take off."

"Okay."

But he didn't leave. We stood there looking at one another for a few more seconds while crickets chirped in the dark. My heart began to beat faster, and I realized I was holding my breath. When he reached out with one arm, I sort of leaned forward, expecting a hug, but all he did was tug one of my curls.

A total big brother move.

"Night, Sugar," he said with a grin.

"Night." Embarrassed, I hurried inside the house.

• • •

My alarm went off at five. Since I couldn't get my left hand wet yet, I skipped a shower, sprayed my head with dry shampoo, and managed to get my hair into a sloppy bun. Getting my uniform zipped was a bit of a struggle, and it wasn't done all the way up, but I figured I could ask for help when I got there. I went for flats since there was no way I could tie the laces on my sneakers.

Putting my makeup on wasn't too bad—thankfully, I was right-handed—and I was able to leave home on time. At least I wasn't scheduled to work in the kitchen. No way would I be able to handle all the chopping, scrambling, flipping, and prepping on the line.

As Dash had promised, my car was in the driveway when I went outside. I reached into the mailbox, and the key was there, along with a note written in plum-colored ink on the back of a Starbucks receipt, which had probably been on the floor in my front seat.

Your check engine light is on. You should get that looked at. Hope your hand is okay. Dash

Sticking the note in my bag, I hurried over to my car. When I started it up and heard the horrendous noise it made, I winced.

On the three-minute drive to Moe's, I wondered when I'd see him next. Cherry Tree Harbor was a small town, so surely I'd run into him, unless he planned to hide out. At the very least, I'd see him at Devlin's wedding, which was three weeks away.

Mabel was coming home for it, and she had asked me to come along as her date. Suddenly I wished I could afford a new dress, something pretty and sexy. Something that would turn Dashiel Buckley's head. Make his eyes pop a little.

Stop it, I scolded myself. *Just because he was nice to you last night and you decided to be friends doesn't mean you should dig up all your old feelings. Leave them six feet under, where they belong.*

At ten to six, I let myself into Moe's back door and called hello to the baker as I walked through the kitchen. I had just stuck my bag and sweater in the office when a text came in from Gerilyn, who was scheduled to waitress during the breakfast shift.

My heart fell as I read it.

Hey I'm so sorry but my mom had a bad fall and broke her hip. I'm with her at the hospital. She'll be fine, but I can't work this morning.

It's okay! I'm so sorry to hear the bad news, and I hope your mom heals fast. I'll get your shift covered today. Let me know how she's doing when you can. Thinking of you!

I sent a few emergency texts to our other waitstaff, but I wasn't too hopeful that anyone would be up and eager to run into work at six in the morning on a Sunday when they hadn't been scheduled. That meant I'd have to cover, and I only had one good hand.

But it would be fine. I've been through worse.

Quickly, I started running through all the usual morning tasks. Doing a POS system check, ensuring the credit card machine was functioning, putting on the coffee, writing out the specials, sanitizing the surfaces. I greeted the cooks, who were firing up the grills and fryers, explaining that service might be a little slow today, but I was going to do my best.

I was checking the condiments at a booth near the jukebox when I heard a knock on the thick glass of the door fronting Main Street. Looking up in surprise—we weren't open for another twenty minutes—my heart tripped over its next few beats when I saw Dash standing there.

I hurried to the door, unlocked it, and pulled it open. "Good morning," I said. "You're up early."

He shrugged. "Couldn't sleep. Figured I'd head over here to grab coffee and something to eat. How's your finger?"

"Not too bad." I held up my bandaged hand. "But I'm short a server this morning, so service might be a little slow."

"Can I help?"

"Doing what?"

"Anything. You name it, I've done it—washed dishes, flipped burgers, waited tables, poured drinks." He went through a pantomime of all his previous restaurant jobs. "It's all muscle memory. And I'm not doing anything this morning. My dad's not even back yet."

I hesitated. "Are you sure?"

"Positive."

"Okay." I swung the door open wide enough for him to enter, then locked it behind him. "It's not the most glamorous job in the world, but if you can pour coffee and take breakfast orders, I can use you."

Dash turned in a circle, looking around the diner. "I haven't been here in a while. Looks the same."

"Nothing ever changes at Moe's."

His eyes scanned the photos on the wall, and he laughed. "What happened there?"

I followed his line of sight to his headshot. "Oh, that. Uh, someone broke in and vandalized your picture."

"Just *my* picture?"

I nodded, pressing my lips together.

"And why didn't you clean it off?"

"I just think you look better that way. It makes your face more interesting."

He laughed. "My face wasn't interesting before?"

"Not really. Average at best." Grinning, I moved past him toward the counter. "So first thing, we—"

"Hey, wait." He caught up to me and put his hands on my shoulders. "You're not zipped all the way."

I went still as he finished the task, heat rising within me. "Thanks. I couldn't reach it this morning."

"All good." His hand lingered at the top of my spine.

Move, Ari, I told myself. "Can I get you a cup of coffee?"

"I'd pay many Bulge Bucks for some coffee."

"What are Bulge Bucks?" I grabbed the pot and filled a thick white mug for him.

"It's what my siblings call the money I made from *Malibu Splash.*"

I laughed. "Sounds like them. Cream and sugar?"

"Nope. This is perfect." He picked up the cup and sipped. "So do I get a cute little uniform like you have?"

"No. But I'll get you an apron," I said, heading for the kitchen. "Then I'll go over the specials with you."

From a closet in the back, I grabbed a clean white apron that said Moe's on the front and brought it to him, watching with amusement as he removed his hoodie, slipped the loop over his head, and tied the string around his waist. Beneath it he wore jeans and a black T-shirt, the sleeves of which hugged his biceps.

"How do I look?" he asked, holding his arms out.

"Like Bulge in season two, episode six, when he worked at the soup kitchen. Or maybe the Halloween episode from season four—the slasher parody—when you played the scary butcher and walked around with that cleaver." I shivered.

"You watched my show?"

I cringed. "I'd like to say no, but I think you'd call my bluff."

"At this point, I might."

"I especially like the musical episodes. But the Christmas special was fun too. You looked great in the Santa suit."

He laughed, shaking his head. "You've watched every episode, haven't you?"

"Let's not talk about it." Suddenly, I realized something. "You know, you're probably going to be recognized in here today. People will be asking for autographs and selfies and stuff."

He dismissed the idea with a shrug of his shoulders. "I'm used to it, but if having me here turns out to be more stressful for you, let me know, and I'll go."

"Deal." But I realized I was kind of excited about having Dashiel Buckley by my side today. Not because he was famous, but because he was *Dash*. "Okay, let's go over the specials."

• • •

Within minutes of opening, I discovered he hadn't been lying about his hospitality skills—Dash was awesome at the job. He took orders quickly and efficiently. He remembered everything I told him about the menu. He kept the coffee cups filled and the plates moving. And he insisted on letting me work behind the counter so I wouldn't have to carry the trays necessary to serve the booths and tables out front.

He was recognized instantly, of course. And everyone wanted not just autographs and selfies, but his attention as well. If they'd known him growing up—like his former fifth-grade teacher or his Little League coach—they wanted to chat all about *we knew you when*. If they were fans of the show—like the teen girls who couldn't stop blushing—they wanted hugs. Even if they'd never seen an episode of *Malibu Splash*, they were excited to meet a real Hollywood actor, one who'd grown up right here in this very town. They asked him dozens of questions about what it was like to be on television, whether he'd ever met this celebrity or that one, and what advice he had for anyone who'd like to get into acting.

Somehow, he managed to find a minute to make everyone feel special, keep up with his work, and make sure I was doing okay. We made it to two o'clock, which was when Moe's closed for a couple hours before opening back up for dinner. After locking the door, I poured out the coffee and wiped down the machine while Dash carried a final tray full of dirty dishes to the kitchen.

"So now what?" he asked when he came out.

"Now I finish up, grab something to eat, and open for the dinner shift. But you can go," I added quickly.

"How long is the dinner shift?"

"Four to nine. We close a little earlier on Sunday nights."

"I'll stay and help you. Austin is coming in with his family for dinner."

"Dash, you should eat with your family." I checked the napkin supply behind the counter. "I have another server coming in at four, and my aunt is coming in to close. You don't have to work."

"I know I don't have to work. I want to." He tugged one of the curls that had escaped my sloppy bun and let it spring back. "Stop trying to get rid of me, Sugar."

I tilted my face down toward the counter so he wouldn't see me smile.

Chapter 4

DASH

*N*ews travels fast in a small town—and on the internet. By the time Moe's opened up for dinner, word had gotten out that I was working there today. Swarms of girls came in, the older ones with friends, the younger ones with their parents. The moms were often just as excited as the kids, and in between making their milkshakes, serving them burgers and fries, and refilling their soft drinks, I must have taken a hundred photos and starred in dozens of videos wearing that apron, setting down a plate with a grin.

Pics and reels from this morning and afternoon had already hit social media and gone viral, garnering thousands of likes and hundreds of shares within a couple hours. My agent was thrilled.

Dash! This organic traction is
fantastic!

Milk called. They want to offer you
a sponsorship. Apparently they
recently fired some loudmouth bull
rider for bad behavior, but they love
your wholesome vibe.

> No to Milk. Let me know if Whiskey
> calls. Any progress on the audition
> for All We've Lost?

Not yet. But I made a call and told
them you'd like to be considered for
Johnny. I'm waiting to hear back.

Who's the girl???

> An old friend. Her family owns the
> diner.

You look adorable together.

> We're not together.

You're hopeless.

I stuck my phone back in my pocket.

Austin arrived with Veronica and his eight-year-old twins,
Adelaide and Owen, who were giddy that their celebrity uncle
was in town. Veronica, a tall, beautiful blonde with a friendly
smile, greeted me with a hug.

"I've heard *so* much about you," she said. "It's so nice to
finally meet you."

My brother hardly took his eyes off her, and they sat close on
one side of the booth. He also kept an arm around her shoulder,
which surprised me.

Ari came rushing over, and from the way Veronica popped up again and embraced her, I could tell they were good friends. When I returned to the table with water for everyone, Ari was explaining the bandage on her hand. "I wasn't being careful enough with my knife, and I sliced my finger."

"Did you need stitches?" my nephew Owen asked.

"I did, and I *hate* needles," she said, wrinkling her nose. "Lucky for me, your uncle Dash stayed and held my hand."

"Did he?" Veronica glanced back and forth between Ari and me, a peculiar smile on her face that made me wonder what Ari had told her about me. "How sweet."

"What's with the apron?" Austin asked me with a grin. "You give up on the whole acting thing?"

"Nope, just helping out," I said, setting the water glasses down. "Ari was short-staffed today—and injured as well."

Veronica laughed. "Well, the internet has certainly taken notice—not to mention the entire town of Cherry Tree Harbor. I've never *seen* this place so busy on a Sunday night."

"Dash is definitely good for business," Ari said with a laugh. "Too bad my parents aren't here to see it."

Adelaide tugged on my apron. "Our teacher is sitting over there. Can we introduce you?"

"We want to ask her if we can bring you in for Show and Tell," added Owen.

I glanced at Ari as the bell above the door rang again, bringing new customers in. "Go ahead," she said with a grin. "It's fine. I think you'll make an excellent specimen for Show and Tell."

• • •

The dinner rush was pretty much over by eight. I poked my head into the office, where Ari sat at the desk, hunched over a binder. "Hey. How's your hand?"

"It's okay. You can go now." She swiveled the chair to face me. "Things are quiet, and my aunt Elena is here to close."

"Are *you* leaving now?"

"I have a few things to do first." She glanced at paperwork on the desk.

"Then I'll wait for you."

She shook her head. "You've been here all day, Dash. Go home."

"I do have to run back and let Fritz out, but then I thought maybe we could grab a beer somewhere." When she hesitated, I reached out and tugged one of those stray curls. "Come on, Sugar. One beer. I'll even buy it."

She laughed, batting my hand away. "Okay, fine. But only because I'm truly enjoying all the photos and videos of you in a Moe's apron on the internet. Have you seen the slo-mo edit of you walking across the diner carrying the condiments?"

I groaned. "Ketchup will probably reach out tomorrow and ask for a meeting."

"What's wrong with ketchup?"

"Nothing. Never mind." I didn't want to complain about my career to Ari. She worked her ass off here day after day. She bartended on weekends. She drove a car that groaned with agony every time you tapped the gas pedal. She was great at what she did and always wore a smile, but I wondered if she was happy or if she wanted something more. "I'll be right back."

"You know what? Meet me at my house," she said. "I want to change out of my uniform."

"Okay." I started to leave the office and turned around again.

"Do you want me to unzip you?"

Her eyes widened. "Huh?"

"Your uniform. Will you be able to unzip it with only one good hand?"

"Oh. Probably not. Do you mind?" Rising to her feet, she presented me with her back. "Just a few inches should do it."

I had many thoughts about giving her a few inches—and then some—but I decided to keep them to myself. We were finally friends again, and it felt good.

Still, I took my time pulling that zipper down, and as the two sides of her uniform parted, I became so distracted by the sight of her upper back and a tiny mole she had just to the left of her spine, I went a little too far. Her nude bra strap appeared. I zipped it back up a few inches, letting my fingers brush her skin.

A shiver rippled through her, and when I dropped my hand, I heard her exhale, as if she'd been holding her breath.

• • •

About half an hour later, I pulled up in front of her house, left my car parked on the street, and waited for her on the sidewalk. It was early May, and the temperature was cool but not cold. The smell of spring here was different from the smell of spring in California. More fresh and green, with a trace of dampness to it.

She came out the front door a minute later wearing jeans and a thick sweater, her hair loose and curly around her shoulders.

"I need a favor," she said as she came down the walk. "I can't tie my stupid shoes."

Laughing, I knelt down and laced up her sneakers in the light cast by a street lamp, then popped to my feet again. "Anything else?"

"Yeah. Can you come over tomorrow morning and wash my hair? Give me a nice smooth blowout?"

"I could try, but I'm not sure you'd get the look you're going for." Unable to help myself, I reached out and touched one of the soft strands hanging by her cheek. "Besides, I like the curls."

Her cheeks bloomed with pink. "Thanks."

My eyes dropped to her lips. They were also pink. Full and round, luscious as a strawberry. Somehow I knew they'd taste as sweet.

It would be so easy. One step forward. A hand on the back of her neck. A tilt of my head. A stroke of my tongue.

She glanced to her right, breaking the spell. "I thought maybe we could walk. It's kind of nice out."

"Sure," I said, stepping back. What the hell was the matter with me? I was supposed to be here working on myself. Somehow I doubted that messing around with Ari DeLuca would show the universe I was deserving of a lucky break.

But fuck, it would be a good time. I had ideas for that mouth.

I zipped up my hoodie a little higher and shoved my hands in my pockets.

At the end of her block, we turned left onto Spring Street, which sloped down toward the harbor. "Hey, did you get my note?" I asked. "The check engine light in your car is on. You should take it in."

"Yeah, I know. I will." She sighed, keeping her eyes on the sidewalk. "I'm just afraid of what a mechanic will tell me. I can't afford any expensive repairs at the moment."

"Austin could take a look at it for you."

"Austin?"

"Yeah. He's pretty good with cars." I had no idea if Austin knew shit about cars, but what I did know was that Ari wasn't going to let me take her car in as a favor. And I didn't feel right letting her drive around in that thing. It wasn't safe. "I'll trade cars with you tonight, and swing by his house tomorrow. Let him take a peek under the hood. If there's anything that needs immediate attention, he can probably do it."

She thought for a moment. "I guess that would be okay. If he's not too busy. But don't let him do it for free."

"I won't." It wasn't really a lie because Austin wouldn't be doing a damn thing. I was going to take her car to an actual mechanic. "Where should we go for a drink?"

"There are a few new places on Main Street," she said. "A wine bar called Lush and an English-style pub called The Mermaid. We could try one of those."

But the bars along Main Street were all closed—it was a Sunday night, after all, and not quite tourist season yet—so we walked three blocks north and ducked into the town's gas station convenience store. There, we bought a six-pack of beer, a bottle opener, and two hot dogs. After warming them in the microwave, we decorated them with condiments, and Ari wrapped them back up in foil while I paid for everything.

"Nice night," said the woman at the register, looking back and forth from me to Ari.

"Perfect for a picnic," I said with a smile.

She stuck the six-pack in a brown paper bag. "Enjoy."

Outside, we headed down toward the harbor and crossed Bayview Road. "Want to go sit by the water?" I asked.

"Sure." Ari glanced toward the marina to our right and Waterfront Park to our left. "Seawall or dock?"

"Let's walk out on the dock," I said.

We skirted around the darkened restaurant at the Pier Inn, where I'd spent many summers working, and walked out onto the dock. The planks creaked beneath our feet as we strolled past sailboats and cabin cruisers and speedboats bobbing in the dark to our right and left. At the end of the dock was a bench that faced the lighthouse.

"This okay?" I asked.

"Sure." Ari sat down and placed the bag with the hot dogs on her lap, unwrapping them to see which was hers—mustard only—and which was mine. "I'm hungry."

Dropping to the bench on her left, I pulled two beers from the pack, pried off the caps, and handed one bottle to her. She placed it on her other side, then set the bag with the hot dogs and napkins between us. "Bon appétit."

For a few minutes, we said nothing, just ate our dinner while listening to the slap of the water against the pilings and the metallic clang of a nearby flagpole. When we were done, we put the trash back into the bag, and Ari walked it over to a bin at the end of the dock.

"So graduates of the Culinary Institute still eat gas station hot dogs, huh?" I asked as she sat down on the bench again.

"This one does."

Smiling, I stretched out my legs, crossing them at the ankle. The moon painted a silvery ribbon on the dark surface of the lake, and the lighthouse beacon flashed at regular intervals. It was familiar and peaceful.

I tipped up my beer. "I can't remember the last time I sat out here like this."

"You probably don't miss it. You've got the ocean and all."

"It's not the same. I do miss it," I said, realizing it was true. "I never thought I would."

"Same. When I was younger, I couldn't wait to get out of here. And I *never* thought I'd come back."

I looked over at her. "What were you going to do?"

"After culinary school, I was going to go to New York or Paris or Tokyo—a huge city with millions of people and a fabulous restaurant scene. I was going to work in famous kitchens for world-renowned chefs before opening up my own place. I would earn Michelin stars and James Beard awards and publish cookbooks and maybe even have my own TV show."

"What made you change your mind?"

"Reality, I guess."

I studied the shimmering water again. A breeze rippled its surface. "Mabel said you lived in New York for a while."

"Yeah." She was silent for a few seconds. "I had a rough time there."

"What happened?"

She brought her heels up onto the bench, wrapping her arms around her legs. "I was recruited by a chef I really admired—I'd met him when he guest taught at my school—to come work in his restaurant. He made it sound like he saw something special in me. Like he would be a mentor to me. He talked about my raw talent and wanting to mold me."

"What happened?"

"At first, it was great. I was thrown in over my head for sure, but he was patient with my mistakes, and I was learning. And then..." She shook her head. "Gradually, he was less understanding. More temperamental. 'Good enough' wasn't going to cut it in his kitchen. I had to be perfect."

"He sounds like an asshole," I muttered.

"He is. But he's also a genius."

I took a swig of my beer.

"And he knew just how to manipulate me. If he gave me even the smallest amount of praise, I felt like a million bucks. I'm already a pleaser by nature, and he just had this extra talent for making me crave his approval. So I did everything he asked me to."

I hesitated, not sure I wanted the answer to this question, but unable to resist asking it. "Do you mean in the kitchen?"

"Yes." She paused. "But also beyond it. I know it makes me sound stupid, but I was really flattered to have his attention like that. And I thought maybe if I gave him what he wanted, he'd let up on me a little."

I said nothing, because I was too busy being pissed.

"But he didn't," she went on. "In fact, he got worse. He told me my ideas were boring, my technique was average, and my palate was unsophisticated. When I'd get upset, he'd say I should be thankful for his guidance. And he had me convinced that *only he* could make me better. But his criticism didn't make me feel talented. It made me feel stupid and worthless."

Fury surged through my veins. I gripped the bottle in my hand so hard I was surprised it didn't shatter. Next time I had to channel rage for an emotional scene, I knew what I was going to think about.

"When I told him I was leaving, he told me I was being an idiot and a child. He told me I'd be nothing without him. But I realized I couldn't feel more worthless than I already felt, and I was homesick anyway. So I came back."

"First of all, you're not nothing," I seethed. "Second, I'm so fucking mad right now, I want to get on a plane and fly to New York just to punch this guy in the face."

She chuckled. "You'd knock him out with one blow."

"You want me to do it? Gimme a name right now."

"Niall Hawke." She put her bandaged left hand on top of my right thigh, as if to keep me on the bench. "But don't bother, Dash. He's an asshole, and I've moved on. I don't even take his calls anymore."

"He still *calls* you?"

For a moment, she was flustered. "Not a lot. Just every now and then—probably when he's drunk. For a while he tried to get me to come back, but I have no interest in him, in that scene, in any of it."

"What *do* you want?"

"I'd like to stay in Cherry Tree Harbor. I know it's not a big culinary scene, but it's home to me." She laughed self-consciously. "I'm a small-town girl at heart. I'd like to have a family someday, raise my kids here. And I don't need a Michelin star or a James Beard award. I just want to make feel-good food—meals that make people happy. I'd like to take classic diner fare to the next level."

"Can you do that at Moe's?"

She sighed. "It's hard. I have ideas, but my parents are so resistant to change. They just want everything to stay the same— the menu, the decor—" She side-eyed me. "Even the photos on the wall."

Chuckling at the dig, I elbowed her gently. "So open your own place. Something different, more upscale."

"I can't do that." She shook her head vehemently. "Moe's is the family business, and my parents are depending on me to keep it alive. I'd never abandon them."

"Would they see it that way?"

"*I* see it that way," she said. "They've done so much for me my entire life, paid for culinary school, encouraged me to chase my dream in New York City, and welcomed me back with open arms when I came home. They say all the time how happy they are that I'll be there to take over when they retire. I can't leave and open a place that would compete with them. It would break their hearts."

I admired her devotion to her family, but it also seemed like a lot of pressure. "You're sort of in the position Austin was in with Two Buckleys. He stayed there for so many years, even though it wasn't his dream, because he didn't want to let my dad down."

"And I bet he doesn't regret it. Family matters most," she said empathically. "But let's not talk about me anymore." She hugged her legs to her chest again. "Let's talk about you. Tell me what's new in Hollywood."

Finishing off my beer, I set my empty bottle back in the cardboard holder and took out another. "Hollywood and I are on a little break from each other."

"How come?"

I uncapped the bottle and took a long drink. "Frustration, I guess. I'm trying to level up in my career and running into a lot of dead ends."

"But you had a huge role on a hit show. You have tons of fans. I saw a bunch of them today."

"Yeah, but Bulge is the only kind of part I'm considered for. I'd love to play a serious dramatic role. Something I can really sink my teeth into. The kind of part that would prove that I'm not just—" I frowned, shaking my head. "Never mind. When I hear myself say these things out loud, I sound like an asshole."

"You're not an asshole to want more challenging work," she argued. "And it's not like you aren't grateful for what you have now."

"I'm definitely grateful," I said. "I might be sick and tired of

Bulge, but he rescued me from obscurity. He bought me a house. A car."

"Hot dogs and beers." Ari clinked her bottle against mine.

"Hot dogs and beers."

Silence fell around us again, but it was comfortable. A breeze ruffled Ari's curls. I wished I could put my arm around her shoulder, tuck her against my side. It had been a long time since I'd wanted to get close to someone. "You know, I've been thinking about you a lot the last couple days."

"Oh yeah? Why's that?"

"My agent dragged me to this psychic healer a few days ago. She looked like you."

She burst out laughing, her feet hitting the ground again. "Wait a minute. Back up. A psychic healer?"

"Yes." I paused with my beer halfway to my mouth. "Her name was Delphine."

"Oh my God." She turned on the bench to face me, tucking one leg beneath her. "I need to know more. Why are you seeing a psychic healer?"

"Because casting directors have said that my work lacks emotional depth, and Izzie—that's my agent—said that I can't make an audience feel things if *I* don't feel things."

"You don't feel things?"

"I *do*," I said, rubbing the back of my neck, "but I don't like wallowing in them or talking about them. And playing Bulge for the last five years hasn't really challenged me to dig very deep into my emotional well. So now that I need that skill, I'm struggling. There's this director—Katherine Carroll. Have you heard of her?"

"Of course."

"I really want to be considered for this particular role in

her next project—it's a movie called *All We've Lost*—but it's a romantic lead, and Izzie said she wouldn't get me an audition unless I went to the psychic healer to clear some negative energy. Open up the emotional channels or something."

Ari quirked a brow. "So what did Delphine do to unclog your channel?"

"She took me into a dark room and told me to sit in the chair across the table from her. Then we held hands so our energies could meet."

Her lips twitched. "And then?"

"And then she told me my energy was fucked because my ego is too big, and my heart is constipated."

"*What?*" Ari dissolved into laughter again.

"She said there was some kind of blockage to my heart energy that was preventing me from connecting to my deepest feelings. Then she said she was going to try to shift some of the energy around and get it moving again, but she couldn't." I tipped my beer up again. "My poor heart energy is all backed up, and she was fresh out of emotional plungers to sell me."

She wiped tears from her eyes. "So what's the solution?"

"According to Delphine, I have to strip down to my purest self and get more comfortable with vulnerability. I need to show the universe that I'm willing to accept its gifts. And my agent thought some time away from the L.A. scene would be good for that."

"Wait a minute." Composing herself, she rested her beer bottle on top of my thigh. "Is this why you were walking around naked yesterday?"

"Yes." I paused. "But I also just like being naked."

She shook her head. "This is ridiculous, Dash. You need a better plan for solving your emotional depth problem."

"I'm all ears if you've got one."

She was silent for a moment, during which I studied the way her hand was wrapped around the neck of that beer bottle on my leg and imagined it closed around my cock, which was in the vicinity and *definitely* aware of her fist.

Then she sat up taller. "You know what? I do have a plan."

"Oh yeah?"

"Yes. I believe I can help you get in touch with your feelings, Dashiel Buckley."

"How's that?"

"I'm going to make a list of my all-time favorite big-feels movies. Then we're going to watch them together and soak in the emotional depth."

"*Soak in* the emotional depth?" I laughed. "I'm not sure that's how it works."

"Oh, but walking around naked is going to help? Listen, these films are going to be a *masterclass* in making an audience fall in love with you." She got to her feet and faced me. "I need to start making my list!"

I watched her start pacing back and forth in front of the bench, the moonlight dusting her hair. "I'm almost afraid to ask what's on this list."

"All kinds of things. *Titanic* for sure," she said. "Possibly *The Lion King.*"

"*The Lion King*? As in the *cartoon*?"

"You're right, maybe we should stick to people." She kept pacing. "*The Princess Bride* is great. *Shakespeare in Love* is a must."

"Shakespeare?" I made a face. "I'm not much of a—"

"We need something classic too. Something black and white, maybe a wartime love story." She stopped pacing and pointed her bandaged hand at me. "*Casablanca.* That's *full* of emotional depth! I mean, that kiss? When she says, '*If you knew what I went through, if you knew how much I loved you…how much I still love you.*' Gah! Just stab me!" She clutched her heart.

Amused by her excitement, I gave up arguing with her and leaned back, draping an arm along the back of the bench. "Okay, professor. Where and when is this masterclass taking place?"

"My house. I'll finalize the list over the next few days, and we'll start the viewing this week. We've got a whole month, right?"

"Right."

She nodded. "I can definitely have you in your feels by then. Finally, reading all those romance novels is going to pay off!"

"Jesus. You're not going to make me read one, are you?"

"No, but I do think all men could learn something from them. Now let me think." She tapped a finger against her lips. "I've got dance class tomorrow night, so let's meet up Tuesday. My place around seven."

"Dance class?"

"Yes. I take an improvisational dance class at Veronica's studio." She grinned. "You should come! It's all about translating feelings into movement. You'd have to wear clothes, of course, but I bet the internet would love it."

I was shaking my head before she even finished the thought. "No fucking way. I'll stick to the movies."

She pointed her bottle toward me. "You better thank me in your Oscar acceptance speech."

I tapped my beer against hers once more. "Deal."

• • •

We walked back to her house, and after some additional prodding, she brought me her car key so I could take it to get checked out tomorrow.

"Thank you," she said. "I appreciate it."

I handed her my phone. "Do you want to give me your number?"

"Sure." She typed it in and gave it back to me, and I handed her the fob to my rental SUV.

"Well, goodnight," I said.

"Night." She lingered on the sidewalk for a second, and I wondered if it would be a bad idea to give her a hug. Could I trust myself to put my arms around her and let her go in an appropriate amount of time? Without any wandering of the hands? Before I had decided for sure, she gave me a little wave and headed up the front walk.

Kicking myself, I walked over to her car.

· · ·

Later that night, I crawled into bed and lay for a while staring at the ceiling. The twin bunks Devlin and I once shared had been replaced by a queen-sized bed, but everything else was the same. I glanced over to the wall where the bunk beds had been and recalled that soft, sweet kiss. Her naked shoulders in the moonlight. The bare chest I'd glimpsed before looking away. Would she consider giving me another chance?

No. Stop it. You hugged it out, you're friends, and that's that.

I thought about her ridiculous plan to help me get in touch with my feelings and smiled. I was probably just going to end up sitting through a lot of chick flicks while she cried, but it was a sweet gesture. It came from the heart.

And maybe if I did more things from the heart, I'd give a more heartfelt performance.

Still, as I lay there staring at the ceiling, I couldn't help wondering about the boundaries of friendship and how far they might stretch.

Chapter 5

ARI

$\mathcal{A}$fter dance class, Veronica and I met up at Lush for a glass of wine. I got there first, snagged a round high-top in the back, and ordered a glass of pinot noir for me and a sauvignon blanc for her—our usual. Veronica came in about ten minutes behind me, and the moment she sat down, she clamped a hand around my forearm.

"Tell me *everything*," she said dramatically.

"Everything about what?"

"About you and Dash! I was dying to ask you about it at the studio but there were too many people around, and Dashiel's name is so well-known. I didn't want to start any rumors flying." She grinned. "But it's obvious something is going on."

"Nothing is going on." I picked up my water and took a sip.

"You're so cute." The smile faded, and her tone grew

threatening. "Now tell me the truth."

I laughed. "Nothing is going on, Roni. It's exactly what I said—he was at the bar when I cut my finger, he took me to the emergency room, then he took me home. I was as shocked as anyone when he showed up Sunday morning and offered to fill in for my absent server."

Veronica sighed like I was testing her patience and tightened her long blond ponytail. "Okay, but for nearly a year now—as long as I have known you, Ari DeLuca—you've done nothing but roll your eyes whenever Dash's name comes up, and once or twice you have alluded to the fact that you're not exactly his biggest fan."

"That's true," I allowed. "But honestly, I was just being immature. I had a huge crush on him when we were younger, and one night I did something stupid that resulted in utter heartbreak and humiliation."

Our wine arrived, but Veronica ignored it. "What did you do?"

"I'll tell you. But please keep in mind, I was sixteen and crazy about him. Don't judge me."

She held up both palms. "Ari, I walked into your diner last June wearing a wedding gown, having just left my fiancé at the altar, and you could not have been nicer. You served me the best burger and fries I'd ever had and told me about the nanny job for Austin's kids. My life was transformed because of that day. I'd never judge you."

"Not even when I tell you I snuck into his bedroom and asked him to deflower me?"

Her eyes popped. "You did not!"

"I did," I said, my face growing hot. "Climbed into bed with him, took off my pajamas, and offered myself up right there on the bottom bunk."

Veronica slapped a hand to her forehead. "What did he do?"

"Jumped out of bed and turned me down. Said we should just forget it ever happened." I shuddered. "Let me tell you, there is nothing more tragic at sixteen than having the boy of your dreams tell you he just looks at you like a little sister."

Her expression was anguished. "God, that's so painful. Then what happened?"

"I snuck back into Mabel's room and sobbed into the pillow."

"Did Mabel know?"

I shook my head. "Not until later. I mean, she knew about my crush on him—it had been going on for years—but I hadn't told her what I was planning."

Veronica took a sip of her wine. "It's probably better that he did the right thing, don't you think?"

"Now I do. But not in the moment. I loved him too much." I picked up my wine glass. "So what else could I do but hate him forever?"

"Nothing. It was the only solution your poor wounded pride could handle."

"Especially after he got all famous. Do you know how annoying that is?" I took a sip of pinot and set my glass down. "The guy who rejected you shouldn't grow up to be a gorgeous Hollywood star," I said. "He should turn into a toad."

Smiling, Veronica lifted her wine to her lips. "So how did you go from wanting him to turn into a toad to working side by side at the diner?"

I sighed. "The night I cut my finger, we sort of hugged it out and decided we could be friends."

"Friends. Hmm." Her mouth, painted with her usual shade of red lipstick, twisted gleefully.

"What?"

"Nothing." She lifted her shoulders. "From what I saw at the diner, you two just seem very…cozy together."

"Cozy?"

"Yeah, you know, just…" Again, she shrugged. "Comfortable. Like you've known each other forever."

"Well, we have. We're kind of like brother and sister." Even as I said it, it didn't feel true.

"Hmmm," she murmured, her tone conveying skepticism. "I don't think so. He was paying a lot of attention to you. I might even say there was *fawning* involved."

My face heated up again. "There was no fawning. He just didn't want me to do too much because of my hand. He's protective—like a big brother."

Veronica laughed. "I'll allow protective. But he was *not* looking at you like a little sister. He was looking at you like he hopes you're the princess whose kiss will turn him back into a man, at which point he is going to take off all her clothes and make up for that time he turned her down."

"Stop it." I laughed, but I felt hot beneath my sweater and peeled it off. "He has never looked at me like that."

She gave me a look that said she knew better. "So then you probably don't have any plans to see him again."

"Not really."

She feigned surprise, the fingers of one hand steepled over her heart. "Oh, you *do* have plans to see him again?"

"Well, we're friends. I'm helping him with something."

"Something like what?"

"Something like developing more emotional depth in his acting so he can be considered for bigger roles." I tried to make it sound businesslike.

"I see." She set her glass down and leaned on the table with both elbows, hands clasped like an executive. "And how are you going to do that?"

"While he's home over the next month, we're going to watch movies I think have big, emotional performances in them. You know, like *Casablanca* and *Titanic*."

Her head fell back as she laughed. "I see. So you're going to cuddle up on the couch and watch some of the most romantic movies of all time. But it's strictly platonic."

"There won't be cuddling." God, I hoped there would be cuddling.

"I have a movie suggestion."

"Which one?"

"*Friends With Benefits*."

I rolled my eyes. "Veronica."

"It's actually more of a prediction than a suggestion."

"That's not going to happen."

"Are you sure?" Veronica arched one brow.

Remembering how Dash had tugged my hair Saturday night on the porch and said goodnight on the sidewalk last night with even less affection, I felt confident nodding my head. "Totally."

...

We left the wine bar out the back door. At first, I didn't see my car in the lot and got excited that someone had stolen it, but then I remembered that Dash and I had traded vehicles. Digging the BMW fob from my bag, I unlocked it.

When the lights flashed on the back of the SUV, Veronica stopped short. "Did you get a new car?"

I laughed. "Are you kidding? In what universe would I be able to afford a car like this? It's Dash's rental."

She turned to me, one eyebrow raised. "And why are you driving Dash's rental?"

"Because the check engine light is on in my car, and he was going to have Austin take a look at it."

Veronica's expression morphed from suspicion to confusion. "Why would he want Austin to look at it?"

"Because according to Dash, Austin is handy under the hood. Isn't he?"

"Not that I know of." Veronica laughed. "I mean, maybe in a manner of speaking, but I'm not talking about cars."

"Seriously?" I stuck my hands on my hips. "Austin doesn't know about engines?"

"I've never seen him work on a car, but I've only been around since last summer, so I suppose it's possible."

"Weird." Opening the driver's side door, I tossed my bag on the passenger seat. "I wonder why Dash would make that up."

"Maybe he didn't," Veronica said with a shrug. "I was running errands all day, so maybe he brought the car by while I was out."

"Maybe." I gave her a quick hug. "Thanks for meeting me."

"My pleasure. I love our Monday night dates."

"Hey, can you do me a favor?"

"Of course."

I played with the key fob in my hand. "When you get home, can you ask Austin about the car thing?"

"Sure." She nodded. "Then I'll text you what he said."

. . .

By the time I let myself into my house, I'd gotten a message from her.

I asked Austin about your car. He
said Dash didn't come by with it,
nor does he have any idea why he
would. Austin said he can change a
tire and the oil, but that's about it.

Hmm. Thanks for letting me know.
Dash must be up to something.

Like what???

No clue.

FAWNING.

Lol stop. I'll keep you posted.

If I had his phone number, I'd have texted him, but I'd only given him mine last night, and he hadn't reached out today.

After a quick shower, I put my pajamas on and brushed my teeth. I was just slipping between the sheets when my phone buzzed on the nightstand. I picked it up and looked at the screen.

Hey. It's Dash. How was your day?

Fine. How was yours?

Good. I hung out with my dad.

Did you take my car over to Austin's?

Actually I didn't have time today.
I'll do that tomorrow.

You will not.

Yes, I will. I'm sorry, today just got
away from me.

You will not because Austin doesn't
know anything about cars.

Three dots appeared, fading in and out.

Veronica told me the truth. Why did
you lie about it?

Because I was worried about you
driving that car around and I wanted
to get it checked out by a mechanic.
I thought you'd say no if I asked.

You were right. Where is my car now?

At Harbor Garage. It will be ready
Wednesday.

I sighed. I was irritated with him, but I was also really touched.

You shouldn't have done that. But
thank you. Can you give me the total?

It's already paid for.

DASH!!!!!!

It wasn't even that much. It was a
faulty gas cap causing the CEL to
come on, and there were just a few
other small things the mechanic
said he could fix in a couple days.

DASHIEL BUCKLEY
I SWEAR TO GOD

I did it for me, okay? I couldn't
sleep if I thought you were driving
around in an unsafe car. And I
really need my beauty rest.

You're making it impossible to be
mad at you.

Good.

Thanks for doing that. I'll pay you
back as soon as I can.

I don't want your money, Sugar.
How about I get to pick the movie
tomorrow night?

No. You are watching Titanic with
me, whether you like it or not. But I
think you'll like it.

Why?

Because I'll feed you. I'm testing
out new recipes.

Does it have iceberg lettuce? (Get
it? Iceberg???)

OMG.

No, there will not be iceberg
lettuce. The dinner is not themed.

I'll eat whatever you make. Can I
bring anything?

Nope. It's all my treat.

Can I strip down to my purest self
in your house?

I laughed, but I also felt a little zing shoot through me when
I remembered him walking into the kitchen naked. Tucking my
lower lip between my teeth, I was trying to come up with a funny
but not too flirty reply when he texted again.

Only kidding. I promise to keep my
clothes on. I can even wear multiple
layers. Don't run away again.

I wasn't running away. I was picturing it.

I hit the blue send arrow before I had time to think it through.
But as soon as I saw the words on the screen, I gasped. "Shit," I
whispered. The dots faded in and out again.

You were picturing me naked in
your house?

It's your fault.
You put the idea in my head.

Does that mean I can picture
you naked at MY house?

No.

Too late.

My breath caught. Was he flirting? Or just trying to poke at me?

This is not a very appropriate
conversation for friends, is it?

Not really.

So I will say goodnight and see you
tomorrow at 7.

Goodnight.

I set my phone on the charger and set my alarm. Then I sank down in my bed, remembering how I used to lie awake at night and fantasize about Dashiel Buckley.

Kissing him. Flirting with him. Wearing that navy UM hoodie he loved, the one that made his eyes look even more blue. Holding his hand in the hallway, even though he was a senior and I was a freshman, and such a thing was *never* going to happen.

I had more suggestive dreams too.

Lying on a couch with him. Running my palm over the front of his jeans. Allowing his hand to slide up my shirt. Feeling his weight on me.

I picked up my Kindle from my nightstand and opened my book, but I found my eyes skimming over the words without actually reading them. My mind was wrapped around a question.

If I could've gone back in time tonight and told sixteen-year-old Ari exactly how her attempt at seduction would play out, I wondered if she'd have taken my advice, found a new crush, and abandoned her mission to give Dashiel Buckley her virginity.

Knowing my teenage self, I had a feeling she'd have told me to go back to the future and leave her alone—that's how sure I was back then that he and I were meant to be. In fact, she'd probably blame me for messing up her dream.

You must have screwed it up, she'd tell me. *It's all your fault. Look at your hair, it's a mess. Is that how you wore it? Ugh! And what's with the giant bandage on your hand? Am I clumsy in the future? Great, just great.*

Then I'd tell her he was coming over to watch a three-hour movie with me tomorrow night. She'd like that.

A second chance, she'd say with satisfaction. Then she'd scowl and point a finger at me. *Don't fuck it up.*

There's nothing to fuck up, I'd tell her. *We're just friends.*

Weren't we?

• • •

For dinner Tuesday night, I made a version of chicken pot pie that had all the comforting, savory flavors of the original dish but included a few French-inspired ingredients—shallots, tarragon, and puff pastry. Everything took me a little longer with only one good hand, but I managed to get it in the oven and grab a few minutes to change into clothes that weren't dusted with flour, spattered with cooking oil, or splashed with chicken stock.

In my bedroom, I pulled on clean jeans and a soft ivory sweater in a light knit. I didn't want to look like I was trying too hard—this wasn't a date or anything—so I didn't put on fresh makeup, and I left my hair alone. Studying my reflection in the mirror, I frowned and added some mascara. Dusted my cheeks with a little blush. Applied some lip gloss.

"Stop it," I whispered to myself, spraying perfume on my neck. My hair. My wrists.

I was fluffing my brows when I heard a knock on the front

door. Tossing the brush in my makeup bag and the bag in the cabinet under the sink, I hurried to the door and pulled it open. "Hi. Come on in."

"Thanks," Dash said, stepping inside. He sniffed and looked at me with awe. "Is that our dinner I smell?"

I laughed and shut the door. "Yes."

"What is it? My mouth is watering so fast, I'm going to drool here in a second."

"It's a fancy twist on chicken pot pie," I said, walking through the living room to the kitchen. "It's just about ready to come out, I think."

"Is it something you want to serve at Moe's?" He wandered over to the stove, watching me pull the large cast iron skillet from the oven.

"I'm going to serve it as a special one day this week. Don't tell my parents." I set it on the stovetop and studied the puff pastry crust, golden and flaky and fragrant. It looked beautiful, and yet I still found myself looking for faults. Was the crust overdone? Had the sauce properly thickened? Were my vegetables chopped consistently? Had I over-seasoned or under-seasoned? Was the balance of savory and sweet correct? Were the textures perfect?

I calmed myself with a deep breath. No one was here to pass judgment on me.

"It's pretty, isn't it?" I glanced at Dash, who was staring at the pie with hearts in his eyes.

"Yes." He leaned closer to sniff it. "Oh my God. How wrong would it be to say I want to bury my face in your pie right now?"

I laughed and punched him lightly on the shoulder. "Very wrong."

"Okay, then I'll just think about it."

On shaky legs, I found my way to the fridge and pulled it

open. The cool air rushing out felt good on my overheated face. "Would you like a glass of wine? I had to open a bottle for the recipe."

"Sure."

The bottle of white Burgundy was on the shelf right in front of my face, but my eyes seemed to be having trouble locating it. All I could see was Dash's head between my legs. His scruff rubbing my thighs. His tongue teasing my clit.

Finally spotting the wine, I grabbed the bottle by the neck and set it on the counter. *This is not a date*, I repeated as I poured two glasses. *This is two friends eating dinner and watching a movie. The only pie being eaten tonight is of the chicken pot variety.*

When we moved into the living room and set up two tray tables, I made sure to place mine at the opposite end of the couch from his.

Sixteen-year-old Ari was still in my head, and she was a fool for Dashiel Buckley.

She always would be.

...

"This is ridiculous. There is totally room on that door for both of them."

"Shhhhh!" I reached over and slapped his arm. "No talking. This is a very emotional scene, so pay attention."

Dash sighed and folded his arms over his chest. His legs were stretched out in front of him and crossed at the ankle. He wore jeans and a black T-shirt he filled out like it was a second skin. For a moment, I was distracted by the fact that I'd seen him naked just the other day, so I knew exactly what that body looked like beneath the clothes. My skin prickled with heat, and I wished I could take off my sweater, but I wasn't wearing anything beneath it except a bra. My eyes wandered to his crotch. My mind went to the dangle.

"Hey. If I have to watch this, you have to watch this."

Mortified, I quickly looked at the screen again. "I'm watching."

A laugh rumbled low in his throat. "Okay."

I kept my eyes where they belonged for the rest of the movie. It was a struggle.

• • •

When the credits were rolling, I wiped the tears from my eyes. "That movie gets me every time."

"Why?"

"Dash! Are you made of stone? The sacrifices they made for each other! She got out of that lifeboat stupid Cal put her in because she didn't want to leave Jack! And he doesn't get on the door because he doesn't want to risk her life. Then when she can barely summon the will to survive, she does it *for him*." I reached for the box of tissues I'd placed on the end table, knowing I'd need them. "All those photos at the end prove that she lived an extraordinary life, even though she had to do it without him."

"Might have been more extraordinary if she'd sold that big-ass diamond," he pointed out.

I sighed heavily. "She hung onto it because it was her only link to Jack—her only evidence that he ever existed. It's not like there were photographs of him. Just her memory. And then—" I fought tears again. "And then she gives her heart to him in the end. She *saved* it for him."

Dash pondered that, then shrugged. "Okay."

"Dashiel! Were you not moved by any of this? I'm beginning to think your agent was right and you don't have any feelings!"

Laughing, he rose to his feet and picked up his empty plate and wine glass. "I have plenty of feelings. But I can't help it if I thought the food was better than the movie."

"I suppose I can't get mad about that," I said, following him into the kitchen with my own plate and glass.

"Dishwasher?" he asked.

"Just put them in the sink. I'll take care of it."

"No, you won't. You did all the cooking, and you've still got a hurt finger. How's it feeling?"

"Okay." I set my dishes on the counter. "I'll be glad when I can get the stitches out. I'm giving you some pot pie to take home for your dad, okay?"

"Do I *have* to give it to my dad?" He opened the dishwasher and began to load it.

I grinned as I portioned out the leftovers into two containers. "You can take both of these. One can be yours, and one can be his. But I'm going to ask him how he liked it, so don't hog both for yourself."

"Don't *you* want any?"

"I'm good. I'll make something else tomorrow."

"If I promise to do the dishes again, can I come back for dinner tomorrow night?"

I laughed as I pressed the lids into place. "Sure. We can watch another movie."

"Can I choose it?"

"Nope. That's not how this works." I set the containers on the table by his keys and hopped up on the counter to the left of the sink as he finished loading the dishwasher.

"So what was your favorite scene in *Titanic*?" I asked.

"I didn't know there would be a quiz."

I nudged his leg with my foot. "It's not a quiz. We're just talking about the movie. We're exploring and comparing our feelings."

"I'm not sure I had a favorite scene. What about you?"

"Hmmm, my favorite is probably the scene where he's drawing her."

"Why?"

"Because he's looking at her the way she wants him to look at her. He's seeing the *real* her, or at least a side of herself she hides from everyone else."

"The naked side?"

"No! The side that's showing her trust in him. She's so vulnerable in that moment."

"Got it."

"But of course, I also like the scene in the car, where she says, 'Put your hands on me.' Or maybe the scene where he gives her the note that says *make it count*." I sighed. "You just know that moment changes *everything*. I love a moment that changes everything."

He reached for the dish towel and began drying his hands. "But if you keep doing the same things all the time and never take a risk, nothing will ever change. For example, I'd be playing shirtless lifeguards for the rest of my life—well, until I got too old to play them. Then I'd be playing the freewheeling, troublemaking uncle with good hair. And then when I aged out of that role, I'd be playing the well-meaning but clueless single dad whose kids end up teaching him all the important lessons in life."

I blinked. "Wow. You've really thought about this."

"In Hollywood, there just aren't that many options once you're a certain age. Unless you're a big movie star." He turned around so he was leaning back against the sink, his hands draped over the edge in a way that made his deltoids bulge against the sleeves of his T-shirt. "Which is why I'm hoping to change my luck. What about you? If you make safe choices all your life, where will you be?"

"Serving up the same old burgers, fries, and milkshakes at Moe's, I guess."

He shook his head. "That's not going to happen."

"No?"

"No. You're going to build a name for yourself. You're going to do your own thing."

"You sound awfully confident about that, Dashiel Buckley."

"As a matter of fact, I am."

And then some force of nature, some gravitational pull, was acting on the muscles in my body, and I found myself leaning toward him slightly. He lifted his chin, tilted his head. Our mouths were so close I felt his breath on my lips. Bells began to chime.

Wait, bells?

Startled, Dash and I jumped apart, and I realized it was the alarm on my phone, reminding me to take my birth control pill. Jumping down off the counter, I located my purse on a kitchen chair, dug around in it for my cell, and turned it off. "Sorry about that."

"No problem. Guess I'll take off," he said, grabbing his keys and the leftover containers.

"I'll walk you out." I put a hand over my fluttering stomach and followed him to the front door on wobbly legs.

He stepped onto the porch, immediately looking down at his

feet. "Soft spot here. You should maybe replace some of these boards."

"Your dad said the same thing," I told him with a sigh. "It's on the list, along with repairing the railing. But first I have to finish painting the guest room. I got it all taped off and primed last week—I even bought the paint—and then I cut myself, so I can't manage the roller."

"I could help you paint," he offered.

I laughed. "Are you *that* worried about your karma? You already accompanied me to the hospital, worked a shift at the diner, and took my car to have it fixed. How did you even get here tonight?" I squinted at the vehicle parked on the curb.

"Borrowed my dad's car. Don't forget agreeing to Show and Tell in Mrs. Fletcher's second-grade classroom at Paddington Elementary."

I grinned. "When is that?"

"Next week. But I'm not offering to do this stuff for good karma, Ari. I'm offering because I genuinely want to help you."

"I appreciate it. I just don't want to monopolize the time you're supposed to be spending with family."

"You are family," he said with a smile that melted my insides. "Anyway, thanks again for dinner."

"You're welcome." Those were the words that came out of my mouth. In my head were others. *Don't go. Kiss me. Stay the night.*

He glanced at my lips and I tasted victory. But a second later, he met my eyes again. "Night, Sugar."

"Night." I tried not to let the disappointment show on my face.

He headed down the front walk, got behind the wheel of his dad's car and drove off. When his taillights had disappeared down the block, I shut the door and wandered into the kitchen. As I finished cleaning up, I tried to calm my racing heart.

"Stop it," I said aloud. "Nothing is going to happen. It's obvious. We're just going to be friends. He wants to come for dinner again because he likes my cooking. He offered to help me paint because he's a nice guy. He said I was family because of my friendship with Mabel. Don't get carried away."

But as I lay awake in bed that night, I desperately hoped I was wrong and Veronica was right. I just wanted to know what it was like to *be* with him. To feel desired by him. To get this *thing* I had for him out of my system once and for all.

Just once. That was all I needed.

Just once.

Chapter 6

DASH

*J*esus Christ, I thought as I drove home. I almost kissed her. I promised myself that I wouldn't touch her tonight. I kept my distance all during that endless, waterlogged movie. I even caught her staring at my crotch, and I *still* stayed on my end of the couch.

There should be a reward for that kind of restraint.

She was so fucking pretty, with that curly hair and those curvy hips and that sweater that looked so soft it would be like hugging a cloud if you put your arms around her. And that mouth. Jesus. The number of times I looked at her lips and thought about them on my dick was fucking obscene.

But it wasn't just physical. She was so different from the women I knew in L.A. So normal and real and down-to-earth. When she laughed at something you said, you knew she really thought it was funny. When you made a ridiculous remark, she called you out on it. When you had a conversation with her, she didn't just talk—she listened.

Everything just felt easy with her.

Except keeping my hands to myself.

You shouldn't go back there tomorrow night, I told myself. *You should just stay away from her house for the next month, because you know what might happen if you keep spending time with her.*

Hell yes, I knew what might happen.

In fact, I thought about it in great detail as I undressed and got into bed. While we were sitting on the couch, I might move a little closer. Put my arm around her shoulders. Pull her onto my lap. Press my lips to hers. Slip my tongue in her mouth. Unbutton her jeans.

My hand moved inside the elastic waist of my boxer briefs and fisted my cock.

I might slide my hands beneath her sweater. I might tug her jeans right off. I might lay her down on the rug and bury my head between her thighs. I might give her an orgasm with my tongue right there on her living room floor.

My erection thickened in my palm as I imagined the way she'd taste. The way her body would tremble. The way she'd say my name. The way she'd beg for my cock.

But this time I'd say yes.

My arm worked furiously, my stomach muscles flexing, my breath coming fast.

This time, I'd strip her clothes off myself. I'd get my mouth on those luscious tits. I'd push inside her tight, wet pussy and fuck her hard and fast, hearing her cry out with every thrust, and then I'd come so hard I wouldn't be able to think or see or even breathe.

You know. Emotional depth stuff.

"Fuck, fuck, fuck," I whispered through clenched teeth, the climax rippling through me.

When I was completely spent, I lay there for a moment, my chest heaving, my conscience spiraling. Was it wrong that I was getting myself off while thinking about my sister's best friend, just like I used to when she was sixteen and sleeping down the hall?

Probably. But damn, it felt good.

• • •

The next morning, Austin picked me up and we went to the gym together.

"Why the hell did you tell Ari I could fix her car?" he asked as soon as I got in his truck.

"Because I didn't think she'd let me take it to a mechanic, and the thing is barely alive," I explained as I pulled the door shut. "It needed serious resuscitation."

"Oh. So where is it now?"

"Harbor Garage. It'll be done later. Can you take me to pick it up?"

"Yeah." He reversed out of the driveway and glanced at me. "That was nice of you. Having her car fixed."

I shrugged. "She doesn't have a lot of extra money right now. And it wasn't much for me." I waited for the Bulge Bucks joke, but he didn't make one.

"I hear you've been hanging out with her."

"From who?"

"Dad. Veronica. The woman behind the counter at the gas station store."

I rolled my eyes. "Jesus. Small towns. I'm not *messing* around with her, if that's what you mean. We're just helping each other out. So you, Dad, Veronica, the gas station lady, and whoever else is all up in my business can just relax. There's nothing going on."

"You sound a little defensive about that." My brother wore a smirk that said *I am the oldest brother and I know everything.*

"Well, I feel like my character is being attacked. Like you guys don't trust me with her."

"She's a nice girl."

"I *know.*"

"And she's practically family."

"I know that too. Which is why I took her car to the mechanic. And why I pitched in at the diner. And why I agreed to go over to her house for dinner last night and taste-test a new recipe for her." Maybe not the whole truth, but not a lie either. And my brothers were easily distracted by food.

"What did she make?" Austin asked.

"Chicken pot pie with some kind of special puffy crust and fancy French ingredients."

"Damn. That sounds good."

"It was."

"I'm hungry."

"Me too. I didn't eat anything this morning."

"After we work out, want to go get some breakfast at Moe's?" he asked.

"Sure," I said, trying my best to sound nonchalant about it, like I didn't care one way or another where we ate our bacon and eggs.

But my pulse picked up when I thought about seeing her again so soon.

...

My insistence that there was nothing going on between Ari and me might have been more believable if she didn't light up at the sight of us walking through the door.

From behind the counter, she grinned and waved. "Good morning! Just the two of you?"

We nodded, and she gestured to a pair of empty stools in front of her. "Have a seat. Specials are on the board."

After settling onto the stools, we looked at the chalkboard behind the counter while she poured coffee for us.

"Creole Eggs Benedict," said Austin. "Is that new? I haven't seen that one yet."

"I just added it today," she confirmed with a smile. "House-made biscuit, spicy pork sausage, poached egg, and my own Creole mustard hollandaise."

"Sold," Austin said.

"Make it two," I added.

Ari laughed. "Coming right up." She set some almond milk in front of Austin before he even requested it and disappeared into the kitchen. I watched her go, admiring the way that little diner uniform hugged her hips. A memory from last night's fantasy floated through my mind.

Fuck. Stop it.

I picked up my coffee and redirected my brain. "Dad says Xander's new house is cool. Where is it?"

"Near downtown and close to the harbor, one of the newer places. We did some reno on it, but mostly it was cosmetic. Paint, trim, things like that."

"Have you seen Ari's new house?" I asked, watching as she passed by with the coffee pot.

"Not yet, but Veronica has. She said it needs work, but it's cute. I guess Dad's been helping her out a little."

I nodded and tried to sound nonchalant. "I told her I'd give her a hand painting a bedroom this week."

The smirk was back.

"How's the new business going?" Another redirect. After working for Two Buckleys Home Improvement with our dad for years, Austin had finally started his own company, making furniture from reclaimed wood.

"Good. I still have a pretty long waitlist, especially for dining tables."

"Xander said you did the bar at Buckley's Pub. It looks great."

"Thanks." He laughed a little, shaking his head. "I lost a bet, so I had no choice but to make it."

I looked over at him quizzically. "What was the bet?"

"That I wouldn't be able to stay away from Veronica after I hired her."

"I can't even believe you took that bet," I said with a snort, recalling how he'd kept that arm around her shoulders at Moe's the other night.

"Yeah, well... I had good intentions."

I took a swallow from my coffee mug and watched Ari crack up delightedly as she poured coffee for someone down the counter. Who was making her laugh like that? Frowning slightly, I leaned forward to look past Austin, glad when I saw it was only old Gus and Larry. Then I kept my eyes on her as she passed in front of me on her way to the kitchen, giving me a quick smile over her shoulder that made my chest get tight, like my heart and lungs were swelling.

When I couldn't see her anymore, I sat back.

And realized Austin was looking at me, one brow cocked.

I splashed some coffee down my throat. "Veronica seems really cool."

"She is."

"Kids like her?"

"They love her. They're the ones who convinced me to hire her—well, plus Mabel and Ari." He frowned. "Also Xander. Maybe Gus and Larry too."

"You didn't want to hire her?"

"She showed up on my doorstep wearing a fucking *wedding* gown. No experience, no references, no skills that would qualify her to be a nanny."

I laughed. "But it all worked out."

"It all worked out."

"So is it serious?"

"Yeah. I'd say so." He set his cup down. "I haven't said anything to anyone about this, so keep it to yourself, but I'm thinking of asking her to marry me. Maybe this summer."

I blinked. "Seriously? That's awesome. I'm happy for you."

"Thanks."

"I always figured you'd get hitched first. I'm still kind of shocked about Devlin."

"I was surprised too," Austin conceded. "I think all of us were, especially because it happened so fast. But when you meet Lexi, you kind of get it. They're good together."

I nodded, observing as Ari hopped up on the back counter to erase the Creole Eggs Benny, which must have sold out. Her uniform rode up a little bit, exposing more of her thighs. She tugged it down, glancing over her shoulder to see if anyone noticed. When she caught my eye, she held a finger over her lips, and I winked.

"What about you?" Austin asked. "Dating anyone?"

"Nah. I don't date much."

"How come?"

"I don't know. I mostly end up at places where there are a lot of industry people, and they're not always the most genuine. Sometimes I'm standing in a room talking to someone, and she's smiling at me, but I can see her looking around, wondering if there's someone more famous or more powerful she should be talking to. It starts to wear you down after a while, and then I'm just like, what's the point?" I shrugged. "But I don't really care. I like being single."

Austin laughed. "Yeah. I did too."

"But it's different for you. You're a lot older, and—"

"I'm not *that* much older," he scoffed.

"Okay, but you have kids. I'm just not at all in that headspace right now. I'm not focused on relationships," I said, watching Ari approach carrying two plates. "I'm focused on work."

She set our breakfasts in front of us. "Here you go. Two Creole Eggs Benny. You have to let me know what you think."

Austin wasted no time in digging in. "I think I'm in love."

She blushed beautifully. "It sold out already."

I took a bite too. "It's really good, Ari. I'm not surprised it sold out."

"Thanks. I'm kind of proud of it."

"You should be," I told her. "You're so talented."

The color in her face deepened. "Thanks."

"Especially since you've learned the difference between salt and sugar," I added.

She burst out laughing and swatted at me with a paper napkin. "Jerk!"

Austin was chuckling too. "I'd forgotten about that."

"Apparently, Dash doesn't forget *anything*," Ari said, giving me the stink eye.

"What can I say?" I shrugged. "I have a good memory."

"Do you still want to come over for dinner tonight?"

"Sure," I said casually, as if I wasn't dying to spend more time alone with her. "If you want me to."

"I'm going to try a sandwich with braised short ribs, maybe served with some crispy truffle fries."

"Can *I* come for dinner tonight?" Austin asked.

Ari laughed. "Absolutely. But you'll have to watch a movie with us. Last night, I made Dash watch *Titanic*. He hated it."

"I didn't *hate* it," I said. "I just don't think I'm the target audience."

"Maybe you'll like tonight better," she said.

"What's the movie?"

She shook her head, her eyes twinkling. "Not telling. Come over about seven?"

"If I came a little earlier, we could get some painting done," I suggested. "What time will you be home from work?"

"I have to hit the grocery store after my shift, but I should be home by four."

"Sounds good. I'll have your car by then too."

"Okay." She smiled brightly. "You're the best, Dash. Thanks."

When she disappeared into the kitchen, Austin put down his fork and picked up his coffee. Took a sip while staring straight ahead.

"What?" I demanded.

"I didn't say anything."

"Your silence implied an opinion."

He finally looked at me, his mouth hooking up. "You said there was nothing going on."

"There's not. We're spending some time together at her house, that's all."

"Watching romantic movies. Having dinner she cooks for you. Painting a bedroom together."

"As friends," I stressed. "She doesn't have any older brothers to help her with the house, and her dad has a bad back."

"I get it. That's nice of you."

But I felt compelled to continue explaining. "She's showing me her favorite romantic movies because I'm trying to improve my range as an actor, and I'm taste-testing new recipes she's trying. She'd like to add a few more upscale items to the menu here, but her parents are resistant."

"Why doesn't she open up her own place?"

"She's too loyal to her parents."

"Can't fault her for that," said Austin.

"No. But it's a hell of a sacrifice."

Ari approached with the coffee pot again, so I stopped talking and picked up my fork.

"So what will you two do with the rest of the day?" She glanced out the window before refilling our cups. "Looks beautiful out there."

"Work," said Austin.

"I promised my dad I'd help him with some spring cleanup in the yard," I said. "We're going to make a run to the hardware store for some new garden tools, then if we really feel like getting crazy, we might hit up the nursery for some new shrubs. Maybe some mulch."

She laughed. "And you want to come over and *paint* after doing all that? You're going to need a back massage."

When she wandered off again, Austin shook his head. "Now I know how Xander felt when he told me how obvious it was between Veronica and me. You and Ari *have* to be worse."

"I told you," I said, my nerves fraying a bit. "We're just friends."

"I know what you told me."

"You don't believe it?"

"Well, I'm trying, but the way she keeps looking over here at you is making it difficult."

I risked a peek at her, caught her staring, and quickly dropped my gaze to my plate.

"Jesus." Austin laughed. "I feel like I'm in the middle school cafeteria. But look, you two are grown-ass adults, and you can do what you want. Just be careful. It's Ari. You know?"

"I *know.*"

"Good. Then I won't say anything more about it."

• • •

Around one that afternoon, I was spreading some mulch in the garden bed that bordered the patio when Xander opened the sliding glass door and stepped outside. In his hand was one of the containers with the leftover chicken pot pie. "Hey," he said. "Where's Dad?"

"I'm not sure, actually." Straightening up, I removed my hat and wiped my forehead with the inside of my arm, leaving a sweaty streak of dirt. It was so hot, I'd taken off my long-sleeved Henley and wore only a white tank. "He keeps disappearing."

"To do what?"

"I don't know." I replaced the hat. "Once he said he had to make a phone call. Twenty minutes ago, he said he wanted lunch. I thought he was just going into the kitchen to make it."

"His car is gone."

I laughed. "Fuck. He ditched me."

Xander dropped into one of the patio chairs and dug into the container with a fork. "Damn, this is good. Where did it come from?"

"Ari made it last night. She sent me home with leftovers for dinner tonight."

"Hope you guys have a backup plan." Xander took another huge bite.

"I'm actually having dinner with her again tonight, and there's a second container Dad can eat. So you're welcome."

Xander was quiet for a moment, and I thought for sure he was about to give me shit for all the time I was spending with Ari. Instead, he surprised me.

"Speaking of Dad, he's been acting a little strange lately."

"What do you mean?"

"Just kind of secretive, I guess."

"Secretive?" I walked over and pulled out the chair across the table from him.

"Yeah. Like last weekend, he supposedly went away on a fishing trip."

"So?"

Xander shook his head and swallowed. "That makes no sense. Where? With who?"

"His fishing buddies?"

"They're all here. Why would he need to leave town to go fishing?"

"I have no idea. I didn't know he was going to be gone. I bumped into Ari in the kitchen the day I got here, and later that night she told me he was away for the weekend, and he'd asked her to look after Fritz."

"That's another thing. Why wouldn't he have asked *me* to look after the dog?"

I shrugged. "Because you're busy with the bar?"

He forked more pot pie into his mouth and shook his head. "I don't buy it. Kelly and I think something else is going on."

"Like what?"

"Well, she's been away from Nashville for the last month. It's the first leg of her North American tour," he added proudly.

"That's cool."

"Anyway, while she's in Nashville, she shares a big house with her mom, Julia. They're close," he said, scraping the side of the container. "When she comes up here to visit me, often her mom comes with her. Sometimes we all hang out together—Kelly and her mom, me and Dad."

I tilted my head, wondering where this was going. "Where's Kelly's dad?"

"Who knows?" He stuck a bite in his mouth. "He's a jackass that abandoned his family a long time ago and only shows up when he feels like it. He's got addiction issues, which Kelly has tried to help him with many times, but he doesn't want to get better. Last fall, Julia finally said enough is enough and threw him out. The divorce should have been final already, but he's contesting a bunch of shit because he thinks he has a right to money Kelly's earned."

I rolled my eyes. "Of course."

"Anyway, Kelly said after the last time they visited Cherry Tree Harbor, which must have been in early March, her mom started to act a little weird."

"Weird how?"

"Like hiding her phone when Kelly would walk in the room, lowering her voice and going into her bedroom while she was talking to someone on the phone, closing the door. Then Kelly would hear her laughing and talking like she was flirting. One time she put her ear on the door."

"And?"

"And she swears she heard her say the name George."

I shrank back a little. "You think Dad has a girlfriend? In all the years since Mom died, he hasn't so much as *looked* at another woman."

"I know. 'It only happens once' and all that."

I cocked my head, squinting at Xander. "But you think that's changed?"

"I do, and I've got proof. When Kelly tours, she and her mom share their location. It's their way of staying connected while Kelly is gone. And over the weekend, her mom was at a resort hotel casino in Detroit called the MGM Grand. She *said* she met some friends for a spa weekend."

I folded my arms and waited for him to go on.

"Just now, I was waiting for this to heat up in the microwave, and that box where Dad keeps all his receipts like it's 1985 was out on the counter. I happened to glance at it."

"And?"

"And there are a bunch of receipts from the MGM Grand in Detroit. Valet parking, restaurant, room."

My jaw fell open. "Seriously?"

Xander plunked the fork into the empty container and set it aside. "It's official. Dad has a girlfriend."

"I think it's nice," I said, once I recovered from the shock. "Do you like Julia?"

"Julia's a little different, but yeah, I like her."

"What's 'different' about her?"

Xander ran a hand over his bearded jaw. "She's just a little out there. But she's sweet, she's high-energy, she's attractive, and she and Dad get along really well. She could be good for him."

"How old is she?"

"Fifty-nine."

"And Dad's what, sixty-six?"

"Yep."

"Good for him." I locked my hands behind my head, leaning back in the chair. "So why's he hiding it?"

"I don't know. He must think we won't like the idea."

"That's ridiculous. We've been telling him for years he should make an effort to meet someone."

"I know. And Kelly is thrilled—she adores Dad and knows he'll treat Julia like a queen."

"Maybe we should—"

The patio door slid open, and our dad stepped outside carrying a white paper bag from a local bakery. "Decided to run into town. I had a hankering for a ham and cheese croissant."

I couldn't help but regard my father differently. Did he look a little younger? A little happier? He'd told me he was going to the gym three days a week, and I thought his renewed energy was due to taking better care of himself. But maybe there was another layer.

"Hey, son," he said to Xander. "Didn't realize you were coming over or I'd have brought extra."

"No problem. I already ate."

Dad set the bag on the table. "I'll just go get us something to drink. Want a water or something, Dash?"

"I'll take a water, thanks." I fished a sandwich out of the bag and took a bite.

"Xander?"

"I'm good."

"Be right back."

We watched him enter the house and slide the glass door shut. "So what's he do, call her while he's in the car or something?" I asked quietly.

"That's my guess." Xander started to laugh. "Poor guy. Sneaking around like a teenager."

"He's been in a great mood over the last few days. I sort of assumed it was because of my surprise visit, but now I don't know."

"Maybe the sap is still rising," joked Xander.

Our dad came out of the house and joined us at the patio table again, setting a bottle of water in front of me. Now it was unmistakable to me—the spring in his step, the glimmer in his eye, the quick humor.

After he'd eaten his lunch, he leaned back in his chair and folded his hands over his stomach. "You know, I've been thinking about taking a little road trip before the wedding."

Xander and I exchanged a glance. "Oh yeah?" my brother asked. "Where to?"

"Oh, I don't know. I might just get in the car and hit the road now that the weather is good. See where the wind blows me." He laughed.

"Want company, Dad?" I inquired, even though I knew what the answer would be.

"Actually, I was thinking of striking out on my own," he said. "Maybe you'd be able to keep an eye on Fritz for a few days?"

"Sure. No problem at all. When are you thinking about hitting the road?"

"Oh, maybe next week sometime. No real plan." On the table next to his glass of iced tea, his phone vibrated. He picked it up and glanced at the screen, a smile overtaking his face. "'Scuse me, boys. I need to make a quick call."

Xander and I watched him hurry into the house and quickly slide the door closed. Then we looked at each other.

"I have a feeling I know what direction the wind will be blowing in the day he leaves," Xander said.

"Same. I'm no psychic, but I predict a southerly breeze that takes him straight to Nashville." I laughed, tipping my chair back again. "So do we say anything?"

"Nah. He'll tell us when he's ready." Xander folded his arms over his chest. "So you're seeing Ari again tonight, huh? What's up with that?"

I let the front legs of my chair hit the ground. "Nothing, and don't start any rumors."

My brother looked delighted at having pushed a button. "You seem testy all of a sudden. Was it something I said?"

"No wonder Dad doesn't want us to know about his friend. All this family does is stir shit up."

"Hey, you're the one who told me she was making dinner for you again."

"It's not *for me*," I said irritably. "She's making dinner, and I'm going to eat it. There's a difference."

Xander smirked just like Austin had. "Sure."

"Listen, I don't need a lecture on how I need to be a gentleman with Ari from you, okay? I already got it from Austin this morning. And you know what? Ari's not a little kid anymore, she's a grown woman, and she can make her own decisions."

"Dude, I wasn't going to lecture you."

"No?"

"No. I was going to tell you flat out that if you're shitty to her, I'll kick your ass."

I laughed. "Much better. Thanks."

Chapter 7

ARI

"I think my dad has a secret girlfriend."

"What?" Positive I heard wrong, I looked over at where Dash was leaning back against the kitchen counter, beer in his hand. He still wore his painting clothes—jeans and a navy Two Buckleys Home Improvement T-shirt that was now smudged here and there with beige paint. "A secret *girlfriend*? Your *dad*?"

"Yeah. So you can't tell anybody."

I mimed zipping my lips. "Okay, but now I need details."

He talked while I put the finishing touches on our sandwiches—braised short rib grilled cheeses with melted gruyère on sourdough, served with au jus for dipping—and waited for the parmesan truffle fries to come out of the oven.

"Oh, I love that for your dad," I said, my heart warmed by the story. "I've met Julia, and she's wonderful. So vivacious and fun. And she's beautiful—long legs, blond hair, great smile."

"I'm happy about it too. I just wish he'd be honest about it. Why doesn't he trust us to know?"

"Do you think he's worried you might judge him?"

"After we all begged him for years to get back out there?" He shook his head. "He couldn't be."

"He never dated anyone after your mom died, right?"

"Never. He always said the same thing—it only happens once."

I peeked at the fries. "Do you believe that?"

"Not sure what I believe."

The fries needed a few more minutes, so I shut the oven and set the timer. "Have you ever been in love?"

"No."

I turned around and faced him. "Really? That surprises me."

"Why?"

"I don't know." It also pleased me, but I didn't want to admit that. "I guess I just assumed you had lots of girlfriends out in Hollywood. I've seen some pictures."

"Don't believe anything you see online. I mean, I'm not saying I've been a monk, but I've never dated anyone too seriously. Feelings have never really been my thing."

I laughed. "That's right. You've been all clogged up for years."

"What about you?" He tilted his head and gestured toward me with his beer. "Ever been in love?"

"I thought so, at the time. But maybe not." I shrugged. "I tend to pick the wrong guys."

"Wrong how? Like they treated you badly?" Dash looked like an angry big brother, like he might go out right this minute and beat somebody up for messing with his kid sister.

"No," I said quickly. "Other than Niall, no one has ever treated me *badly*. They just weren't right for me. We didn't want the same things."

"What do you want?"

"Nothing crazy." I picked at a loose thread in my oven mitt. "I just want to feel like someone thinks I'm worth the time and effort a relationship takes. Sometimes I think I was spoiled by my parents' marriage. I grew up seeing them work together, live together, raise me together. Not that they never fought, because they did—all the time. But at the end of the day, they put each other first."

"Yeah, your parents are a tough act to follow."

"I just want someone to *be there*. Be in it with me. You know?" My timer went off, and I tried opening the oven door with my injured hand. "God, I can't *wait* to get these damn stitches out."

"Here, let me do that." Setting his beer down, he plucked the mitt off my right hand, slipped it on, and opened the oven.

After he set the fries on the stovetop, I poked at them with a spatula. They looked and smelled delicious—browned at the edges, fragrant with truffle oil and parmesan. And yet, I found myself studying them with a critical eye, knowing Niall would comment scornfully on the inconsistent thickness of the fries. Maybe he'd force me to throw them out. Maybe he'd berate me in front of everyone else on the line and I'd have to dig my fingernails into my palms so I wouldn't cry.

Stop it, I admonished myself. *You're not there anymore. You're here, with someone who doesn't expect you to be perfect and would never make you feel bad.*

Dash leaned over the tray and inhaled. "God, that smells good. My mouth is watering. But that always happens when I'm around you."

I smiled. "Oh really?"

"I meant at your house," he said quickly. "When you're cooking."

Ignoring the butterflies in my stomach, I concentrated on plating our dinners. When I turned around, it was obvious he'd been staring at my ass. He quickly raised his eyes to mine, but his guilty expression gave him away.

"Everything's ready," I said, grabbing the beer he'd opened for me from the counter. "Let's eat."

• • •

"So? What did you think?" I asked after the final scene of *When Harry Met Sally* concluded, and Harry Connick, Jr. was crooning my dad's favorite tune over the credits.

"Fucking delicious. The best sandwich I have ever had."

"Dash!" I poked his leg with my foot. "I meant the movie, not the food."

"I liked it. That was way better than *Titanic*," he informed me. "You should have led with that one."

"It's not way better, it's just different. And if you're trying to improve your range as an actor, I feel like it's necessary to study a variety of performances."

"Okay, fine."

"So what was your favorite part?"

He thought for a moment, rubbing a finger beneath his lower lip. "There were a lot of good scenes with just the two of them. The dialogue was great, the back and forth. What about you?"

"Well, I love the last scene, where he runs through the street on New Year's Eve and shows up at the party to tell her he loves her, but it's not good enough until he lists all the things he loves about her. It just shows how well he knows her, and that all her little quirks are lovable to him."

Dash nodded. "Perfect ending, I agree."

"But I really love the scene where she fakes the orgasm at the diner. I wish someone would do that at Moe's. I've always wanted to name a special 'What She's Having,' but my mother won't let me."

He grinned. "What would it be?"

"Good question. I've thought about this a lot."

"Have you?"

"Yes. See, what she's actually eating during that scene looks like a very plain turkey sandwich, so I could either jazz that up, or I could do something with apple pie à la mode, which is what she orders at the beginning of the movie and makes it all complicated."

"Is that what you're like when you go to a restaurant?"

"Me?" I shrank back. "Hell no. I'm the *least* picky person at the table when I eat out."

"Why? I'd have thought you'd have crazy high standards."

"I do if I'm cooking or serving the food. If I'm just out for a good time, you can pretty much bring me whatever, and I'll eat it. I'm a cheap date. My favorite thing ever is carnival food."

"Seriously?"

"Yes! Funnel cakes, corn dogs, deep-fried whatever on a stick. Take my money and put it in my mouth."

He laughed. "Good to know."

"I just had an idea…" I tapped my lips with one finger. "You know what would be good? Some kind of twist on a corn dog with the Creole mustard I used in the eggs benny special today." My mind wandered for a moment as I thought about flavors, textures, presentation.

"That does sound good." He finished off his beer and set the bottle on the tray table, next to his empty plate. I was still thinking about carnival food when he spoke again. "So tell me something. Have you ever faked it with anyone?"

Surprised, I shrugged. "Sure."

"Because the guy didn't know what he was doing?"

"Right, but he thought he did, and it was obvious he was waiting for it to happen and just getting more frustrated by the minute—like it was my fault."

Dash cringed. "That does not sound like a good time."

"What, having sex with me?"

"No!" He thumped my shoulder. "Being with that dumbass you had to fake it with."

"You already rejected me once, Dash. You can stop doing it now," I teased.

"Listen, I rejected you for your own good."

"Jerk!" I leaned over to give him a shove, and the next thing I knew, he tackled me, throwing me onto my back and pinning my arms above my head, his body sprawled over mine.

"You're the one who brought it up," he said, his voice deep and playful. "I thought we were never allowed to talk about it."

"We're not." I squirmed beneath him, although I loved the heaviness of his weight on me. It was every bit as thrilling as sixteen-year-old me had imagined. "We're supposed to forget it happened."

"Impossible. I'll never forget it."

I stopped moving. His mouth hovered above mine in the semi-darkness, the silvery light of the TV screen illuminating one side of his face, leaving the other in shadow. "You won't?"

"No." He'd dipped his head, and his mouth was on my neck

now. He was *kissing my neck*. "I still think about it."

"Me too." I tried to swallow, but the touch of his lips on my throat seemed to have disabled the mechanism.

"Maybe we need a do-over." He left a trail of searing-hot kisses on my skin, clavicle to jaw. "We could give it a better ending."

"Dash," I whispered. Before I could say another word, his mouth was on mine. Warm and firm and salty from the French fries. His lips opened, and his tongue stole into my mouth. My heart thumped hard enough for him to feel it, like it wanted to escape my body and jump into his before I could snatch it back again. Was this really happening? I arched my back and struggled to free my hands so I could touch him, make sure he was real.

But he must have thought I was struggling to push him away, because he sprang back and popped to his feet as if someone had yanked him off me. "Sorry. Jesus. Did I hurt your hand?"

"No." I sat up, my pulse a jackhammer in my head, my body yearning for his weight again.

"Are you sure?"

"Yes." I tried to smile. An invitation. "I'm fine."

He looked away and ran a hand over his hair. "My brothers."

"Your brothers?" I frowned. "What about them?"

"They basically told me to behave around you."

"They did?"

He laughed, but it sounded forced. "Yeah. They don't trust me with you. Apparently for good reason."

"Dash, that's ridiculous."

"Anyway, I should get going." He grabbed his empty plate and beer bottle from the nearby tray table and made a beeline for the kitchen.

I sat there for a minute in the dark, seeing the kitchen light come on, hearing the faucet run. *Damn you, Buckley brothers. I'm not a kid.*

Sixteen-year-old me held up a hand. *Please. This is no one's fault but yours. You could have at least changed out of your sweatpants after painting.*

Disappointed, I grabbed my dishes and headed for the kitchen.

Dash was at the sink. "I'll load the dishwasher for you."

"Don't worry about it. I'll do it later. But let me give you some braised short ribs to take home for your dad."

"Okay." Dash backed off while I worked, standing all the way across the room. "He was looking forward to his chicken pot pie tonight. Good thing you sent two helpings because Xander ate one of them this afternoon."

"Did he like it?" I kept my face turned away from him so he couldn't see how flushed I was. How could he act so normal? I felt like I'd just been through an earthquake, like the ground was still shaky beneath my feet.

"He inhaled the entire thing in about three minutes, so I'd say yes."

"Good." After I pressed the lid onto the container, I set it on the table and then took our empty beer bottles out to the recycling bin on my back porch. When I returned to the kitchen, he was zipping up his hoodie.

"Thanks for dinner," he said.

Trying not to feel like I'd just been rejected a second time, I stayed about five feet from him. "You're welcome. Thanks for helping me paint the guest room—and for having my car fixed. I wish you'd let me pay you back."

He shook his head. "I don't want your money."

I nearly asked him what he *did* want. Instead, I grabbed his

SUV key fob from my purse and held it out. "This is yours."

"Thanks." He took it from me and toyed with it. "I promised Austin's kids I'd take them out for pizza tomorrow night."

"Sounds like fun." I wrapped my arms around myself.

"You could come along if you want."

"That's okay. You enjoy a night out with family."

"Okay." This time, he didn't say I was family too. "Then I guess I'll see you around."

The silence around us was thick and cold as chilled butter.

"Ari, I'm sorry again about—about what I did."

"Don't be."

"I…" He struggled for words. "I like being friends with you."

"I like being friends with you too."

"So are we good?"

I forced a close-lipped smile. "We're good."

He was out of the house before I could say another word.

. . .

Two days went by.

We didn't talk at all on Thursday, even though I thought of him every other minute and spent the evening alone, wishing I'd taken him up on his invitation to have pizza with Austin's family. Instead, I baked an apple pie—always the most popular dessert at Moe's—and tried to think of ways I could deconstruct it or play with the theme. A waffle? Some kind of crumble? Apple pie bread pudding?

But as I tasted it, trying to let the flavors inspire me, all I could think about was the taste of Dash's kiss.

On Friday, I left Moe's a little early and got my stitches out, and even though I still had a bandage on my finger, it was a relief to be able to use my hand a little more. As I got ready for my shift at the pub, I wondered if he'd stop in tonight.

Just in case, I left my hair curly, the way he liked it. I pulled on jeans that made my butt look cute. I wore lipstick and perfume and my best push-up bra beneath my fitted Buckley's Pub T-shirt.

All during my shift, I kept my eye on the pub's front door, anticipation rising with each passing hour.

By nine, my hopes plateaued.

At ten, they began to sink. I asked Xander in the most casual tone I could muster if he thought Dash was coming by tonight. I was only working until eleven because I had to open the diner in the morning.

"I'm not sure what he's doing," Xander said. "Earlier today he said he might, but he must have ended up somewhere else."

I nodded and went back to pouring beers and mixing cocktails, but the butterflies that had been fluttering in my stomach all night were gone. If he'd told Xander he might come up here, that meant he thought about it and decided against it. It meant he'd gotten a better offer. It meant he didn't care whether or not he saw me tonight.

Distraught, I turned on the tap and berated myself as the tall glass filled. Why was I still so hung up on Dashiel Buckley? What was it about him that got under my skin? Was it because I was lonely and he felt safe? Did I just want a hot famous guy to pay attention to me?

Maybe it was this fourteen-month dry spell. I hadn't been with anyone since I walked away from Niall, and sex was starting to feel like a distant memory. Not that it had ever been that good with Niall—he was as narcissistic in bed as he was everywhere else.

Dash would be so different.

He was generous.

He'd listen to me.

He'd talk to me.

He'd care.

Give it up, Ari. It's never going to happen. He just wants to be friends.

I finished up my shift and went home, falling into bed tired and cranky, determined to stop thinking of him like that once and for all.

And then he texted me.

Chapter 8

Dash

*W*hat? It was an innocent text.

At least, it was supposed to be.

I was just checking in with her. As a friend.

A friend who'd been thinking about her nonstop since I left her house two nights ago. A friend who'd forgotten his manners and kissed her. A friend who'd gotten himself off the last three nights in a row while fantasizing about her.

I told myself it was wrong. I told myself a guy shouldn't think about his friends that way. I even stayed away from the bar tonight because I'd been afraid that if I saw her, I might say something stupid like, *We should hang out later.* Or walk her out to her car at the end of the night and give her a hug. Put my tongue in her mouth. My hands on her ass. My ideas in her head.

I had dinner with my dad tonight, and we'd watched some

baseball before he snuck into his bedroom, where I heard him laughing behind the closed door.

Bored and frustrated, I searched for "Niall Hawke chef" on the internet. Scrolling through the results, I skimmed some articles and looked at photos. By all accounts, he was a difficult, temperamental perfectionist with a lot of talent I decided he didn't deserve. In every picture, he looked either angry or smug, but he definitely wasn't big. Satisfied I could definitely kick his ass if it came to it (and I truly hoped someday I'd have the chance), I ended up falling asleep on the couch. I woke up about midnight and dragged myself upstairs to bed.

But I still couldn't get her off my mind. I wondered if she'd gotten home from work yet. If she was still awake. If she was thinking about me.

After undressing and slipping between the sheets, I reached for my phone.

Hey.

Hey.

You home yet?

Yes.

How was work?

Fine.

Are you tired?

A little.

I frowned. Was she upset with me? Fucking hell, I shouldn't have kissed her. I was about to apologize again when she sent another text.

I thought maybe you'd come up to
the bar tonight.

I was going to.

Why didn't you?

I wasn't sure it was a good idea.

Why not?

I hesitated before replying but decided to be honest.

Because I would have
been coming to see you.

It took her a while to respond.

And that's a bad thing?

It could be. If we're
going to stay friends.

Because friends don't hang out
when one of them is working?

I exhaled, my thumbs hovering over the screen. I was either
about to blow this up or take it to the next level.

Because friends don't think
about each other the way
I think about you.

Seconds ticked by.

How do you think about me?

I am not sure I should
answer that question.

Answer it.

Next level it was.

Naked.

In bed with me.

Begging for my cock.

Why would I have to beg?

Because I'm not done fucking
you with my tongue.

Three dots fading in and out.
One erection surging to life beneath the covers.

Oh.

All that time for oh?

I wasn't sure how a friend
should reply to that.

A friend should tell me to fuck off
and never talk to me again.

So a friend shouldn't tell you she's
in bed. Or that she wishes you
were here.

Not if she knows
what's good for her.

What else wouldn't a friend do?

> A friend would not tell a friend
> to put her hand between her
> legs and touch herself the
> way he wants to touch her.

How is that?

> Slowly and softly. Like he's
> stroking her with his tongue.

She didn't reply, and my cock jumped as I imagined she was unable to type because she was doing what I said. But I had to make sure.

> Should I go on?

Please.

> Lick your fingers. Spread your legs.

My breath was coming faster now. My blood rushed hot and quick through my veins as I pictured her following my every command.

> Put your hand between your thighs.
> Rub your fingertips over your clit.

> Go slow.

> I would take my time.

> I want your pussy soaking
> wet for me.

I want to bury my face between
your thighs and devour you.

Dash

The taste of your pussy.
God. I can't get enough. So sweet.
Sugar on my tongue.

God

I want to make you come so hard.

Dash

I want to hear you say that.

And then it was Ari who took it up a level.

Call me.

I did as she asked without thinking.

"Say it again," she whispered instead of hello.

"I want to make you come so hard." I kept my voice low, my tone firm. "I want to bury my face between your legs and fuck that sweet little pussy with my tongue until you can't take it anymore."

"Oh, God." Her voice cracked softly. "Keep talking."

"You like hearing me say these things?"

"Yes."

My adrenaline surged as I pictured in vivid detail all the things I wanted to do to her. "Can you feel my fingers sliding inside you? Do you like it when I suck your clit? Do you want to come on my tongue?"

Her answers were little more than muffled sighs.

"God, the things I want to do to you…" I closed my eyes and imagined her body beneath me. The arch of her back. The smell of her skin. The softness of her thighs against my face and the grip of her hands in my hair. I slid one hand beneath the waistband of my sweatpants and fisted my cock. "I'm so fucking hard."

Her breathing was quick and heavy.

"I want to feel your pussy tighten around my fingers. I want your legs to shake. I want to hear you say my name."

"Dash—don't stop—"

"Come for me. Right now."

As her cries grew more intense and high-pitched, I stroked my cock and imagined her working herself into a frenzy while she thought about me.

"Oh my God. Dash." She was quieter now, her breath still audible but slowing down.

"Did you do what I said?"

"Yes."

"All of it?"

"Every single thing. You should know by now I can't say no to you."

My cock thickened in my fist. "Good girl. Are you wet?"

"Yes."

"God, I want to fuck you."

"That can wait. I want to make you come with my mouth."

My breath caught. "You want to suck my cock, you greedy little thing?"

She gasped, and for a second I was afraid I'd gone too far. But then…

"Yes," she said. "That's exactly what I want."

I shoved my underwear down my legs and kicked it off.

"Get on your knees for me, Sugar. Tell me exactly what you would do."

"I would take your cock in my hands. I want to feel how big it is. How hard it is." She paused. "I've thought about this before."

I groaned softly as I worked my hand up and down my erection. "You have?"

"Yes. I would lick you slowly. Tease you with my tongue. I would take just the tip in my mouth and suck it while I stroked you with my hands."

Goddamn, I could feel it. "More," I growled. "Take more of me."

"Shhhh," she scolded. "I would tell you to be patient. Then I would slide your cock between my lips and back out again, taking a little more each time, but never as much as you want me to."

I grimaced with frustration, as if I could actually feel her taunting me.

"When you were all worked up, I'd take you all the way in, so deep you hit the back of my throat. I'd use my hands. I'd suck you so hard." She lowered her breathy voice to a whisper. "I can taste you."

I groaned a little louder. Pumped my arm a little harder.

"You put your hands in my hair. You hold my head and fuck my mouth. I put my hand between my legs and touch myself while I think about how much I want to make you come."

"Ari," I choked out through clenched teeth. "Why are you so good at this?"

"Because I've thought about you like this so many times. You don't know how badly I want to feel you throb between my lips and taste you dripping down my throat."

"Jesus," I whispered. Then I was grunting as the orgasm surged through me, unfurling from the base of my spine in hot, rhythmic pulses. In the dark, I felt my hand grow slick.

When the muscles in my lower body relaxed, I opened my eyes. "One sec," I told her.

"Okay."

In the bathroom, I took a minute to clean up, my head spinning with the knowledge that Ari had just given me the most intense orgasm I've had in a long time, and she hadn't even been in the damn room.

Which was unfortunate. Because I'd be ready to go again in about twenty minutes and would have given anything to have her in bed beside me.

Was that allowed? What were we doing? Where could this go?

I crawled back into bed and picked up my phone. "Hey."

"Hi."

"I was just wondering. Are we still friends?"

"Why wouldn't we be?"

"I don't usually tell my friends to get on their knees and suck my cock."

"Sir! I don't know what you're talking about."

I laughed. "Never mind. I must have been mistaken."

"I should say so. This was simply a goodnight chat between friends."

"That was definitely my intention when I texted you."

"Was it really?"

I paused. "No."

"Good." She laughed softly, and it made me want to wrap my arms around her and breathe her in, feel her skin on mine. "Well, I'm working early. I should get some sleep."

"Maybe I'll come in for lunch."

"Do it. I have a new special for you to taste."

"There's only one thing I really want to taste."

"Goodnight, Dash."

"Night, Sugar."

. . .

I woke up the next morning to an empty house and a note from my dad on the kitchen table telling me he'd decided to take his little road trip, but instead of driving, he was flying down to visit a friend in Tennessee. Laughing, I took a picture of it and sent the shot to Xander.

I stepped out into the yard with the dog, and it was so nice out, I decided to go for a run. After changing into shorts and a T-shirt, I laced up my running shoes, put Fritz on the leash, and headed out. As I jogged the streets of the neighborhood where I'd grown up, I remembered different things from my childhood—the lemonade stand Devlin and I had on the corner (he was the CEO, I was the employee), the house that gave out the best Halloween candy (full-sized Snickers bars), the races my brothers and I used to run from one end of the block to the other (yes, I came in last. Every fucking time, because those assholes had never let the youngest win).

It really was a great place to grow up. If I had a family like my brother Austin, I'd live here. You had sun and the lake in the summer, you had snow and ski hills in the winter, and fall here was the prettiest season I'd ever seen anywhere. I could understand why Ari had wanted to come back.

I still couldn't believe what we'd done last night. When I opened my eyes this morning, the first thing I'd done was check my phone to make sure I hadn't dreamed the whole thing. But those texts were there, ending with *Call me.*

Then it wasn't just words on a screen. It was her voice in my ear. Every time I thought about the things she said, my body ignited.

Now that we'd broken this barrier, did that mean we could keep going? Would it be a mistake? Or just a great fucking time? I didn't want to mess with her feelings—Ari was always going to be part of my family, and the *last* thing I wanted to do was hurt or mislead her, creating an awkward situation for years to come.

But the *first* thing I wanted to do was get naked with her.

Could we enjoy some sort of friends-with-benefits arrangement while I was home? I'd never slept with anyone I'd known for so long or considered a close friend, so I wasn't sure how that worked.

When I got home, I took a shower, wrapped a towel around my hips, and checked my messages. Nothing from Izzie or Ari, but there was one from Devlin asking me to give him a call. I tapped his number.

"Hello?"

"Hey." I smiled at the sound of my brother's voice. "How's everything going?"

"Good. Busy. I hear you're in Cherry Tree Harbor."

"Yeah, I came home a little early to spend some time with Dad, although he hasn't been around much." I laughed. "I think his social life is busier than mine."

We took a few minutes to get caught up, and Devlin filled me in on finishing up the renovation at Snowberry. "It took a little longer than we expected to get it all done, but it was worth the wait."

"I'm excited to see it, and to meet your wife," I told him. "Although I still can't wrap my brain around the fact that you're married."

Devlin chuckled. "I know. Speaking of my wife, there's something we'd like to ask you."

"Name it."

"Since you're the best man, would you mind giving a toast at dinner after the ceremony?"

"I'd be honored," I said. "And I won't even mention all the times you said you'd rather eat dog shit than get married."

"Go ahead and mention it. Lexi loves that I was anti-marriage before her. She feels a huge sense of accomplishment."

I laughed. "She should. I never thought I'd see the day. But I'm happy for you."

"Thanks, brother. I can't wait to introduce you to her." Devlin's voice grew quiet and serious. "She's the best thing that's ever happened to me."

. . .

After Devlin and I hung up, I took advantage of having the house all to myself and wandered around naked for a while. I thought maybe it would show the universe or God or whatever higher power Delphine had access to that I'd taken her advice to heart.

Strolling from room to room, I looked at old photographs, watching myself change from a tow-headed toddler into a sandy-haired kid into a teenager who finally grew into his ears. I saw the way my older brothers grew up to resemble our dad and the way Mabel and I took after our mom.

I looked at the corner where we'd always put the Christmas tree. The window I'd broken when I accidentally threw a baseball through it. The couches where we all sat during family game nights. I smiled when I thought about the way we all used to accuse Mabel and Ari of cheating at Pictionary because they seemed to communicate in some kind of silent language. One of them would start scribbling, and it would take the other one less than five seconds to guess the correct answer, even though what had been drawn looked *nothing* like a pirate or a platypus or whatever the thing was supposed to be.

At one end of the living room were some built-in bookcases, and I spied my senior year high school yearbook on one shelf. I pulled it down and opened it up, the spine cracking. On the front flyleaf, a bunch of my friends had signed their names, and some (mostly girls) included little messages like *always stay sweet* or *have a great summer.* I flipped to the back, and Ari's name caught my eye.

Dash, thanks for always driving me and Mabel around and being like a big brother to me. Good luck in L.A. but don't forget about everyone back home. There is more I want to say but I can't. Maybe someday. Love, Ari DeLuca

She'd dotted the i in her name with a little heart.

I skimmed through the senior portraits in the front of the book—there I was in full color, wearing a suit and tie, hair freshly cut, grin confident. I'd been voted Most Talented, which was noted beneath my name. Then I skipped to the freshmen pictures, which were at the back and smaller, shown in black and white. Laughing a little at my sister with her crooked bangs and glasses, I scanned the next page and found Ariana DeLuca. Her curly hair was long, held off her face with a headband. Her eyes looked wide and her lashes were thick. She was smiling brightly, innocently, and I felt like the biggest pervert on the planet for—

"The fuck are you doing?"

I looked up to see my brother Xander standing in the doorway to the living room.

"Doesn't anybody knock around here?" I shielded my crotch with the yearbook.

"I have a key. Why would I knock?" He stuck his hands on his hips. "A better question is, why are you naked in the living room?"

"I'm getting more comfortable with my vulnerability," I said, like it was obvious.

"Well, I was coming by to see if you wanted to go get some lunch, but you'll have to put your vulnerability away."

"Why, is it making *your* vulnerability feel bad?"

Xander narrowed his eyes. "You wish."

. . .

Xander wanted to go to Moe's—he'd heard about the braised rib grilled cheese from our dad and hoped it would be on the specials menu—and I didn't argue.

The diner was full when we got there. While Xander gave his name to the hostess and told her we'd wait outside, I searched for Ari but didn't see her anywhere. Disappointed, I followed my brother out to the sidewalk.

While Xander checked his messages, I glanced at the poster taped inside Moe's front window advertising a spring carnival nearby. A quick look at the dates told me it was happening this weekend. Recalling what Ari had told me about carnival food, I wondered if there was any way I could surprise her with a quick trip either today or tomorrow.

Xander slipped his phone into his back pocket.

"Hey, is Ari working at the pub tonight?" I asked.

He nodded. "I think she starts at five. By the way, you didn't tell me you had her car fixed."

"Because it wasn't a big deal."

The sun was in his eyes, and he squinted at me, crossing his thick, tattooed forearms over his chest.

"You can quit with the bodyguard routine," I told him. "Ari doesn't need you to protect her from me. If you don't believe me, you can ask her."

"Relax, brother. I'm just curious about the situation." He shrugged. "I get bored when Kelly is gone."

"Where is she this week?" I asked.

"Texas. Then Phoenix and Salt Lake City. And the following week, she has a bunch of California shows."

"If she wants to stay at my house while she's there, she's welcome. I can give you the codes for the gate and the front door. Might be more comfortable than a hotel."

"You sure that's okay? I think she'd like that."

"Of course. Extend the offer."

"Thanks." He took his phone out again and started typing. "I wish I could fly out and surprise her."

"Do it."

"I can't. I'm taking time off for Devlin's wedding, and I shouldn't be away from the bar that much. I just won't see her for a couple more weeks, and it sucks."

"Is she coming to the wedding?"

He shook his head. "She can't. She doesn't have a public show that night, but she's got some kind of private appearance in L.A. the record label said she had to do."

"That sucks. The long-distance thing must be hard."

A shrug of his shoulders. "It isn't ideal, but music is her dream. And anything I can do to make her dreams come true, I'm going to do it—even if that's just making her feel okay about the separations."

"And it's worth it?"

He gave me a funny look as he put his phone away again. "Fuck yeah, it's worth it. I can't imagine my life without her. I don't want to."

His words made me think of what Devlin had said about Lexi being the best thing that ever happened to him. I wondered if maybe some kind of relationship gene had skipped over me. I've never had those feelings for anybody. Not even close.

"Buckley? Party of two?"

We turned toward the door, where the hostess, a high school girl, had stuck her head out and called our name. "That's us," Xander said.

Inside, she led us to a booth toward the back, and we slid in on opposite sides. Again, I looked around for Ari and didn't see her. After placing menus on our table, the hostess said our server would be over in a minute to tell us about the specials. Then she turned beet red and smiled at me. Her name tag said Kinsey. "Sorry to bother you, but I love *Malibu Splash*. Would it be okay to take a selfie?"

"Sure."

Kinsey pulled out her phone, aimed it at us from just the right angle, and snapped a couple shots. "Thanks," she said, still blushing furiously as she hurried back up front.

Our server, whose name tag said Gerilyn, came over a few minutes later and told us about the lunch specials—I recognized the chicken pot pie and the grilled cheese, but there was also a BLT on house-made sourdough served with truffle aioli.

"Braised short ribs grilled cheese, please," said Xander with obvious excitement.

"I'll try the BLT," I said. "Is Ari here by any chance?"

"She is," Gerilyn said, "but she's giving someone a tour of the diner right now and then they're doing an interview."

"Who is it?" I asked, sitting up straighter in the booth.

"I forget his name, but apparently, he's a pretty big-deal food writer. Evidently, he came in here one day earlier this week incognito and tried one of her specials." She grinned. "He said he couldn't stop thinking about it and showed up again this morning asking if he could interview her!"

"That's awesome." My chest filled with pride for Ari. "Was she excited?"

Gerilyn laughed. "She was freaking out."

"I can't wait to hear about it."

"I'll send her over when she's done. Now what can I get you guys to drink?"

• • •

While we waited for our sandwiches, I decided to get my brother's take on the friends-with-benefits situation. "Hey, can I ask you something?"

"Hang on." Xander was looking at his phone. "Kelly just texted back. She said she'd love to stay at your house and she's asking for your number so she can call you and get all the information."

"Great. Send her my contact info."

"Thanks." He tapped his screen a couple times and set his phone down again. "Now, what was it you wanted to ask me?"

I tried to sound casual, even though Xander would know in less than half a second why I was asking. "Have you ever had, like, a friends-with-benefits kind of arrangement with someone?"

"Nah." He leaned back in the booth, stretched one arm along the top. "Those things are a myth, like dragons or comfortable dress shoes."

"What makes you say that?"

"Because sooner or later, one of you starts to feel things. If you're so into someone that you want to sleep with them again and again, there's good chemistry there. And in my experience, it's impossible to keep that chemistry from changing things."

I considered that. "Even if you both agreed at the beginning it was all in fun and there were no strings attached?"

"Yes. Because somehow, strings get created. And people get attached."

I nodded, watching Ari appear from behind the counter and greet some people at a table up front. She looked so happy. Was it selfish of me to hope the light in her eyes had at least *something* to do with last night?

"Are you listening to me?"

Realizing Xander had said a few things I hadn't heard, I refocused on him. "Sorry. I got distracted for a second. I'm listening."

"Look, I'm not trying to tell you what to do," Xander said. "But let me tell you what *not* to do."

"Isn't that the same thing?"

My brother leaned forward and spoke quietly. "Don't sleep with Ari unless you're prepared for one or both of you to get attached."

"I won't," I said.

Sitting back again, Xander studied me shrewdly. "Yeah, you will. But at least I warned you."

A few minutes later, she made it back to our booth, her face glowing with excitement. Without hesitation, I jumped up and threw my arms around her, lifting her right off the ground. "I heard the news—congratulations!"

She clung to me, and I probably held her for a moment too long before setting her down. When she looked up at me, her expression was a mix of pride and rapture. "Dash," she said breathlessly. "This is the craziest thing."

"Do you have a minute to sit and tell us about it?"

"Maybe a couple," she said. When I slid into the booth again, she dropped down next to me and shook her head. "I still can't believe it."

"So who's the guy?" Xander asked. "A food critic?"

"His name is Hugo Martin," Ari said. "He's originally from New Orleans, and his restaurants have at least a dozen Michelin stars between them. He's written like five cookbooks, had a show on Culinary Central, and now he's considered a major food influencer—he's got millions of social media followers. He loves traveling around and finding out-of-the-way places with great food."

"How did he hear about Moe's?" I asked.

"He's got a cousin who bought a summer place up here, and he's in town visiting. He came in on Wednesday and didn't say anything, of course, so I had no idea who I was serving!"

"It's probably better that you didn't."

"Totally. I'd have been so nervous." Ari laughed. "I probably would have hidden in the kitchen."

I smiled at her flushed cheeks. "So he came back today to meet you?"

"Yes. Well, first he ate," she said with a grin. "I thought it was kind of weird that he was sitting alone at the counter and ordered two lunch specials, but after he introduced himself, it made sense."

"What did he order?"

"The chicken pot pie and the grilled cheese."

"And he loved them?"

She nodded, her eyes bright with happiness. "He loved them. Or at least he said he did."

"How did the interview go?" Xander asked.

"Great. He said he's going to write something up and post it in the next couple weeks." She shook her head. "I still can't believe it. It just goes to show you never know what opportunity might be around the corner. One moment can change everything."

Beneath the table, I found her hand and squeezed it.

Chapter 9

Ari

*A*ll day, I felt like I was floating.

First there was the insane thing with Dash that happened last night on the phone. From the second we hung up, I'd been on cloud nine. All through the night, I'd wake up and check my phone, just to see those text messages again.

Naked.

In bed with me.

Begging for my cock.

Every single time, my toes would curl beneath the covers. And when I got to the part where he'd told me to touch myself like he wanted to touch me, my insides whooshed all over again. I'd done everything he'd told me to. I wanted to please him, even if he wasn't there.

Then he'd called me—good God. That low, sexy voice right in my ear saying all those filthy things, telling me he was hard, instructing me. I'd never been so turned on in my life. The orgasm I'd given myself with his encouragement had been better than any I'd ever experienced. It had loosened up all my inhibitions and my tongue, and I heard myself saying things to him I'd never said to anyone. Describing my hottest fantasy about him. Telling him every little thing I'd do.

I still couldn't believe I'd had the nerve. I wasn't exactly shy, but I'd never been bold enough with anyone else to talk that way. Dash just did something to me.

Was he ever going to do it in person?

Focus, Ari, I told myself, reaching for the coffee pot. *Don't get lost in dreams right now.*

But as if that wasn't enough, having Hugo Martin eat something I created and say it was a marvel of flavor and texture also had me pinching myself.

When the gentleman sitting alone at the counter told me his name, my knees had trembled. He'd looked a little familiar, but my head was in the clouds, and I figured he was just a local I'd seen before. Once he took off his hat and met my eyes, I recognized him.

Right away I glanced at the two specials I'd brought him, noting they were both only about one-third eaten. I wasn't sure what that meant—had he liked them? Found them delicious and inspired? Or, like Niall, would he be unimpressed with my efforts and deem them mundane and unsophisticated?

"I hear you're the creative mind at Moe's Diner," he said. He was in his fifties and spoke with a gruff but kindly tone.

"Yes." My voice came out high-pitched and squeaky, so I

took a breath and tried again. "My name is Ari DeLuca."

"A pleasure to meet you, Ms. DeLuca," he said with a genuine smile. "I have thoroughly enjoyed everything I've eaten here. Classic comfort food with a dash of elegance. Bravo."

I gasped and put my hands to my cheeks. "Thank you so much! I wish my parents were here. They own the diner, and it's been in my dad's family for generations."

"That's what I heard. I love a family-run restaurant off the beaten path. Will they be around tomorrow? I'm in town one more day."

"No. They're on a cruise for their thirtieth anniversary," I explained.

"Well, maybe I could do a quick interview with you while I'm here and then get a few quotes from them via email. How does that sound?"

"Great," I said. "Would you like a little tour of the place? When we're done, I'll get you an email address for my mom and dad."

"Perfect." He put his hat back on his head and came around the counter. "Lead the way."

• • •

After showing him around the kitchen, we used the office for a quick interview, which he recorded on his phone. We exchanged contact information, and he took a few photos, which made me wish I'd paid more attention to my appearance this morning. I'd been in a complete Dash-induced daze.

When Hugo left, he thanked me again for a wonderful meal and promised to be in touch. I was catching my breath in the kitchen when Gerilyn came in and told me Dashiel and Xander Buckley were seated at table eight. With my heart singing and my feet barely feeling the ground beneath them, I raced out into the restaurant, as excited to see Dash as I was to tell someone about the news.

And the really crazy thing? He seemed just as excited to see me. He jumped out of the booth where he was sitting and scooped me up in his arms. Then he invited me to sit for a minute and tell him and Xander about Hugo Martin. While I was talking, he grabbed my hand beneath the table, and when I got up to leave, he suggested we do something to celebrate my big day.

"Let me take you to dinner," he said.

My heart thumped hard. "That's really sweet, but I can't. I have to be at the pub at five."

"You can come in a little later," Xander offered.

"Are you sure? I hate to leave you short-staffed."

"I'm sure." He waved a hand. "Go celebrate. Make Dash spend some of his Bulge Bucks on you."

I laughed. "Thanks, Xander. I'll be there by seven, I promise."

"What time are you done here?" Dash asked.

"I should be home by three."

"I'll pick you up at four."

"For dinner?" I laughed. "Are we getting an early bird special?"

"No, but that's all I'm going to tell you." Under the table, Dash put a hand on my leg. "I'll see you later."

Reluctantly, I slid out of the booth and went back to work, fully aware that this was the most magical day of my life.

And it wasn't even half over.

• • •

"So where are we going?" I asked as Dash backed out of my driveway.

"It's a surprise."

"Dash!" I laughed. "What if I'm not dressed right?"

He glanced at my work clothes—black pants and Buckley's Pub top (worn with push-up bra). "You look perfect in everything."

My whole body tingled. "Thank you. But you better not be taking me anywhere fancy."

"I'm wearing jeans and a flannel, Ari. I haven't trimmed my beard in over a week. We are not going anywhere fancy."

Actually, I didn't care where we were going. Dashiel Buckley had picked me up in his car and we were going somewhere together that was not the E.R. Everything about this was amazing.

"So my dad took off on a mysterious road trip," he said.

"Oh yeah? To see Julia?"

"That's what Xander and I assume. His note mentioned visiting a *friend* in Tennessee."

"Sweet old George. I hope he has fun."

"Me too. But I hope he realizes he can tell us what's going on. We'd all be happy for him."

"He might just need a little more time to come to terms with it himself, you know?"

"Yeah," Dash said slowly. "That's a good point."

"He's been alone a long time, and probably not because he wanted to be. He did it out of respect and love for your mom. And getting beyond the past can take a lot of emotional work."

"True." He glanced over at me. "And speaking of the past."

"Oh, God. What?"

"I found my senior year high school yearbook this morning."

Covering my face, I groaned. "Don't tell me. I wrote something embarrassing in it."

"It wasn't embarrassing. It was sweet. I don't remember ever seeing it before."

"That is because you paid *zero* attention to me in those days, Dash. Meanwhile, I had the crush of the century on you." Sighing, I shook my head, dropping my hands into my lap. "So what did I write?"

"You thanked me for being like a big brother. You wished me luck in L.A. and told me not to forget anyone back home."

I laughed and pointed to my chest. "Meaning me."

"And you wrote you had more to tell me but you couldn't. Maybe someday, you said."

"Maybe someday I will appear in your bedroom and offer myself up as a parting gift," I joked. "But you will not want this gift, so perhaps you should start locking your bedroom door."

"Are you kidding? Of course, I *wanted* the gift. You were sixteen and hot as fuck."

"What!" I shrieked. "You said you thought of me like a little sister and didn't have those feelings for me!"

"Ari, you weren't even legal," he pointed out. "You'd never had sex before. We were in my *dad's* house, and my *sister* was sleeping down the hall. Believe me, I tried to reason away all those things, but I couldn't do it. I couldn't be that guy." He glanced at me. "No matter how much I wanted to."

"I guess that makes me feel a little better," I said, the past rearranging itself slightly in my head. "I was convinced you turned me down because I wasn't pretty or sexy enough for you."

"I was just trying to be a good guy."

"Your dad raised you right, Dashiel Buckley." Grinning, I reached over and patted his leg. "I should really take those devil horns off your headshot."

"After last night, maybe you should leave them." Then he reached for the volume on the stereo and turned it up.

• • •

Fifteen minutes later, we were still in the middle of nowhere. "Where on earth are we going to dinner around here?" I asked when Dash turned off the highway.

He smiled. "Your first clue is coming up."

That's when I spotted the Ferris wheel. As we got closer, I saw a Superloop and Zipper against the blue sky. Then a sign for the Spring Carnival appeared, directing cars to turn right for parking. When Dash turned right, I clapped my hands. "Are we going to the carnival?"

"I wanted you to have your favorites today. Funnel cakes and corn dogs, right?"

"Don't forget deep-fried junk food on a stick," I said gleefully. "This is a perfect way to celebrate. Thank you!"

Dash paid for parking and we found a spot. After we got out of the car, he tugged a baseball cap on his head and slipped on a pair of sunglasses, making himself less recognizable. And while part of me liked the idea that people would see us together and look at me with envy—*if Dashiel Buckley likes her, she must be someone*—another part wanted him all to myself.

We walked across the matted grass and weeds toward the fairgrounds. "I didn't think about getting dirty," he said, looking at the dust already collecting on my black pants. "Is this okay?"

"Are you kidding? I don't care about a little dirt." I inhaled the scent of fried dough, grilled hot dogs, and fresh popcorn. Music from the carousel drifted toward us, punctuated by screams from riders on the Superloop or Zipper. Colorful neon signs and strings of party lights glowed in the afternoon sun. I twirled in circles, arms out, face to the sky. "This is the best day ever!"

He laughed at my exuberance. "I'm glad."

After Dash bought us wristbands, we decided to hit all the thrill rides first. He was recognized every time we waited in line and sometimes as we walked from one attraction to the next, gamely posing for selfies and signing everything from phone cases to popcorn boxes. After about an hour, we wandered over to the food stands and got some dinner—cheesesteak for Dash and a corn dog for me, a basket of fried pickles to share, and a couple cans of Vernor's. We carried everything over to a picnic table inside the tent and managed to eat without being approached by fans.

"You know what you should do?" he asked, cracking open his ginger ale.

"What?" I popped a fried pickle in my mouth, savoring its salty crisp outside and firm, tangy inside.

"A food truck. You could do catering for parties, special events, weddings, street fairs—anything."

"I've thought about it. It won't work." I ate another fried pickle.

"Why not?"

"It's a huge investment up front and no guarantee it will pay off."

"Have you even looked into it?"

I opened my ginger ale. "Not in detail."

"You could even keep it connected to Moe's, but do different things." He took a bite of his sandwich. "Moe's on the Go."

"My parents would never go for it, Dash. They wouldn't understand the appeal. And they'd see it as a distraction from the 'real Moe's.'" I made little air quotes with my fingers.

"You could teach them about the concept. How food trucks are the new shiny thing."

"They hate new shiny things," I reminded him. "Plus, food trucks are like fifty grand at a minimum. I don't have fifty grand."

He shrugged. "Maybe I do."

"*No.*" I dipped my corn dog in mustard. "Don't even think about it."

"Why not?"

"Are you serious?" I took a bite and studied him incredulously. "Anyone would tell you loaning that kind of money to a friend to start a business is a terrible idea."

"Anyone?" He turned around and tapped the shoulder of a woman behind him. "Excuse me."

The woman, who might have been about my mom's age, turned around, her expression slightly annoyed. However, when she saw Dash's handsome face, she brightened up. "Yes?"

"I wonder if you could help me settle a little argument I'm having with my friend here." He gestured at me. "Do you think it's a bad idea to invest in a friend's business?"

"What kind of business?" the woman asked.

"A food truck."

"What kind of food truck?"

"Diner food, but a step up. What do you call it again, Ari?"

"Elevated comfort food," I said, giving him a murderous look.

He smiled. "That's right. Elevated comfort food."

The woman looked thoughtful. "Like gourmet sliders or something?"

"Exactly." Dash snapped his fingers. "And fancy grilled cheese sandwiches made with braised short ribs. Truffle fries. Craft milkshakes. Things like that."

The woman's eyes grew wide. "That sounds amazing. I think it would be a good investment."

"Thank you." Dash sent me a triumphant look before turning his charm on the woman again. "What's your name?"

"Lisa."

"Thank you, Lisa. You've been a big help."

Lisa looked like she'd just been handed a check for a million dollars. "You're welcome."

Facing me again, he picked up his cheesesteak. "So it's settled? You'll let me invest in your food truck?"

Laughing, I shook my head. "I don't have a food truck. But I appreciate your confidence in me."

"It's not just me, Ari. Look how you impressed that food influencer. Look at your parents' faith in you. Look at your training and your experience and your feel for Cherry Tree Harbor. You *know* what people like."

I ate silently for a moment, Niall's voice creeping into my head, dripping derision and scorn. "But I also know other things—like what it feels like to go after something and fall short of expectations."

"Will you at least talk to your parents about it?"

"No."

"Then I'm not telling you where the mustard is on your face."

Embarrassed, I shielded my face with my hands. "Dash! Tell me!"

"Your chin," he said, laughing. Then he grabbed a paper napkin, reached across the table, and swiped at my jaw. "There. It's gone."

"Thank you." But I picked up another napkin and wiped my face a second time.

"You don't trust me?"

"I trust you. Mostly."

He grinned and sat back in his chair. "Then you should listen to me. Give this food truck idea some thought, okay? That's all I'm asking."

"Fine," I said, mostly to change the subject. "I will."

When we were done eating, Dash bought me a funnel cake, which I nibbled on as we wandered from one game booth to another. He did his best to win me a prize while I cheered him on, and eventually, he succeeded at some kind of bean bag-toss Tic-Tac-Toe challenge—I ended up walking away with a giant stuffed bear.

"What are you going to call him?" Dash asked as I hugged him tight.

"Bulge, of course."

He groaned. "Of course."

I checked the time on my phone. "I hate to say this, but we should probably head back. It's already going on seven."

"Xander said there was no rush."

"I know, but I still need to grab my car, and I should probably change my shirt." I glanced down at my chest. "I got powdered sugar all over it."

"It suits you," he said with a grin. "But sure. We can head out. Maybe I'll come sit at the bar while you're working tonight."

I smiled. "That would be fun."

As we started walking toward the parking lot, he slipped his hand into mine. With the bear he'd won tucked under my left arm and the fingers of my right hand laced with his, I tipped my head against his shoulder for a moment. At that moment, I wasn't even sure my *wedding day* would compare to this one.

I wished it never had to end.

• • •

I watched the carnival lights grow blurry in the sideview mirror as we left them behind. "Thank you so much for celebrating with me today," I said. "That was so much fun."

"You deserve to be celebrated." He was silent for a moment, his eyes on the road. "And speaking of fun."

"Yes?"

"Last night."

My heart skipped like a flat stone over a still lake. "You had fun last night?"

"Fuck yeah, I did."

"What did you do?" I studied his handsome profile, an amused smile on my face.

His mouth twitched as he glanced my way. "I was texting with this girl I know, and things got kind of hot."

"Really?" I rested my elbow on my stomach and my chin on my knuckles. "Tell me about it."

"Well, it's a little tricky, because this girl, I've known her forever. She's my little sister's best friend, and she's my friend too. But last night, I said some things to her that were borderline inappropriate."

"Borderline inappropriate, oh dear."

"I told her I think about her naked."

"My, my."

"I believe I mentioned wanting to hear her beg for my cock."

I feigned clutching my pearls. "Heavens to Betsy!"

"And I *may* have let something slip about wanting to fuck her with my tongue."

"Hmm. Well." My blood was simmering. "Yes, I can see where that might have muddied the waters of friendship a bit."

"Well, that's only the first part of it." He reached over and put his hand on my thigh, sliding it toward my crotch as he spoke.

"Then I told her to lick her fingers and spread her legs. I told her to touch herself. Right here." He rubbed me through my pants, sending that simmer toward a roiling boil. "I told her I wanted to make her come."

I could barely breathe. "And what did she say?"

"She told me to call her."

"Did you do it?"

"Yes. That's where things got really crazy." His fingertips were moving in slow circles that had my legs tingling.

I glanced out the window, thankful we were alone on this stretch of highway. "Crazy how?"

"I told her all these things I wanted to do to her. And she told me things she wanted to do to me."

"Did she? Like what?" One of my hands gripped the edge of my seat. The other was flattened against the center console.

"She said she wanted to make me come with her mouth. She wanted to taste me dripping down her throat."

"Oh," I managed. Speaking was becoming a bit of a problem.

"It surprised me." Dash took his hand away, and I closed my legs and pressed my hands between my knees. "I don't really know her like that."

"Do you want to?"

"Of course I want to. I'd like to take her home right now and learn everything about her. The way she tastes. The way she sounds. The way she moves." He exhaled. "But I can't."

"Why?"

"Number one, she'd get fired from her job, and it would be all my fault. Number two, it might ruin our new friendship, which is not a thing I want to do. Number three, I'm supposed to be here in Cherry Tree Harbor working on myself, so the universe will think I'm worthy of its gifts. I'm not sure abducting my sister's best friend so I can fuck her with my tongue will help to purify my soul."

Arousal fluttered between my legs, and I squeezed my thighs together, craving the pressure. "Probably not."

"I mean, it would be fun, don't get me wrong. But there's definitely a cost."

"Several costs," I said. "Her job, your friendship, the purity of your soul. It's all at risk."

"True." He glanced at me, his mouth curving into a grin that made me want to tell him to pull over and climb into the backseat so we could ruin our friendship here and now, hard and fast. "Although I am not feeling particularly pure right now."

"No?"

"No." His eyes were on the road again. "I want to do very bad things to you, Sugar."

My core muscles contracted involuntarily. "Dash."

"Hm?"

"Better not come up to the bar tonight."

"You trying to get rid of me?"

"I'm trying to save your soul."

Chapter 10

DASH

I dropped Ari off at her house and watched her hurry inside. The urge to follow her had my hands gripping the wheel hard, but I knew she was already late for work, and if I went into that house, she wasn't leaving again until I got my fill.

Which would take a while.

Back at the house, I let Fritz out, refilled his food and water, and pondered what to do with myself the rest of the night. What I wanted to do was go sit at the bar at Buckley's Pub and flirt with Ari. Make her laugh. Drive her a little crazy. Take her home at the end of the night.

Would it have terrible consequences?

I loved how things were and didn't want them to change. I just wanted to see her lips around my cock. Fuck her ten different ways. Ruin her for all other men.

I squeezed my eyes shut. I was not a good person.

In an effort to cool off a little, I shot a quick text to Austin, thinking maybe I'd go hang out at his place for a while. Get my mind off Ari. Play video games with the twins. Have a beer with my oldest brother and talk shit about Xander. But Austin replied that they'd taken the kids to a movie and wouldn't be back until later.

Flopping onto the couch, I sent a message to my dad asking if he arrived at his friend's house okay. A few minutes later, I got a message in return.

Hi Dash, it's Dad.

I had to laugh. We'd told him many times he didn't need to identify himself when texting one of us, but he did it every time.

I arrived safe and sound. I hope
you had a good day. Say hi to Fritz
for me. I'll be home on Tuesday.
Love, Dad

Shaking my head, I told him to have a good time and Fritz said hello back. I debated giving Mabel a call, but given her close relationship with Ari, I didn't really want to talk to my sister right now. But the longer I sat here in this quiet, empty house, the more anxious I got.

My phone buzzed again, and I expected another message from my dad, but it was from an unknown number.

Hi Dash, it's Kelly.
Are you with Xander?

Hey, Kelly.
Nope, he's at work. I'm home.

Great. Can I call you?

                                        Of course.

I had just enough time to save her contact info before the call came in.

"Hello?"

"Hi, Dash. How are you?"

"I'm good. How's the tour?"

"It's going well. A lot of work, and I'm exhausted, but shows are packed and the energy is great."

"That's awesome. And I'm glad it will work out with the house."

"That's why I'm calling. I don't really have a private appearance in L.A. the night of the wedding. I'm flying to Michigan so I can come, but it's a surprise for Xander."

"No shit!" I smiled. "He's gonna love that."

She laughed. "He better. Anyway, I just wanted to let you know, and to say thank you for the generous offer."

"No problem. So what day do you get in?"

"Thursday. Then I'll drive up to the wedding with you all on Friday."

"Do you need a ride from the airport?"

"Transportation is all arranged, but thanks. God, I'm so looking forward to a couple days off. And I love Cherry Tree Harbor. I miss it when I'm gone—it's so quiet and peaceful and charming. It already feels like home to me." She laughed. "Plus, Xander is there."

"He's definitely here," I said, remembering his stern words for me across the table. "But I won't say a word about the surprise. I'll tell him we connected about you staying at the house."

"Thanks, Dash. I appreciate it. And I'll see you in a couple weeks!"

"See you, Kelly. Take care."

Bored again, I scrolled through some mindless bullshit on my phone. I turned on the TV and flipped through the channels. I wandered into the kitchen and opened the fridge, but I wasn't hungry. When I shut the door, I saw a Moe's Diner magnet. I pictured Ari behind the bar in one of those tight black Buckley's Pub shirts that showed off her tits. Smiling as she poured drinks and made every guy there want her.

But she wanted *me*, didn't she?

Xander's advice was knocking around in my head like a pinball. *If you're so into someone that you want to sleep with them, there's good chemistry there. And in my experience, it's impossible to keep that chemistry from changing things.*

Was he right? Was a successful friends-with-benefits situation merely a myth? Xander *had* been known to talk out of his ass.

Then I remembered something else.

He'd said not to sleep with the friend *again and again*, right? Because that's where the trouble was. If you kept doing it.

Doing it just *once* on the other hand...that would be different.

Once was casual. Once was fun. Once would not create strings or attachments or unrealistic expectations. As long as both parties were in agreement that the show had a limited run, there wouldn't be any issues. Strings were not formed in one night.

Maybe *once* was the answer.

Once will never be enough.

"Fuck it," I said.

I grabbed my keys.

• • •

She arrived home at ten-thirty.

Parked across from her house, I saw her turn onto her street and watched her car disappear up the driveway. After giving her a couple minutes to get inside, I knocked on her front door.

When she opened it, she wore her work clothes and a smile. "Hi."

"You shouldn't open your door so late at night without asking who it is first."

"I knew it was you."

"How?"

"I saw your car parked across the street, stalker." She nodded in that direction. "Have you been sitting there all night?"

"Maybe."

"Doing what?"

"Thinking things through," I said, stepping into her house and shutting the door behind me.

"What things?"

I started moving toward her, forcing her to walk backward into the living room. "Delphine never said I had to be *alone* when I stripped down to my purest self. She just said I had to get more comfortable being vulnerable."

"Interesting."

I unzipped my hoodie and worked it off, dropping it on the floor. "And is there a more vulnerable act than sex?"

Her back hit the opposite wall, and she flattened herself against it. "I can't think of one."

"Me neither." I braced my hands above each of her shoulders. "I mean, you're literally laying yourself bare in front of someone."

"Yes." Her voice was a whisper.

"Asking them to fulfill your deepest desires."

She licked her lips. "Yes."

"Telling them exactly what you want to do to them. Or what you want them to do to you." Bending my arms at the elbow, I pressed closer to her, letting my lips brush hers as I spoke. "Maybe even begging for it."

She bunched a hand in the front of my shirt. "Yes."

"It's still a risk, of course." I put a hand on the curve of her waist, moved it up her ribcage until it covered one lush, round breast. My cock surged, bulging against my fly. "Such an extreme act of vulnerability might cause damage to a friendship."

"I—I don't think it has to," she stammered as I moved my mouth down her throat, teasing her pert nipple with my thumb through the thin, stretchy material.

"I don't either." I slipped my hand beneath her shirt and unhooked her bra with an easy flick of my fingers. "Especially if it only happens once."

"I agree." Her hands moved to the button on my jeans. "It might even make our friendship better."

"We can finally put the past to rest." I slid both hands up her shirt, beneath her bra, filling my palms with her perfect tits.

"The past is *very* tired," she murmured, dragging down my zipper. "Let's send it to bed."

I picked my head up and looked down at her. "You're sure?"

She slipped a hand inside my pants and curled her fingers around my cock. "Yes."

Our mouths came together, greedy and demanding. Head slanted, lips open wide, I stroked her tongue with mine, reveling in the sweetness of her taste, the sound of the soft little moans coming from the back of her throat, the points of her nipples beneath the pads of my thumbs. My cock thickened inside her grasp as she worked her fist up and down.

Desperate to get my mouth on her skin, I yanked her shirt

over her head and tossed it aside. She dropped the bra from her arms and I whipped off my shirt before slipping my hands beneath her ass and lifting her up. With her back against the wall, she wrapped her legs around my waist and cradled my head in her hands as I feasted on one breast and then the other. Threading her fingers into my hair, she panted as I licked and sucked, swirling my tongue around each stiff peak before drawing it into my mouth. Her thighs tightened around me.

"Dash," she whispered, her hands closing into fists, making my scalp tingle. "My bedroom. Now."

No argument here—this time I wasn't stopping. I carried her into her room and tipped her backward onto the bed, those dark curls spilling onto the white sheets.

"I forgot to make my bed," she said sheepishly.

"Don't care." I yanked off her shoes. Peeled off her jeans and her socks. When she wore only a tiny pair of black panties, I stopped with one knee on the bed and stared at her. Her skin appeared golden and luminous in the soft glow of her bedside lamp. "Fuck, you're beautiful."

"I'm not." She put her hands on her head. "I've been working all night. I look awful."

"You're even more beautiful than you were at sixteen. And much sexier." I ran a hand up the inside of one leg from her calf to the apex of her thighs. Caressed her through the warm, damp lace, sliding the length of my index finger along the seam of her pussy. "Did you really do all the things I asked you to last night?"

"Yes."

"Show me."

"Show you?"

"Yes. With your hand. Your fingers."

She took an adorably deep breath, like she was working

up her courage. Her hand slid down her stomach but hovered just below her belly button. "I don't think I can do it with you watching."

"Not even if you know how hot it makes me?" I took her by the wrist and moved her hand lower, slipping her fingers beneath the edge of the lace. "Let me watch you." When she began to move her fingers in a circular motion, I groaned with appreciation, my hand instinctively reaching into my pants to fist my cock. "That's it. You're so fucking hot."

Bending her knees, she brought her heels to the mattress and lifted her hips slightly. My eyes nearly popped from my head when she brought her free hand to her chest and played with one dark pink nipple, rolling it between her fingers.

"Fuck yes." After a few strokes, I took my hand from my pants and edged her panties aside. Eased one finger inside her, and then another. She was hot and soft and snug, and my cock ached with jealousy. "You're so wet. I can't wait to get inside you. Feel this tight little cunt on my cock."

She gasped, like my words had shocked her. But I could tell she liked them, because her fingers moved faster over her clit. Her pussy got even more slick on my fingers.

"But first, I need to taste you." I moved from the bed to the floor and dropped to my knees, hooking my arms around her thighs to drag her closer to the edge of the mattress. From there I tugged her soaked panties over her knees and off her feet before slinging her legs over my shoulders.

"Oh, God," she said weakly. "I'm feeling very...vulnerable."

I lowered my head between her thighs and breathed in the sultry, seductive scent of her. Dragged my tongue up the center of her pussy in one long, decadent stroke. Lingered at the top, teasing her clit, which was swollen from her touch. "You taste so fucking sweet," I told her. "I could eat this meal every night."

"Dash." She slid one hand into my hair. "That feels—so good. Even better than my fantasies."

I loved that she'd fantasized about my mouth on her. I wanted to be the best she ever had. I buried my face between her thighs, fucking her with my tongue, making her writhe and moan and pant above me. I slid my fingers inside her again, as far as they'd go, sucking her clit while her insides tightened around my hand. When her hips began to buck with abandon, I prayed to God I'd found the secret little spot that would make her lose control.

She tightened her hand in my hair. Added the second. "Oh, God. Don't stop."

Stopping hadn't even entered my mind, because as soon as I made her come with my tongue, I was going to make her come again with my cock, which was about to explode in my pants. I'd already decided *just once* did not apply to her orgasms. The legs over my shoulders pulled me closer, and her noises grew more high-pitched and frantic until her body was spasming around my hand and her clit was beating a delicious little rhythm on my tongue.

"Dashiel," she panted. "That was—I can't even—oh my God." One leg slipped off my shoulder. "I want—I need—"

Rising to my feet, I shucked off my jeans and boxers and wrapped my hand around my aching cock. "What do you want? What do you need? I'll do it all."

She propped herself up on her elbows and watched me, her breath fast and heavy. "I want you to fuck me. I need you inside me."

Before I got carried away and did something stupid, I felt around on the rug for my jeans and pulled my wallet from my pocket. I'd stuck two condoms in there before I left the house—

pilfered from a box I'd found in the bathroom cupboard that Xander must have left behind.

I owed that asshole a favor.

I was about to tear the wrapper when she sat all the way up and reached for it. "Let me," she said. "I want to."

But that's not what she did. After taking the condom from me, she set it on the bed beside her and wrapped both hands around my erection. Hooked her heels around the backs of my calves and pulled me closer. "But first," she said, swirling her tongue around the tip of my cock. "I want to hear you tell me I'm a good girl."

I sucked in my breath. My abs tightened, and my thigh muscles clenched. "Yeah?"

"Yes." She looked up at me with wide, dark eyes. "Just like last night."

I inhaled and exhaled slowly, struggling for control as she did to me exactly what she'd described on the phone—licking me slowly. Sucking just the tip while her hands worked up and down my shaft. Teasing me.

"More." My hands curled into fists at my sides. "Take more."

She eased her mouth down about another inch and then backed off again. "You're so big," she murmured. "So thick. I don't know how much more I can take."

"Try."

Lowering her head once more, she stopped with her lips about halfway down, sucked greedily for a moment, then pulled me from her mouth and looked up at me. "Like that?" Her tone was sweet and innocent. Her thighs open wide. Her pussy drenched.

Every muscle in my body was twitching with need.

"More," I growled.

She bobbed her head a few times, taking more of me past her lips with each stroke, but never all the way.

"Ari." My jaw clenched. "Take it all."

She obeyed me, sliding her mouth all the way down my cock until I felt myself at the back of her throat. Groaning, I put my hands in her hair, keeping it out of her face as she sucked me hard and deep, like she couldn't get enough. Instinctively, my hips thrust toward her hot, wet mouth. She moved one hand to my ass and grabbed on, her nails digging into my skin.

"Fuck," I choked out, barely able to speak as I watched my cock pump in and out of her gorgeous lips. "You're such a good girl."

From the back of her throat came a strangled sound of delight, of need, of gratitude—which drove me even closer to climax. But I didn't want this to end, not without getting inside her. Taking her by the shoulders, I pushed her back, pulling out of her mouth.

"What's wrong?" she asked breathlessly, wiping the lower half of her face with the back of a hand, which turned me on even more.

"Nothing." I held her at arm's length. "But you keep doing that, you're going to make me come."

"That's the idea," she said, trying to get her hands on me again.

"Stop." I spied the condom by her hip and picked it up. Tearing it open, I worked it onto my cock before she could talk me out of it. "A good girl does what she's told."

A smile snuck onto her lips, and she leaned back on her elbows. "So tell me. What is it you want me to do?"

Slipping an arm behind her knees and another around her back, I lifted her up and set her down lengthwise on the bed.

Then I stretched out on top of her, settling my hips between her thighs. "I want you to let me make up for saying no eight years ago," I said, easing my cock inside her, inch by inch. I fucking loved how wet she was for me. "I want you to wrap your legs around me, take me in deep. I want you to say my name and beg me to fuck you harder. I want you to leave claw marks on my back and come all over my cock. Can you do that?"

"Yes," she breathed, eyes closing as I filled her, stretched her.

I put my lips at her ear. "Good girl."

Chapter 11

ARI

*C*ould this actually be happening?

Was Dashiel Buckley really in my bed right now? His words in my ear? His hands on my skin? His hips moving over mine in the dark?

Like the rest of this day, it felt like a dream.

But when I inhaled, it was his scent. When his lips seared mine with a kiss, it was his taste. When I ran my hands over his shoulders and down his back, grabbing his ass as he rocked into me, steady and deep—it was his body.

His cock was hard for *me*.

I was beyond giddy with it. I had already made up my mind I would not *think* about any of this. I would not obsess over what it meant, I would not look ahead to the future, I would not read anything into what we did here tonight. I would just enjoy it.

Knowing this was a one-time-only thing, I wanted to savor every sound, revel in every texture. The ragged breaths. The hot smooth skin. The flexing muscles. The rub of his scruffy jaw on my chin. The sensation of his cock gliding in and out of me. I ran my fingers through his hair, kissed him with feverish longing, lifted my hips to match his slow, sinuous rhythm.

But my desire was greedy, and eventually my patience wore thin. My body craved more heat, more friction, more pressure, more *him*. My muscles and bones were knotted with tension and desperately needed to unravel. I twined my legs around his, digging my heels into the backs of his thighs. "Dash," I sighed against his lips. "Fuck me harder. Give me more."

"You want more, Sugar?" He drove into me with one powerful, hard stroke, burying himself so deep I gasped. "Is that what you asked for?"

I couldn't talk. I might have squealed. He plunged into me roughly several more times, and I closed my eyes as my body absorbed the impact, as the pain mingled with the pleasure. Then he slid all the way home and stayed there for a moment, angling his hips a little differently and thrusting faster, rubbing my clit with the base of his cock.

"Yes," I whimpered, opening wider, raking my nails across his back. "Yes. Dash—*yes*." Every nerve ending in my body was on fire. The bed was on fire. My *house* was on fire.

"Fuck. You're so tight. So wet." His voice was gasoline on the flames, which were now an inferno. "I want you to come for me."

Whether he wanted it or not, it was happening. My body had tightened to the point of pain, my stomach muscles contracting, my legs clamped around him. And then my world exploded in one seismic eruption, tremors emanating from my core and rippling through my body. I was still deep in their throes when

Dash's climax hit, hearing him grunt with every stroke, feeling him thicken and throb within me. He crushed his lips to mine as my insides gripped him again and again.

For a long moment, our mouths shared a breath, our bodies shared a pulse, our hearts shared a rhythm.

I suddenly had the feeling I would never be the same.

• • •

"I'm thinking Delphine was right about this whole walking around naked thing," Dash said, returning to my bedroom with two glasses of water, wearing not a stitch of clothing. "I feel really good right now. You should try it."

I had on a T-shirt I'd grabbed from a drawer and pulled over my head after he'd left the room, although I hadn't bothered with underwear. I laughed as I took the glass he handed to me. "You just had an orgasm. Maybe that's part of it."

"Maybe." He stood by the side of the bed and took a few gulps of water. Illuminated by the lamp on my nightstand, he looked like a god, or a bronze statue of a god. Weight in one hip, arm lifted, biceps bulging, muscles working as he swallowed. Even the goddamn dangle was hot. I watched him and thought for the millionth time how beautiful he was.

He lowered the half-empty glass. "Why are you looking at me like that?"

"You're nice to look at." Crossing my bare legs at the ankles, I leaned back against my headboard and took a sip.

His eyebrows rose. "No more average at best?"

"Suddenly I'm seeing you in an all-new light. Those orgasms are powerful things."

He downed the rest of the water and set the glass on my nightstand. "Speaking of which." He flopped onto his side across the foot of my bed, propping his head in one hand. "How serious were we about that *just once* business?"

"I don't know," I said, my toes tingling. "We sounded serious."

"We did, didn't we?" Brow furrowed, he reached out and rubbed my foot. "There were *reasons*."

"There were," I agreed.

"I'm just having trouble remembering what they were, exactly. Why they mattered."

"Well, I can't think at all if you're going to rub my feet like that," I said as his thumb worked beneath the ball of my foot.

Immediately he moved closer so he could use both hands. "Your feet must hurt all the time. You're on them day and night."

"Oh, God." I moaned softly as he massaged my sore arch. "What were we talking about again?"

"Orgasms."

"I might have another one right now."

He laughed. "Good."

My eyes closed as he rubbed one foot and then the other. "You know, if acting doesn't work out, you'd make a great massage therapist. You have amazingly strong hands."

"Thanks," he said, working his way up my calf muscle. "But there's only one person I'd put my hands on this way."

"You wouldn't make a very good living at it with only one client."

"Nope. And I'd never let her pay." His hands moved up to my thigh. "So as I was saying. I think we may have been too hasty in setting a time limit on our exploration in vulnerability."

"You could be right."

His fingertips brushed me intimately, stroked me shallowly.

"I mean, I really feel like it's working." He brought a finger to his mouth and closed his lips around it. Pulled it out. Then he eased it inside me, using his thumb to rub my clit. "Don't you?"

My nipples tightened and poked through the thin, faded pink cotton of my shirt. "Yes," I whispered, my body humming and alive with need. "It's definitely working."

"In fact, I think we've only scratched the surface of all the possible benefits of this enhanced friendship." He added a second finger, keeping his eyes locked on mine.

"Yes," I agreed, because apparently that's the only word I could come up with when Dash's hands were on me.

"But we should probably keep this to ourselves."

"Most definitely."

"Of course, a question remains."

"Question?" I panted.

"The question," he said, fucking me slowly with his fingers, "of whether two people can *stay* friends when they add these kinds of benefits."

"I think they can." I understood his concern. "Nothing has to change, Dash. No expectations here."

"None here either." He paused. "Well, maybe one."

"What's that?"

"I expect that when I tell you to do something, you'll do it."

"Try me."

His sexy mouth curled up on one side. "Take off your shirt."

I pulled it over my head and tossed it to the floor.

When I lay back again, Dash moved up alongside my body and lowered his mouth to one breast. His wet fingertips moved expertly over my clit as he circled the taut peak of my nipple with his tongue. "Good girl. Now I want you to come for me just like this."

Already I was sinking into that feeling again—the buzz beneath his hand intensifying, the tension in my body rising, the hunger for him gnawing at my insides. I reached between his legs, capturing his cock in my fist, thrilling at the way it swelled and thickened for me. In no time at all, he brought me right to the brink again—the combination of his mouth sucking and his fingers rubbing hard and fast causing me to combust within minutes, his name a desperate plea on my lips.

He wasted no time in jumping off the bed and going for his wallet, pulling out a second condom. I lay there panting, the sheets fisted in my hands, while he tore open the packet and rolled it on. When he returned to the bed, he lay back and pulled me on top of him. "I want to watch you ride me," he said.

Straddling his hips, I glanced over my shoulder at the lamp. It was one thing to be on top—it was another to be watched while you did it. I didn't have much experience with this position, and suddenly my nerves were getting to me. I was hot and sweaty, and my hair had to be a fucking mess at this point. My cute smokey eye makeup was probably verging on panda territory. "Could I turn out the light first?"

"Absolutely not." He grabbed my hips as he looked up at me. "You're too fucking gorgeous for the dark, Sugar."

His words gave me the confidence I needed. Lifting myself up slightly, I positioned the tip of his hard cock between my legs and lowered myself down slowly, each inch stealing another breath. When he was buried as deep as I could take him, I closed my eyes.

"Oh my God." His grip on me tightened. "You have no idea how beautiful you are. How good this feels."

Placing my hands on his chest, I rolled my hips over his, gratified by his agonized moans and the tortured expression on his face. Gradually, my self-consciousness eased, and I moved with more abandon, rocking my body harder, arms flung over my head.

Dash cursed and growled, his hands roaming from my breasts to my thighs to my ass, his fingers digging into my flesh. "Fuck, fuck, fuck. I can't look at you or this will be over too quickly." For a moment he turned his head to the side and squeezed his eyes shut, but a second later, he peeked. "Goddammit, I can't look away!"

I laughed and teased my nipples with my fingers, enjoying the tormented groan that came from the back of his throat. He was so fucking hot and yet so adorable at the same time. Seeing him fall apart beneath me was better than any praise I'd ever gotten before in my life, and I'm someone who *lives* for approval. Suddenly, I was glad he'd turned me down eight years ago, because I never would have been able to enjoy this the way I was right now—I would have been a nervous wreck, silent and stiff beneath him.

Now? Watching his ab muscles ripple as he thrust up beneath me, his skin glistening with sweat, his hungry eyes locked on my body, I felt like a goddess.

Falling forward, I licked his lower lip. He slid his hands into my hair and kissed me deeply, his tongue seeking mine. I rocked my hips faster, grinding against him, my core muscles tightening deep within.

"Goddamn," he growled against my lips, his hands sliding down to my ass. "I love how you fuck me. My good girl."

If I had any inhibitions left, his words obliterated them. Bracing my hands on his chest, I allowed myself to completely lose control, my cries loud enough to shatter my bedroom windows, my hands clutching his shoulders hard enough to leave bruises. Dash was just as loud, his grip on me just as tight. He told me to come with him, and I obeyed.

Sapped of energy and strength, I collapsed on top of him, head on his shoulder. He embraced me, and I closed my eyes. If ever there was a moment I wished I could stop time, this was it.

I wasn't just a good girl.

I was his.

. . .

"You're welcome to stay," I said as Dash pulled on his jeans.

"I wish I could. But I've got Fritz at home." He zipped up and slipped the button through its hole. "And you have to get up early anyway, right? You're working in the morning?"

"Yes." I yawned. "I have to get up at five."

"Then I should definitely go." He came over to the bed where I was curled up on my side and kissed my forehead. "Because you're down to getting only a few hours in. And if I stayed, you'd get no sleep at all."

I smiled. "Probably not."

He bent down and tied his shoes. "I think the rest of my clothes are in the living room."

"I can walk you out," I said, attempting to sit up.

"No." He put a hand on my shoulder. "You go to sleep. I can find my way out."

"I have to lock the door anyway." Dragging myself off the bed, I tugged the pink shirt over my head and followed him to the living room. Switching on the light, I laughed when I spied his T-shirt over by the wall and his hoodie halfway between the wall and the front door.

He put them on, not bothering to tuck in the shirt or zip the hoodie. At the front door, he pulled me into his arms once more. "Sorry I kept you up."

"Liar," I said against his chest.

"You're right. That is a lie." He loosened his arms and pressed his lips to mine. "I'll talk to you tomorrow."

I nodded. "Night."

"Night." He took a few steps off the porch, then turned around and came back to me. Putting a hand on the back of my neck, he rested his forehead on mine. "Ari, I just want to tell you…you're amazing."

Despite my exhaustion, every nerve ending in my body lit up like the Fourth of July. "Thank you."

"And I wouldn't change a thing about tonight."

"Me neither."

He picked up his head and met my eyes. "Or about you."

Smiling, I touched his cheek. "You better get out of here, or I'm not going to let you leave."

With one last grin, he backed off and headed down the walk.

After shutting the door and locking it behind him, I stood there for a moment with my forehead pressed against it. I heard his engine come to life, the sound fading as he drove down the street.

I pinched my arm. Then my leg and my side and my cheek.

But this day still didn't seem real.

• • •

I was a zombie the next morning at work, but I was the most cheerful zombie you can imagine. Every time I thought about the previous twenty-four hours, my heart would skip and my insides would turn cartwheels. When I caught a glimpse of myself in the diner's bathroom mirror, I cringed for a second—bags under my eyes, bun sloppier than usual, the lower half of my face chafed a bit from Dash's scruff.

But then I smiled. Because the girl in the mirror looked tired but completely happy. And I couldn't remember the last time I'd seen her that way.

I made it through my shift and went home, ditching my shoes and crashing hard face down on the couch in my diner uniform. Bone-weary, I fell into a deep sleep the second my eyes closed.

My dreams were good.

Chapter 12

DASH

I knocked on Ari's front door around six o'clock, a bag of groceries under one arm and a scrap of paper in my pocket I hoped would change everything.

She didn't answer, but she'd left the garage door open, and I'd seen her car parked inside. I knocked again, a little harder this time. A full minute later, the door opened.

I smiled as she blinked at the fading sunlight. It was obvious she'd been asleep. Still wearing her diner uniform, she had sleep lines on her face, the bun on the top of her head was listing precariously to one side, and that might have been drool on her lower lip.

She wiped at it with the back of her wrist. "Hey."

"Hi. Were you sleeping?"

"Yeah." She touched her hair. "I must look like I've been

through it."

"You look beautiful. Can I come in?"

"Of course." She stepped back so I could enter, and after she closed the door behind me, I set the grocery bag down and scooped her in close for a hug. She smelled like maple syrup and bacon.

"Sorry to wake you," I said.

"It's okay. I need to get out of this uniform."

"I can definitely assist with that."

She laughed. "No acts of vulnerability until I take a shower."

"That's fine. While you're doing that, I'll make dinner for us." I picked up my grocery bag and headed for the kitchen.

"You're going to make dinner?" The surprise in her voice was evident as she trailed me through the living room.

"Yes. You're not the only one who knows how to cook, Miss Fancypants Culinary School." I set the bag on the counter and pulled out a package of meat, two potatoes, and a bag of broccoli rabe. "Can I use your big iron skillet?"

"Yes. Cupboard to the left of the oven." She peeked into the bag to see what else was in there. "Are those steaks? Is that burrata? What's the lemon for? Ooooh, pinot noir, my favorite."

"Stop it." I took her by the hips and swung her toward the door. "You are not allowed to help. Go take your shower."

"But—"

"Go." With my hands still grasping her waist, I marched her out of the kitchen and sent her toward the bedrooms and bathroom. "I've got this."

She turned around and took a few backward steps. "Thank you."

"And when you come back, I have some cool news for you."

Her eyebrows shot up. "Did you hear back from Izzie? Do you have an audition for Katherine Carroll?"

"No. The cool news is not about me." I smiled at her. "It's about you."

. . .

While she was in the shower, I prepped the steaks for searing and preheated the oven for the baked potatoes. I wasn't an accomplished cook by any means, but all my time in restaurant jobs had taught me a few things. And I'd once had a housemate in L.A. who was a chef—in fact, he won this ridiculous reality TV show called *Lick My Plate*, which featured good-looking contestants who sometimes worked shirtless in the kitchen. The rest of the actors who lived in the house—at times, there had been four or five of us—gave him *so* much shit about it.

The funny thing was, he was actually from Michigan and didn't live too far from Cherry Tree Harbor. Just a couple hours or so. I lost touch with him after he left L.A., which had been right around the time I'd been cast as Bulge, but I knew he'd moved back home, and later I heard he opened up a restaurant. I'd managed to get his number from a mutual friend, and this morning I'd reached out.

"Hey Dash, good to hear from you," he said. "You calling from your infinity pool overlooking the ocean? Or maybe the screening room in your Hollywood mansion?"

I laughed. "Not even close. I'm back at my dad's house in Cherry Tree Harbor walking his dog."

We caught up for a few minutes—turned out Gianni was married with two kids and a third on the way. He and his wife lived near her family's winery, Abelard Vineyards, where he ran a French restaurant called Etoile and she was the tasting room manager.

"Wow," I said. "Two kids? And another one coming? You've been busy."

"I have," he said, laughing. "But life is good. So what can I do for you?"

"I'm back in town for my brother's wedding, and I reconnected with an old friend who works at her parents' diner but is interested in mobile catering—a food truck, specifically." Okay, it was a slight stretch of the truth, since I was really the one who was curious about mobile catering, but whatever. "I wondered if you had any experience in that area."

"Sure," he said. "We actually have a food truck at Abelard we use for events—festivals, tastings, wedding vendor expos— that kind of thing. It's a good investment."

"You think so?"

"Yeah. There are a lot of benefits. Startup costs are a lot lower compared to a restaurant. Food trucks are popular with younger demographics. You've got better flexibility and convenience. As long as you have your niche figured out—"

"She does," I interrupted. "Her parents' diner—it's called Moe's—has been around forever, and she likes taking the tried-and-true dishes served there and coming up with ways to make them a little more upscale."

"That's cool," he said. "I know Moe's Diner. Great place. And she'd have the name recognition to help her out."

"So what does a food truck cost?" I asked. "Any idea?"

"It depends. Cheap end—a used vehicle, let's say—maybe like twenty grand. Top of the line, brand new custom truck could run you a hundred-fifty, easy."

"I don't think she wants top-of-the-line or anything. She'd probably be fine with used if it was in good condition."

"That would probably be best to start out. Then she'd just have to invest in the exterior customization."

"Any ideas where I might find trucks for sale?"

"You know, it's funny you called me today because I just had a conversation with Ellie's dad last week about getting a bigger truck for Abelard this summer. We did a lot of mobile business last year. If he agrees with me that we need to expand, our current one would be up for grabs."

"Really?"

"Yeah. It's not huge, but it's fucking *nice*."

A female voice in the background. "Gianni Lupo! The kids are in the room!"

"Sorry, babe," he said.

"Any way I could see it?" I asked. "If your father-in-law agrees to sell?"

"Sure. You can come see it anytime. Let me talk to him again and see what he thinks."

"Any idea what the price would be?"

"No, but I'll find out. He'll be fair."

"Thanks, Gianni. I really appreciate it."

"No problem." He paused. "So are you dating this girl?"

"No. We're just friends," I said quickly. "But we kind of grew up together. She was my sister Mabel's best friend, so I've known her forever. I'd like to help her out."

"Cool," he said. "Well, if you've got time while you're home, come for dinner at Etoile. Just let me know what night you want to come, and I'll get you in."

"I'd love to do that. Let me talk to her."

As I put the potatoes in the oven, I wondered if I should tell

Ari upfront about the possibility of buying Abelard's truck or if I should just take her to dinner at Etoile and surprise her. Would she be upset with me? Was she really against the idea or just nervous to take a chance on herself?

I put a pot of water on the stove to boil and started trimming the ends off the broccoli rabe.

"Okay, I'm clean."

I turned around to see her entering the kitchen, her hair damp and curly, her face free of makeup. She wore gray shorts and a matching cropped sweatshirt, and thick fleece bunny socks on her feet. "Cute," I said.

She looked down and rocked back on her heels. "Thank you. Now what can I do to help? I'm not good at sitting still in the kitchen and letting other people do the work, so you have to give me *something*."

I grabbed the bottle of pinot noir and handed it to her. "You can open this and pour us some wine."

As she opened a drawer and pulled out the opener, I went back to my dinner prep. "Want to hear my cool news?"

"Yes."

"I spoke to a friend of mine, a chef who runs a restaurant called Etoile at—"

"You're friends with Gianni Lupo?" She sounded impressed.

"Yeah. We lived in the same house years ago in L.A."

"Wow. I didn't know that." She placed a glass of pinot noir on the counter next to the cutting board, on which I was slicing cloves of garlic. "Are those crushed pistachios?"

"Yes." I set the knife down and took a sip of wine. "I gave him a call because I wondered if he had any insight into food trucks."

"Dash!" She was clearly exasperated. "Why did you do that?"

"Because I was curious. And I wanted to learn more about it."

"You could have Googled it."

"I did that before I called him." I gave her a quick kiss. "I'm very thorough."

She leaned back against the counter next to me. "So what did he say?"

While oil heated in the iron skillet, I told her about my conversation with Gianni. "So if his father-in-law says the truck is for sale, maybe we can go see it."

She watched me sear the marbled New York Strips but said nothing. Her expression was a mixture of trepidation and skepticism, her brow furrowed.

"You're making me nervous with that face," I told her. "Are you worried I don't know how to cook a steak?"

Her pinched forehead relaxed. "Sorry. It's not that. I trust you to cook dinner. And I appreciate your confidence in me. But it won't do me any good to go see that truck—I can't buy it."

"All we're doing is looking at it." I added butter, cloves of garlic, and sprigs of rosemary to the skillet, watching it carefully. "What's the harm in that?"

"What if I fall in love with it?"

"Then we figure out a way to make it work. We convince your parents to buy it. Or you apply for a loan. Or you accept my offer to invest in you." Removing the steaks from the skillet, I placed them on the cutting board to let them rest and dropped the rabe into the boiling water. "You have options."

"Maybe." She was silent a minute. "But I also have doubts."

"You can't let doubt cloud your good energy, Ari," I told her. "It will build and build, and before you know it, you have to walk around naked to cure yourself."

She laughed. "Are you trying to get me to take my clothes off right now?"

I wrapped my arms around her and kissed her temple. Her hair smelled like the beach. "I'm trying to make my friend believe in herself. But if you want to get naked, I will not stand in your way."

She laughed. "Thanks, but I'll keep my clothes on for now."

"Are we watching a movie tonight?" I asked, draining the vegetables.

"Yes. I have a great idea—*Dirty Dancing*."

"I have a better one. Dirty talking."

Behind me, she slipped her arms around my waist. "We can do both."

$$\cdots$$

By the time the movie finished, the food was gone, the wine bottle was empty, and Ari was sound asleep with her head in my lap.

She was so fucking cute. I brushed her hair back from her face and remembered a dozen moments from last night—her legs over my shoulders, her mouth wrapped around me, her hips swiveling over mine. My cock jumped at the memory, and I felt it begin to swell. I was dying to do it all again, but I didn't have the heart to wake her.

And unfortunately, Fritz was going to need to be let out soon, so I had to get going. When I reached for my phone to check the time, she stirred and sat up.

"Sorry," she said, rubbing her face with both hands. "Did I miss the ending?"

"You did. They danced. She didn't do the lift at the show, but it was fine."

She smiled. "Did you watch the whole thing?"

"Yes."

"You're not lying to me, are you?"

"I watched the entire thing, I promise. Give me a quiz."

"What does Johnny say to her when he asks her to dance in the final scene?"

I rolled my eyes and poked her shoulder. "Give me a hard one, at least. 'Nobody puts Baby in the corner.'"

"Good job. You passed." She put her arms around my neck, and I pulled her onto my lap. "Thank you for making dinner tonight. It was delicious."

"You're welcome." I pressed my lips to hers. "I know it wasn't corn dogs and deep-fried-whatever on a stick, but I tried."

"It was even better than carnival food, and I appreciate it." She pulled my head down, and our mouths met again. The kiss grew deeper and more intense, our tongues meeting, her hands moving into my hair. I slipped a hand up the back of her sweatshirt and groaned when I realized she wasn't wearing a bra. Moving it around to the front, I covered her breast with one hand, feeling the nipple change shape beneath my palm. With a reluctant moan, I tore my lips from hers. "I hate to say this, but I can't stay much longer. I have to let Fritz out."

"Oh." She sucked in her breath as I caressed the hardened nipple with the tip of my thumb. "We could be quick."

"Or you could come home with me," I suggested, rubbing my lips against hers.

She went still. "I don't have to work tomorrow. I suppose I could."

"You don't sound too sure about it."

"I just wasn't sure how many sleepovers were allowed with our arrangement."

"Well, I checked the by-laws of the Friends with Benefits Association, and it turns out we can have sleepovers at will." My cock was getting harder at the idea of spending the entire night with her.

She laughed. "And your dad is still gone?"

"Yes. Until Tuesday."

"Okay then," she said, kissing me once more. "I'll come home with you."

• • •

Back at my house, I sent Ari upstairs while I let Fritz out and locked up. She was already in bed when I entered the darkened bedroom, and my body was hot with desire for her. "Give me two minutes," I said, yanking my shirt off and throwing it on the floor before going into the bathroom.

After brushing my teeth, I grabbed the box of condoms from the cupboard and brought them out with me. After sticking it in the drawer of the nightstand, I turned back the covers and crawled into bed. Reaching for Ari, I pulled her close—she was warm and soft and smelled like summer, some combination of flowers and the beach.

I buried my face in her neck and inhaled. "I love the way you smell."

"Good." She giggled, wrapping her arms around my head. "I was lying here thinking about the last time I was in this bedroom. Things didn't go my way."

I slipped one hand between her legs and kissed my way

down her chest. "That was then. This is now."

"I like now," she whispered as I sucked one nipple and rubbed gentle circles over her clit.

"Me too," I told her as I moved my mouth down her belly, tasting her summery skin. "Me. Too."

Chapter 13

ARI

I woke up first.

Blinking, I propped myself up on one elbow, momentarily confused by the unfamiliar surroundings. But when I heard the deep, regular breathing beside me, memories came rushing in like the tide, and I settled onto the pillow again.

Closing my eyes, I tried to fall back asleep—the pale pink light filtering in through the blinds told me it was early—but my body was used to getting up at five, and I'd gotten a lot of sleep after work yesterday. So I lay there for a few minutes, my body sore but relaxed, my mind skimming over details from the previous night.

He'd cooked me dinner. He'd reached out to a friend— Gianni Lupo!—about me. He wanted to help me start my own business. He'd agreed to watch *Dirty Dancing* with me and stuck with it all the way to the end, even though I'd passed out on his lap halfway through. He was just so damn sweet.

I rolled to my side and looked at him, my stomach fluttering. He was on his back, head turned toward me, chest exposed. God, he was beautiful. I wondered if I'd ever look at him and not experience that weightless feeling, like I was cresting the steepest hill on a rollercoaster. His eyes were closed, thick lashes fanning over his cheeks. His jaw was finely chiseled beneath the scruff. And his mouth. His *mouth*. Not just the shape of it, but the words that tumbled from his lips in the dark. I'd never known words could be so powerful.

His eyes opened. "Hey."

"Hey."

"Sleep okay?"

I nodded.

"I was just dreaming about you," he said.

Beneath the covers, my body hummed with joy. "What about me?"

He turned onto his side to face me. Bringing a hand to my mouth, he brushed my lower lip with his thumb, tugging it down slightly. "This."

• • •

"I've got Show and Tell today," Dash said as the sweat was cooling on our skin.

"That's right. It's Monday." I propped my head in my hand. "What time is that?"

"I have to be there at one. What time is it now?"

I picked up my phone from the nightstand. "Seven."

"Damn, that's early."

Laughing, I put my phone down again. "You can go back to sleep. I'm going to make some coffee."

"I'm up," he said, but by the time I came out of the bathroom, he was fast asleep again. Leaving him be, I threw on Dash's discarded T-shirt from the night before and tiptoed downstairs.

After letting Fritz out, I filled the coffee maker with water for a full pot and measured out the grounds. While I was standing there waiting for it to brew, I gathered the front of Dash's shirt in my hands and brought it to my face. Inhaling the scent of him sent a shiver throughout my entire body. I closed my eyes and lost myself to the feeling—I was light as a feather, floating through air. I was—

"Oh, shit. Ari?"

Whirling around, I opened my eyes and realized I was half naked in the Buckleys' kitchen and Xander had just come in the back door, which would have given him a nice clear view of my ass. "Xander!" I dropped the shirt and tugged down on the hem. I had no underwear on beneath it.

"Sorry," he said, turning immediately for the door again. "I'm doing some work on the house this morning and needed a tool from my dad's basement. I'll come back later."

"No, it's okay," I said, running for the stairs, holding the shirt down in the back. "I just put on a whole pot of coffee. I'll go wake Dash."

I hurried up the stairs and burst into his bedroom, throwing myself on the bed. "Dash!" I whispered frantically, pounding on his naked shoulder. He was buck naked, lying starfish-style on his belly. "Wake up! Xander is here!"

"Huh?" He picked up his head. "What?"

"Xander is here, and I think he saw my butt."

Confused, Dash flipped over and sat up. "Xander saw your butt?"

"It's possible." I took a breath and put my hand on my stomach. My heart was racing. "I was downstairs in nothing but your T-shirt and he came in the back door and might have glimpsed my rear."

"He never fucking knocks," Dash grumbled, getting out of bed. "Is he still here?"

"He was going to leave, but I told him to stay. Coffee is on."

Dash messed around in his bag and yanked on underwear and jeans. "Okay."

"Dash." I sat back on my heels. "This means he knows about us."

"Yeah." He pulled a black T-shirt over his head.

"I'm sorry."

Right away, he came over to me and tipped up my chin. "Hey. You have nothing to apologize for. Xander is the one that barged in here, and besides, he knew about us anyway."

"He did?"

"Well, he suspected it would happen, although he thinks it's a bad idea."

"He said that?"

Turning toward the mirror over the dresser, he ran his hands through his messy hair, frowning at his reflection. "He's convinced that friends-with-benefits doesn't work, because even if the friends agree at the start about remaining just friends, sex changes things."

"Changes things how?"

"He says someone always gets attached, and it ends badly."

"Oh." I vowed right then and there I would not get attached.

This would not end badly.

"But he doesn't know us. You and I are the only two people whose opinions matter on this subject. We know who we are and what this is."

"Right," I said. But I felt like Xander *did* know us.

Dash turned around and looked at me. "Our friendship is none of Xander's business. But neither is your ass, so put on some clothes, and we'll go downstairs and tell him to fuck off if he's going to be judgmental."

I laughed and jumped off the bed. "Deal."

• • •

Xander was sitting at the table with a cup of coffee when we came downstairs, but other than a quick exchange of looks between the brothers—Xander's said, *Dude, you didn't listen*, and Dash's responded, *Yes, I did but you were wrong*—no mention was made of the fact that I'd obviously spent the night.

Or that Xander had seen my derriere.

After a few minutes, he disappeared into the basement to look for some kind of screwdriver, and Dash leaned back in his chair. "See? All good. What are you up to today?"

"Not much. Some house stuff."

"I was going to ask you if you wanted to go to Show and Tell with me, but it's okay if you're busy."

My eyebrows shot up. "Are you kidding? I'm never too busy for Show and Tell."

And later that afternoon, when I stood in the back of Mrs. Fletcher's classroom watching Dash interact with twenty-one second graders, I knew I'd made the right choice.

Owen and Adelaide introduced him and took turns telling their classmates about their uncle, the famous actor. But when the teacher asked if anyone had ever heard of Dashiel Buckley before or watched *Malibu Splash*, not a single hand went up.

"Really? No one?" Mrs. Fletcher asked. "He's probably the most famous graduate of Paddington Elementary!"

"But if we've never heard of him, is he really that famous?" one kid asked.

"Does he play football?" asked another.

"Is he on TikTok? Because I'm not allowed on TikTok."

I covered my mouth and stifled a laugh.

But the kids loved the games Dash suggested they play— charades and story building and something called Mirror, Mirror in which he faced them and had to mimic their movements and expressions. I noticed how he drew even the shy kids into the games without forcing them. The students had so much fun, they didn't even want to go out for recess and fussed when Mrs. Fletcher said they had to go outside, Show and Tell was over.

He was so good with them, got right down on the carpet, read them a story with very animated voices, and gave out high fives and hugs when Mrs. Fletcher told the kids they had to let him go.

"He's a natural with children," she said to me as the kids lined up to say goodbye. "Are you planning to have kids?"

"Me?" I was confused for a second, and then I realized she assumed Dash and I were a couple. "Oh, we're just friends."

"You're not together?" Her jaw dropped, and she placed a hand on her chest. "Oh, I'm sorry, I thought for sure you two were an item when I saw him with you at Moe's the other night!"

"No." Heat rushed my face, and I'm sure my cheeks were turning red. "He was just helping me out."

She chuckled as one of the kids hopped onto Dash's back. "Well, he'd make a great dad."

"He would," I agreed.

Eventually, all the kids said their farewells and made their way out to the playground. Out in the hallway, Mrs. Fletcher thanked Dash profusely for coming. "The kids love anything to do with performing," she said. "You even got some of the most reluctant ones out of their seats participating."

"It was a teacher at this very school that got me into acting," said Dash.

"Was it really? Who?"

"Her name was Ms. Walsh," said Dash. "First grade."

"Oh, yes." Mrs. Fletcher nodded. "I remember Jessica Walsh. She got married and moved to Indiana. She was a great teacher."

A student with two long braids poked her head back into the room. "Mrs. Fletcher, can we bring the big jump ropes out?"

"Sure, honey. You can grab them from the closet." She turned to us again, shaking both our hands. "Thanks again for coming and sharing your gift with the children."

Dash and I signed out in the office and headed outside. "I didn't know that about you," I said as we walked to his car. "That a teacher got you into acting."

He opened the passenger door for me. "Yeah."

"Was there an elementary school play or something?"

"No." He went around to the driver's side and got in.

"So what was it?"

He turned on the engine but left the car in park. Staring straight ahead out the windshield to where the kids were playing on the playground, he spoke quietly. "I'd stopped speaking."

"What?" I turned to face him. "You stopped speaking?"

"Yes. After my mom died. I stopped talking at school."

"Oh, Dash." My heart splintered, and I put a hand on his leg. "That's so sad. I'm sorry. God, I just want to cry right now."

He gave me a quick smile. "It was a long time ago. No need to cry."

"So what did the teacher do?"

"She made up a game where I played a character, a pirate squirrel or something. I think she realized that I wasn't talking because people kept asking me if I was okay. And that I didn't want to answer because I wasn't."

"Of course not." I rubbed his thigh.

"I knew if I started talking as myself, I would cry. So Ms. Walsh gave me this character to be, which let me feel something else. Think about something else." He shrugged. "It felt good. I would talk as long as I was in character."

"What a great teacher," I said appreciatively.

"She was." He was quiet for a minute, his eyes still on the kids at recess.

"So then you started speaking at school again?"

"I don't think it was light switch fast, but yes."

"And the love for acting stuck?"

"Yeah. It did." He put the car in reverse and backed out of the parking spot.

"You were amazing with those second graders," I told him.

"I like kids." He turned out of the school lot. "So what now, Sugar? Am I taking you home? Or do you want to hang out?"

"I want to hang out, but I should get some work done at the house. I have to work the rest of the week."

"What kind of work at the house?"

"I need more storage for my pots and pans. I only have the one little piece of wall free right next to the door, so I thought maybe I could mount some pegboard and use hooks."

"Pegboard?" Dash frowned. "What about something nicer? Like wood planks or something. You know what? Let's ask Austin. We're right by his house, and I bet he can tell us where to get some cool reclaimed wood. He might even have some scrap that will work."

"Dash, you don't have to spend all your time at home working on my house."

"I don't mind. I like a project." He made a U-turn and headed for Austin's house, which was just up the block. "And it's distracting me from the fact that I haven't heard back from my agent yet."

"Still no word?"

"Nope. She texted me yesterday to remind me she'll be out of town next week, but her assistant will be around if anything comes up."

"But the part you want hasn't been cast yet, has it?"

"Not that I've heard," he said, pulling into Austin's driveway. "So keep your fingers crossed."

· · ·

Austin thought old fence pickets might be cool on my wall, and he did have some lying around. "They need to be sanded and stained, but that's not too big a job."

"Does Dad have a sander in the basement?" Dash asked.

"I think he does, but you can also do the sanding and staining here if you want." He gestured to the garage behind him, which functioned as his workshop. "Do you have measurements? You'll need to cut them."

I shook my head guiltily. "Nope. I'll have to run home."

"Go do that and come back. We'll get them cut, and you can sand and stain them this evening."

"Sounds good, although I might have to miss dance class tonight." I laughed. "Think the teacher will forgive me?"

"You don't have to miss it," Dash said. "I'll sand and stain them for you while you're at class."

I turned to face him. "Dash."

"I told you—I need a project to take my mind off things," he insisted, taking me by the shoulder and nudging me down the driveway. "Now let's go measure your wall."

• • •

Later that night, Veronica sat down at our high-top table at Lush and studied my face at close range. "You're glowing."

"Don't be silly. I'm just flushed from class."

She rolled her eyes. "That is not a sweaty dance class flush. That is an I've-been-banging-my-best-friend's-older-brother-all-night radiance."

I inhaled and held my breath for a moment, then gave up and let it out. "Okay. We banged. But you can't tell anybody!"

"Eeeep!" She clapped her hands. "Tell me everything."

"There's not much to tell. Things sort of heated up over the phone last Friday night, and then when I got home from the pub Saturday night he was parked across the street from my house."

"Obsessed much?" she teased, picking up the glass of wine I'd ordered her.

"He's not *obsessed*," I argued, my face tingling with pleasure.

"Oh no? He barely talked about anything other than you last Thursday night when we all went out for pizza."

"Really?"

"Yes. He went on and on about how talented you are, all the things you've been cooking for him, how you're fixing up your house and he helped you paint."

"He also fixed my car and won't let me pay him back for it. And right now he's sanding and staining wooden planks for my kitchen."

"I know. I ran into him before I left the house." She smiled coyly. "So is this a serious thing?"

"No." I took a sip of my pinot. "It's just for fun while he's in town."

"I guess the geography *would* be a bit of a problem," she said with a sigh. "But what a bummer. You guys are so cute together."

"Dash isn't interested in a relationship anyway."

"He said that?"

"Not in those exact words, but he said something about wanting to avoid attachments."

She nodded slowly. "Ah."

"But it's fine. At least he was honest about it. I know upfront what this is. And he's so good to me, Roni," I said, shaking my head. "The last guy I was with did nothing but tear me down. When I moved back home, I couldn't get out of bed for a month."

"Oh my God, that's awful. I never knew that."

"It was before you came here. And I don't ever talk about it. But Dash is the complete opposite of that guy. He could not be sweeter or more helpful or encouraging. And the sex…"

A slow smile crept onto her red lips. "And the sex?"

My eyes closed, and I tried to think. "Words are failing me."

Veronica laughed. "It's that good?"

"Good doesn't begin to scratch the surface. Hot seems inadequate. Mind-blowing is completely insufficient. The stars collided, Veronica. I saw them. I heard them. I felt them."

She smiled. "You deserve it."

Chapter 14

*A*fter eating an early dinner at Austin's with him and the kids, I spent the evening alongside him in his workshop, sawing and sanding and staining the wood planks for Ari's kitchen.

The garage door was open, and we could hear the kids playing in the backyard while we worked. It reminded me of my childhood, of running around the neighborhood with my brothers and friends until the streetlights came on, when my dad would drag us all inside to clean up and go to bed. Even the scent of the air was the same—clean and woodsy.

The work reminded me of my childhood too. While I'd never been as handy as Austin, our dad had made sure we knew the basics of carpentry, and we'd all tagged along on jobs with him to earn a little extra allowance here and there. I didn't often work with my hands anymore, and I realized that I enjoyed it. It required skill and patience, strong hands and a good eye, but it wasn't a performance. You didn't have any lines. And the only thing you had to feel was the desire to do the job well.

Austin wasn't really a talker, so we mostly worked side by side in silence, which was fine with me. I knew he was probably itching to ask me what was going on with Ari and why I was doing all this work on her house, but he refrained, and I was grateful. I had the feeling that, like Xander, Austin would not think our arrangement was wise. Xander hadn't said anything out loud in the kitchen today, but I could tell by his expression that he thought we were making a mistake.

Eventually, Austin left me alone in the garage and herded the kids into the house for showers and snacks before bedtime. By the time he came out, I'd finished applying the stain.

"Looks good," he said, assessing my work.

"Thanks."

"You'll mount it on the wall and add the hooks tomorrow?"

I nodded. "Yeah. I'll swing by and grab everything in the morning. Then Ari can show me where she wants the hooks."

"How are things going with you guys?"

"Fine. It's casual," I added, although it didn't really *feel* all that casual when I was with her. "We're just hanging out."

"Veronica said she's coming to the wedding?"

"As Mabel's date," I said quickly. My phone buzzed in my pocket, and I pulled it out to look at the screen. It was a text from Ari.

How did everything go?

> Good. I'm about to leave Austin's.
> Can I call you in a minute?

Sure xoxo

. . .

I called her on my way home.

"Hello?"

"Hey. How was dance class?"

"Excellent. Very freeing. You should have come."

"I freed myself with some manual labor."

She laughed. "I appreciate it."

"I was thinking of mounting the planks in the morning, but I assume you have to work."

"I do. I can either leave the door open when I leave at six or get you a key tonight."

Most likely, it was perfectly safe to leave the door open in Cherry Tree Harbor for a few hours on a Tuesday morning, but option B meant I got to see her sooner. "I can swing by and grab a key. Are you home?"

"Yes. Just got out of the shower."

My entire body warmed. "I'll be there in a few."

Less than five minutes later, I knocked on her front door. She pulled it open wearing a hot pink satin robe. It was short and belted loosely at the waist, revealing a deep V of bare skin between her breasts. Her feet were bare, her hair was wet, and she smelled like the beach again. "Hi. Come on in."

I stepped into the house and shut the door behind me. Immediately wrapping her in my arms, I buried my face in her hair. "You always smell so fucking good. What is that?"

"My shampoo, maybe?" She looped her arms around my waist and inhaled. "You smell good too."

"Me? I smell like sweat and wood stain. Maybe a little sawdust."

"Mmmm. I like it." She tipped her head back. "Very manly."

I dropped a kiss on her lips. "I can't stay."

"Okay."

I kissed her some more, tasting mint from her toothpaste. "You're ready for bed."

"Mhm."

My mouth worked its way across her jaw and down her throat. "And I have to go take care of Fritz."

"Yes."

My hands slid down her silky back and squeezed her ass. "I should just get that key and go."

"Sure."

I untied her robe, and it fell open, revealing her nakedness beneath. My cock twitched. "Fuck. Maybe I have a minute."

She laughed. "I don't think you do."

I slipped my hands inside the robe and caressed her hips. "Yes. I definitely have a minute."

"But the dog."

"He's fine." My hands stole up to her breasts and I kneaded them gently.

"I have that key right here."

"Key?" I bent my head to her chest and took one perfect pink nipple in my mouth.

"Yes, the key to my—"

I cut her off with a hungry kiss, pinning her back against the door. Suddenly I was ravenous for her, and I couldn't wait another minute to taste her. Dropping to my knees, I slung one of her legs over my shoulder and buried my face in her pussy, breathing in the sweet, honeyed scent of her, licking her soft, sensitive skin, fluttering her clit with my tongue.

She gasped and moaned, filling her hands with my hair. I slid a hand up her thigh and eased two fingers inside her, stroking her the way she liked, tilting my head this way and that to feast on her like a man starved.

In no time at all, she was riding my hand and my face, crying out with abandon, her pussy clenching around my fingers. With an agonized growl, I rose to my feet, my tongue swiping one pebbled nipple on my way. Her leg dropped to the floor, and her hands went right for my fly. Within seconds, I was poised to enter.

"Fuck," I said. "Do you have a condom?"

"No," she said breathlessly. "But I don't care. I'm good if you are. I'm on the pill."

"I'm good." I grabbed her behind one thigh and hitched her leg up, then pushed my cock inside her, groaning at the snug, sublime fit. Slowly, I thrust upward, pulled back, then thrust again.

"Oh, God," she whispered, clinging to my neck. "You feel so good."

It was good—so good I couldn't speak. And I couldn't hold back. Some primal instinct took over, and my deliberate pace quickly turned into an all-out sprint. I raced toward the finish line, fucking her hard and fast, my hips flexing in short, quick jabs that knocked her back into the door and lifted her right off the ground.

Her arms and legs wrapped around me. I gripped her thighs hard. My legs began to tremble. I could smell sweat and sex and the sweetness of her skin. Then I was coming inside her, my cock buried deep, my body yearning for more, harder, faster, deeper, *yes, take it, take it, take it, take it…*

When my senses returned, I was still holding her up, our bodies still linked. "Jesus. Are you okay?"

"Yes." She laughed softly. "I might walk a little funny tomorrow, maybe have a bruise or two on my back, but I'm okay."

"Sorry. I don't know what came over me."

She nipped at my jaw. "I didn't mind. But I need a minute, okay?"

"Okay." Carefully, I set her on her feet and pulled out. She went straight for the bathroom, shutting the door behind her, and I felt bad, like maybe I should have followed her and cleaned up my own mess. Next time, I'd make sure to offer.

God, I hoped there would be a next time. In fact, I wanted to stay the night with her. Or invite her to come home with me. I wanted to fall asleep with her naked body wrapped in my arms and wake up to kiss her goodbye in the morning when she left for work.

What the actual fuck?

I zipped up my pants and told myself to calm down. Was this what Xander had been talking about? Did good sex create strings? Was this what it felt like to grow attached to someone? This feeling that you'd never grow tired of them, that you just wanted to be with them all the time, and when you were apart you couldn't stop thinking of them and things you wanted to do for them?

The bathroom door opened, and Ari came out, her robe tied again. My heart thundered in my chest, and I had to take a deep breath and stick my hands in my pockets so I didn't throw her over my shoulder and carry her into the bedroom.

She went over to a little table against the wall by the door and picked up a key. "For you," she said. "Not that I expect you to come over here and do work. You don't have to."

I took the key and tucked it into my pocket. "I know."

"Can I make dinner for you tomorrow night?"

"That sounds good."

"What should I make?"

"You choose."

"Okay." Smiling, she slipped easily into my arms once more, pressing her cheek to my chest. "You better go. I bet Fritz is lonely."

"Yeah." I kissed the top of her head, and when she tilted her head back, I lowered my lips to hers. "I'll see you tomorrow."

Leaving her house was a lot harder than it should have been.

•••

The following morning, I picked up everything I needed from Austin's around eight and let myself into Ari's house by nine. I took a quick break for lunch around noon, running home to grab a sandwich and let Fritz out, and went back to Ari's to finish the job. By two o'clock, the wood was mounted on the wall and looked pretty fucking good, if I said so myself. I couldn't wait for her to see it.

Feeling a sense of accomplishment, I was just about to head home and clean up when my phone buzzed with an incoming call. I was hoping it was Izzie or Ari, but I wasn't disappointed when I saw it was Gianni Lupo.

"Hey, Gianni."

"Hey, Dash. Good news."

"Yeah?"

"My father-in-law agrees that a bigger truck would be a good investment, and he's willing to sell the current one."

"Awesome. Got a price?"

"I'm still working on that. Obviously, I want to give you a good deal, but I just have to make sure my father-in-law doesn't lose money. I need to do a little research."

"Of course," I said. "No problem."

"Do you want to come see it? Make sure she's even interested?"

"Yeah." I thought quickly. Ari's parents would be home from vacation later tonight, and she'd want some time to talk to them. "Maybe one day next week?"

"Sure. It's probably easiest to get you in for dinner on a Wednesday night. Would that work?"

"That's perfect," I said. Mabel would be home Thursday, and Friday we'd all head to Snowberry Lodge for the wedding.

"Got a time preference?"

"I think you're about two hours from here, and Ari gets out of work around two, so anything after five works fine."

"Cool. I'll text you."

"Thanks, Gianni. I really appreciate this."

"No problem. Looking forward to seeing you."

Grinning, I locked up Ari's house and headed out. Doing things for her just felt fucking good.

Chapter 15

*D*ash called while I was putting the finishing touches on our dinner—a Moroccan chicken tajine I thought would go perfectly with *Casablanca*, which was the movie I'd chosen for tonight. I'd stopped at the little gourmet market on the way home from the diner and picked up preserved lemons and green olives for the dish, and I'd also made Moroccan bread called khobz from scratch. I couldn't wait for him to taste everything.

"Hello?"

"Hey. How are you?"

"Fantastic. I cannot stop looking at the antique wood on my wall." Turning around, I admired it again and smiled. "It's so beautiful, Dash. Thank you so much for doing that today."

"You're welcome. You just have to show me where you want the hooks and I'll get them in."

"Perfect."

"I just wanted to tell you I'm running a little late. I ended up driving to Snowberry this afternoon."

"Oh, nice! Did you meet Lexi?"

"Yeah. She seems great. Dev seems really happy, and the renovations are incredible. It hardly looks like the same place."

"You didn't have much time there. We should have rescheduled dinner so you could have stayed longer."

"Nah. I'm good."

Smiling, I leaned back against the counter. "I hope you're hungry."

"I'm always hungry. Especially for you."

I laughed. "I'm not on the menu."

"That's what you think."

· · ·

By the end of *Casablanca*, we'd pushed the tray tables aside and lay stretched out on the couch together, Dash behind me with an arm resting on my hip. When the credits were rolling, I flipped around to face him. "Well? Did you like it?"

"Yes," he said. "But it surprises me that you like so many movies where the couple doesn't end up together."

I thought for a moment about the movies we'd watched so far. *Titanic*, *When Harry Met Sally*, *Dirty Dancing*, *Casablanca*. "Huh. You're right. I've only shown you one that ends in happily ever after. That's weird."

"Maybe you don't believe in happily ever after."

I slapped his chest. "Bite your tongue! I read nothing but romance novels, and they always end in happily ever after. You know what I think it is?"

Dash's hand was sliding up my ribcage. "What?"

"I think these movies I shared with you are romantic, but they're not necessarily romances."

"What's the difference?" He scooted down and lifted up my shirt.

"Well, a romance ends with the couple together and happy, and in the movies I showed you, the journey was more about how we're changed as a result of love, even if that love can't last forever."

"Tell me more." Reaching around my back, he unhooked my bra.

"Are you even listening?"

"Yes." He pushed my bra up and put his mouth on my breast. "I swear."

"Well, Rose had to learn to stand up for herself to live the life she wanted, and Jack taught her to be brave and take chances."

"Also to spit." He stroked my nipple with his tongue.

"Baby needed to grow up, and Johnny's lessons weren't just about dancing."

"Does that mean I can make a joke about the horizontal mambo?"

"And then Rick makes Ilsa get on the plane, because he's learned not to be selfish. He puts humanity above his own feelings. It's about sacrifice. What we'll do for the people we love." I paused. "Sometimes we have to give them up. Not every love story can have a happy ending."

"Speaking of happy endings," Dash said, sliding the side of his index finger along the seam of my jeans.

"Dashiel Buckley!" Grabbing fistfuls of his hair, I pulled his head back. "Is sex all you can think about?"

"Yes." He shifted on top of me. "Right now, sex is all I can think about."

Laughing, I widened my knees so his hips were sandwiched between my thighs. "At least you're honest."

"This is what happens when you make me feel so comfortable just being my stripped-down self, Ari." He shimmied down my body, undid my jeans and yanked them off, along with my panties.

I sighed. "You're impossible."

"I'm also ready for dessert."

"I have *actual* dessert. Want some ice cream?"

"No, thank you," he said, lowering his mouth between my legs. "All I want is pure Sugar."

My eyes closed as his tongue swept up my center. "I have that too."

. . .

I ended up on my knees in front of him on the couch, his jeans at his ankles, my head in his lap, his hands full of my hair.

"Fuck," he rasped. "You're such a good girl to take it all like that."

Every inch of my skin tingled, and my clit fluttered. I went harder at him, and within minutes, he was filling my mouth. When I felt the last pulses of his orgasm subside between my lips, I swallowed and picked up my head, grateful for oxygen.

His jaw hung open, his eyes closed. His chest still rose and fell with accelerated breaths.

"How was that for a happy ending?"

"That was *much* sexier than the ending of *Casablanca*." He opened his eyes, relaxing his grip on my hair. "Did I hurt you?"

"No." I smiled and wiped my mouth with the back of my hand. "I love your hands in my hair."

"You should let me braid it sometime."

"Stop it, you can't braid hair." I sat back on my heels so he could pull his jeans up.

"Want to bet? I'll prove it. Turn around."

I turned around and he moved to the edge of the couch so his knees bracketed my shoulders. I'd showered after work this afternoon, and my curls had dried in soft ringlets. He ran his fingers through them, and I closed my eyes.

"Okay, first I make three sections and now I cross this one over," he narrated, "and then that one. And then this one again."

I pictured the plait forming as he worked his way down between my shoulder blades, a look of concentration on his handsome face. "How did you learn to braid?"

"Someone taught me."

"Who?" I asked, feeling the sting of jealousy. Was it someone he'd dated?

"Her name was Catrina. She was a patient on the oncology floor of a children's hospital where I was doing a visit for the Wishing Tree Foundation."

"What's that?"

"An organization that grants wishes to kids with terminal illnesses but also arranges visits from celebrities."

"I didn't know you did that." My heart absorbed the sweetness of him like a sponge soaking up water. "It must be hard."

"It's hard to see kids suffering, yes. But it's not about me. And I'm good at keeping those feelings buried. Lots of practice."

I thought of a six-year-old boy who didn't speak for months. Who only spoke again when he could inhabit another character. "But is that...healthy? To always keep those feelings buried?"

"Probably not. But you do it for long enough, you get used to it." His hands stopped moving in my hair. "Done! But how will it stay in so I can show you?"

"Here. Give me the end." I reached over one shoulder and took it from him. "I need to look in the mirror."

He followed me to the bathroom and watched as I pulled a hand mirror from a drawer and turned around to check his work in the mirror over the sink. "Well? How did I do?"

"Perfect," I said, studying the loose braid he'd fashioned. "I'm very impressed. And I'll never doubt your skills again."

"Good." He tapped my nose.

Smiling, I tucked the hand mirror back into the drawer and wrapped an elastic around the end of the braid. I didn't want to take it out yet.

He leaned against the bathroom doorframe, watching me. "Do you want me to go?"

"No," I said honestly.

"Do you want me to stay?"

As if I'd ever turn him down. As if I were even capable of it.

"Yes," I said, even though I understood the danger posed by spending night after night in his arms. "I want you to stay."

• • •

"I have a surprise for you," he said as we quickly cleaned up the kitchen.

"You do?" I snapped the lid on a container of leftovers and stuck it in the fridge. "What is it?"

"I'm taking you to dinner at Etoile next week."

I gasped. "Really?"

"Yes. Our reservation is at six-thirty on Wednesday. But it's a bit of a drive, and there's something we have to do before dinner, so we have to leave around four." He closed the dishwasher and faced me. "Is that okay?"

I narrowed my eyes. "What's the something we have to do?"

"I'm not telling."

"I have a funny feeling it involves a food truck."

His muscular shoulders twitched. "Maybe. Maybe not."

"Dash." I pummeled his chest gently with two fists. "I haven't had a chance to think about it yet. Or talk to my parents. And I'm certainly in no position to commit to buying."

"You don't have to commit to anything. I just want you to meet Gianni and see the truck. And then we'll enjoy dinner at his restaurant. I'm sure it will be good, and you've earned a night off from cooking."

"I've been dying to go there," I confessed. "I've heard nothing but great things."

"See?" He tucked a lock of hair behind my ear. "We'll have a good time."

I grinned, already thinking about what I'd wear on this dream date with Dashiel Buckley at a romantic French restaurant.

"I love putting that smile on your face," he said, running his thumb over my lips. "It makes me feel so good."

• • •

In my bedroom, we undressed and got into bed on opposite sides but immediately met in the middle, my head on his chest, his arms around me.

"I keep thinking about what you said," I whispered.

"About what?"

"Burying your feelings. It makes me sad."

He brushed his fingers up and down my back. "I just don't like inviting people in that way."

"But why? What do you think would happen?"

"I don't know. I guess I just don't think it's anyone's business what I feel."

"Even if it would help your acting to be a little more vulnerable?"

His hand kept moving on my back. Up and down. Up and down. "I sometimes worry that I won't be able to turn it off. Like, if I feel anything too deeply, I'll feel everything too deeply. And I have memories that hurt."

I pressed my lips to his chest. "I know. But you also have a gift. You can make people *feel* things just by speaking words on a page."

"Maybe."

"You can, Dash. Everyone knows what it's like to fall apart. That's why it's so moving when we see it happening to a character we care about. Don't hold yourself back."

"You sound like Delphine."

I picked up my head and smiled at him. "Sorry. I get worked up thinking about this because I know how talented you are. I want the world to know it too."

He laughed softly. "Thanks."

"I just think it's so incredible to have that kind of power—you can tell stories that make people feel less alone. You can move them to laughter or tears. You can make people fall in love. All I do is cook stuff."

"Stop it." His voice was serious. "You have a gift too. And I'm not just talking about cooking. You see the best in people, and you know how to bring it out. You make everyone around you feel good about themselves. Especially me."

I tilted my head. "Are you just saying that because you like my blowjobs?"

"No. I mean, I love them, obviously, but I'm saying it because it's true. I feel more comfortable being myself around you than I ever have with anyone else."

"Really?" My heart sang in my chest.

"Yes. I don't know what the fuck it is—maybe it's because I've known you for so long—but I feel... I don't know. Safe with you."

I grinned. "Look at you talking about your feelings. Delphine would be so proud."

"Smart-ass." He spanked me lightly, and I kissed him, tipping onto my side and slinging a leg over his thighs.

"Will your dad worry when you don't come home tonight?"

"I sent him a text and told him I was staying somewhere else."

"Where did you say you were?"

"Ari, I'm twenty-seven. I don't have to explain my whereabouts to my father. Plus, I think he's so wrapped up in his secret love affair, he's oblivious to me. I wish he would just tell us about her." He ran a hand over my ass. "Not that I'm telling anyone about my lady friend. I'm keeping her all to myself."

"What are we going to do when Mabel comes home next week?"

"I don't know. Do we have to tell her?"

I chewed my lower lip. "I'm not good at keeping secrets from her. Plus, she *knows* me. She'll guess, even if I don't tell her."

"Is she going to make me give you up?"

"I don't think so." Between us, I felt his cock stirring, and I reached down to sheath it with one hand.

"Well, as long as she doesn't give me a bunch of shit about it, I don't care if she knows."

"Okay."

He rolled on top of me. "And now I don't want to talk about my dad, my sister, or my feelings anymore."

"Works for me," I said, wrapping my legs around him. "But can I say something about *my* feelings?"

"Sure."

"I feel safe with you too. I always have."

"Good." He lowered his lips to mine in the dark.

Chapter 16

My parents were at the diner in the morning when I arrived. As soon as I saw their car parked in its usual spot, I got excited to see them and hear about their trip. If it felt right, I thought I might casually broach the idea of a food truck and see how it went over.

I found my dad in the office and knocked on the open door. "Hey, Dad! Welcome back!"

He turned and rose to his feet with more difficulty than I'd have liked. "Angel! It's so good to see you and be back home."

I moved into his arms and gave him a bear hug. "Did you have fun?"

"Yes, but vacation is tiring."

"Tiring! You were on a cruise! It was supposed to be about rest and relaxation." I held him at arm's length and studied his complexion. At least he had a little more color in his face from the sun.

"Well, there were excursions and activities and shows and all kinds of things to do on the ship." He smiled, his eyes shining. "We got an email from that food writer. Mom answered his questions. Sounds like you really impressed him, angel."

I laughed nervously. "I hope so. Hugo Martin is a big name. It will be great publicity for Moe's."

"I'm so proud of you." He sank slowly into the chair again and winced, gripping his trapezius muscle on the left side.

"Dad, what's wrong?" I dropped to one knee beside him.

"Nothing." He rolled his shoulder. "Just a little joint pain. We old folks have to deal with it."

"Should I get you some Ibuprofen or something?"

"No, no." He smiled through the discomfort. "Don't worry about me. I'm okay. It was that plane ride yesterday. Those seats are getting smaller, I swear. And they weren't comfy to begin with." He waved me out of his office. "Scoot. Go get ready for the first shift."

I found my mom behind the counter, and after greeting her with a hug and complimenting her tan, I asked about Dad. "He doesn't seem rested," I said with concern. "And he said he's having some joint pain?"

"His shoulder was bothering him a little this morning when he woke up." She frowned. "And I don't know why he wouldn't be rested. Almost all he did was sleep on the ship."

"He needs to go to the doctor," I said emphatically. "As soon as possible."

"I have tried, Ari. You know your dad."

"I think we both have to try harder, Mom."

"So everything was good around here?"

"Everything was fine. Business was good." I fussed with the bottom of my apron. "Dad mentioned you heard from Hugo Martin."

"Is that the fellow who emailed us asking questions about you for his blog?"

"Yes," I said, quickly deciding against trying to explain to her what a food influencer was. "He came in while you were away and loved it. And he has a huge audience. It will be great for Moe's."

"That's wonderful, honey." She continued wiping down the coffee machine. "Although he mentioned a few dishes that didn't sound like anything like what we usually serve at Moe's. People might be confused about what kind of place it is."

"They won't," I said. "Everything is good at Moe's. But that reminds me. There's something else I wanted to ask you about."

"Oh?"

I took a breath. "What do you think about a Moe's food truck?"

"A food truck? Like an ice cream truck?"

"Sort of, but it would have a little kitchen in it, and we'd serve Moe's Diner food out of it. We could call it Moe's on the Go." I smiled brightly. "Isn't that cute?"

"But why would anyone need Moe's on the Go when they can just come to the diner?"

"Well, it would be more like catering."

Immediately she shook her head. "Your father and I have stayed away from catering. It's a tough business. And it distracts from the restaurant."

"The menu would be a little different," I said tentatively, scratching my thumbnail along a tiny chip in the marble counter.

"Different how?"

"Well, it would be kind of like my own thing. I could offer a more upscale menu than we serve here. Gourmet sliders, truffle fries. Things like that."

"Truffle fries!" She looked up at me in dismay. "Do you know how expensive truffles are?"

I took a breath. "That was just one example."

She was silent as she started cleaning again, appearing to concentrate hard on sanitization.

"Food trucks are fun, Mom," I said. "It's really the up-and-coming thing. I think people would love to have Moe's cater their parties."

"Who'd drive this truck around?"

"I would."

She began swiping a cloth over the coffee machine. "By yourself?"

"Well, I might need a helper for parties. I bet Gemma would do it," I said, naming my sixteen-year-old cousin. "She always works at Moe's during the summer."

"How much would the catering truck cost?"

"I'm not sure. Maybe around fifty grand?"

She stopped moving and blinked at me. "Fifty grand! We don't have that kind of cash lying around."

"I could apply for a loan," I suggested.

She opened the register and began counting the cash. "That's a lot of money to borrow. What happens if this venture doesn't work out? How will you pay it back?"

"I haven't thought about that," I admitted. "I guess I'd have to sell the truck."

"I don't know, Ari. I remember how devastated you were when you came home from New York after things didn't work out there. You barely got out of bed for a month."

I shook my head. "This wouldn't be like that."

"But it's a risk. And it could fail and leave you and the diner worse off."

"You think I'll fail?" My stomach turned over.

She shut the register drawer, paused for a moment, then turned to look at me. "Of course not. I'm sorry, darling. I don't mean to shoot down your ideas. I'm worried about your dad and the business and just feeling a little overwhelmed after being gone for ten days."

"It's okay, Mom. Forget I asked. It could be a terrible idea."

She touched my shoulder. "Give me a chance to catch up a little and talk to Dad, okay? Maybe we can work something out."

The door to the kitchen swung open, and my father appeared, rubbing that sore shoulder. "Judy?"

"Yes, dear."

"Do we have any Advil here?"

She put her rag down and moved toward him. "Yes, in my purse. I'll find it for you. And then I'm taking you home."

"But—"

"No arguments, Dad." Under the diner's bright lights, I could see the pallor beneath his tan. "Do what Mom says."

He jerked a thumb at me and addressed my mom. "Look who's the boss now."

"That's right." I folded my arms over my chest. "I've been the boss for ten days, and I'm going to stay the boss for one more. You're fired. Go home."

My dad chuckled as my mom put an arm around him, shepherding him back toward the kitchen.

I stood there for another minute or two, fidgeting with the hem of my apron and thinking about what my mother had said. *That's a lot of money to borrow. What happens if this venture doesn't work out? How will you pay it back?*

When the kitchen door swung open again, my mother looked at me with surprise. "What's wrong, honey?"

"Nothing. I was just—I'm really worried about Dad."

"He'll be fine," she said. "I'll get him all tucked into bed and come back shortly."

"Okay, but don't mention anything to Dad about the food truck idea, okay? I get it—it's just not the time."

"I won't say a word," she said, pretending to zip her lips. "Now what do you say we get some specials on the board? Got anything new to add this morning? One of your fancy French toast recipes?"

"No." I opened the drawer and reached for the chalk and eraser. "We can just stick to the old favorites today."

• • •

After my shift, I went out to my car and texted Dash.

> Hey, I brought up the food truck idea to my mom and she doesn't think it's the right time. We don't have to drive all the way down to Etoile next week.

Are you trying to get out of our dinner date?

> No, but we could have a less expensive dinner around here. Or we can cook at home.

I don't care about the money. I've
got Bulge Bucks. And I still want to
look at the truck.

Dash. There's no point.

I have strong feelings about this,
Ari. And you're the one who said
I shouldn't keep burying them.
We're going.

LOL okay fine. Are you still
coming over for dinner?

Yes. What movie are you
torturing me with tonight?

I was thinking about
Shakespeare in Love.

Is it sexy?

Actually, yes. It is.

Happy ending?

For you, always.

Then I will come.

And so will you.

Probably twice.

Laughing, I dropped my phone into my bag. My stomach,
which had been aching all day, suddenly felt fine.

He always made me feel better.

• • •

For dinner, I decided to make spaghetti and meatballs. While I cooked, I told him about the conversation with my mom.

"So she didn't give it a hard no," Dash said, slicing cucumbers for salads.

"I guess not. We sort of agreed to table it for now, until we know what's going on with my dad. Something definitely seems off with him, and I don't want to add to his stress level."

Dash glanced at me. "I thought it was just his back."

"Now his shoulder hurts too. And he doesn't seem to have much energy. His color is bad. My mom is trying to get him to see his doctor, but he never wants to go."

"My dad was like that too, and then after the heart attack two years ago, he started taking his health more seriously. He got on the right medications, started exercising, eating better…he's like a new man. With a new girlfriend."

I smiled, stirring the sauce. "Anyway, my mom said it's just not the time to take on such a big, expensive risk."

"You think it's about the money?"

"Mostly." I turned the heat off beneath the pot. "But she also mentioned the emotional risk. She brought up how depressed I was after New York. I know it was hard for them to see me like that."

"Sure, but she can't protect you from ever making a wrong move or being hurt," Dash argued. "That's part of life."

"I know. I just don't want to upset them. Here, taste this." I lifted the spoon from the sauce and blew on it, then held it out.

He slurped it up. "Damn, that's good."

I smiled. "Thanks. Family recipe. This was the first thing I ever learned to cook on my own."

"Your dad taught you?"

I nodded, and suddenly my eyes filled with tears. Dash set down his knife, came over, and wrapped me in his arms.

"Hey, it's okay. Everything will be okay." He kissed my temple. "I promise."

I circled his waist with my arms and buried my face in his strong, sturdy chest. "Sorry. I was just thinking about all the time he spent with me in the kitchen as a kid. I want him to be there for my kids too, you know?"

"He will be." He stroked my back.

Eyes closed, I inhaled the scent of him, which mingled deliciously with basil and garlic and fresh bread. "Thanks. You always make me feel better. I wish we didn't live so far apart."

"I'm not leaving yet, Sugar. I've got another two weeks."

"I know." But I didn't like thinking about any kind of deadline or expiration date. I just wanted to be with him while I could.

Even if every kiss, every touch, every night together would make the goodbye worse.

• • •

The following Wednesday, Dash knocked on my front door just before four o'clock.

"Jesus," he said when I pulled it open, his eyes wandering over me from head to toe. "You look fucking amazing."

"Thank you." I'd torn my closet apart looking for the right outfit—was this dress too dressy? Was that top too cropped? Did this skirt flatter my ass?—and in the end decided on a short black off-the-shoulder dress with long sleeves that hugged my curves but wasn't obscenely tight. I'd twisted my hair up and left a few loose strands around my face, and on my feet were strappy black sandals that might have been a little summery for the cool temperature but I didn't care.

And judging from the look on Dash's face, he didn't give a damn either.

He put his hands on my waist. "Is it too late to change my mind about staying in tonight?"

I laughed as I pulled the door shut behind me. "Yes. You look good too, by the way." He wore a charcoal suit and a blue shirt that brought out the color of his eyes. His jaw was freshly shaved, and his hair had the perfect tousle to it.

"Thank you." He glanced down. "I had to wear my wedding suit because it was the only nice thing I brought home. You're going to get tired of looking at me in it."

"Not likely," I teased, as he took my hand and led me off the porch. "But I'll let you know."

The scenery on the drive to Abelard Vineyards was stunning. Through the passenger window of Dash's car, my eyes drank in the gently rolling hills of Old Mission Peninsula, which sloped down to the sparkling blue water. Surrounding us were blossoming cherry orchards, lush green forest, and rows of grapevines. Abelard was one of several wineries on the peninsula, built by a French American named Lucas Fournier and his wife, Mia. Their daughter was now married to Gianni Lupo.

"He's got two kids now," said Dash. "And his wife is pregnant. I can't believe it."

"You don't want kids?"

"I don't know. Maybe someday, but I don't feel qualified at this point in my life. There's too much I want to do first. I think Abelard should be coming up on the left here shortly."

A moment later, we turned onto a tree-lined gravel driveway that curved around in front of a gorgeous stone villa that looked like it had been plucked right out of the French countryside. Parking for Etoile was around to the side, and I stared, slack-jawed, at the château as we pulled around it. It looked like a fairy tale.

When we got out of the car, I inhaled. The air was just as seductive as the view, perfumed with spring flowers. Dash came around and took my arm, and I smiled up at him, grateful for the assistance on the gravel in my heels.

As we walked along the path to the restaurant's entrance, we passed a group of older women who looked like they might have been friends enjoying an afternoon of wine tasting. "Gorgeous couple," said one, while another stumbled over her own feet staring so hard at Dash. I couldn't blame her.

Dash held the restaurant door open for me, and I stepped inside. It was a cozy, intimate space—I counted only nine tables, all but one occupied—lit by tabletop candles and wall sconces that cast a gentle glow. The scent of freshly baked bread, garlic, and herbs filled the air, and I inhaled appreciatively. Then Dash's hand was resting on my lower back, guiding me toward the hostess stand, and my breath was caught in my lungs.

The hostess smiled when Dash gave his name. "Gianni said to let him know when you arrived. Wait right here, please."

"Nice, huh?" Dash was looking out the restaurant's windows, which framed the sun sinking behind the vineyard, casting a golden glow over the vines and painting the clouds in pastel watercolors. But I could hardly appreciate the scenery because his entire arm was now hugging my waist, his hand sitting on my hip in a proprietary manner. Like I was his.

It was easy to pretend I belonged to him. We'd spent every

single night together for the last week. We woke up next to each other. We kissed goodbye in the morning and hello in the evening and fell asleep entwined in each other's arms.

"Dash!"

We turned at the sound of a male voice to see a guy wearing a white chef's coat striding toward us, a grin on his face. He was handsome and familiar—I'd seen him on *Lick My Plate*—thick dark hair, full mouth, strong jaw.

"Gianni, hey." Dash let go of me and the two men hugged in the way guys do, with quick thumps on the back. "Good to see you. Been a while." He gestured to me. "This is Ari DeLuca."

Gianni held out a hand. "Nice to meet you. I hear you might be interested in a food truck."

I laughed nervously. "Possibly. It's very nice to meet you too. I've heard wonderful things about Etoile."

"Thanks for getting us in," Dash added.

"Anytime. I hope you enjoy it." Gianni stood with his hands on his hips. "So should we take a look at the truck before you eat?"

"Yes," Dash said. "Lead the way."

His hand returned to my back as we followed Gianni outside.

• • •

"So have you thought more about it yet?" Dash's grin was mischievous across the table, candlelight flickering in his eyes.

"Dash! It's only been twenty minutes since the last time you asked."

"That interior is fucking incredible."

"It is." The truck's custom kitchen was a dream—all stainless interior, fridge and freezer, 24-inch griddle, two fryers, four burners with oven, refrigerated prep table, four sinks, and six-foot concession window—not to mention the exterior speakers and Bluetooth sound system.

"The price is good too."

"I still can't afford it." The asking price was just over forty thousand.

"I can."

I took another bite of my ratatouille, pinning him with a stare. "No."

"Why won't you let me invest in you?"

Because it will tie me to you for years to come. "Aside from not wanting to take your money, I cannot see my parents getting on board."

Underneath the table, he nudged my foot with his. "You can't see them where, in your crystal ball? Maybe they'll surprise you."

"My parents never surprise me."

He set down his fork and leaned back in his chair, studying me.

"What?" I asked, growing uncomfortable.

"Do you really not want this? Or are you just looking for excuses not to take a risk on yourself or do something that's just for you?"

I was saved from having to answer that question by the appearance of a beautiful, dark-haired woman at the side of our table.

"Hello. You must be Dash and Ari." She was petite, wearing a pencil skirt and pink blouse, and her hair was fashioned into a neat French braid, which trailed over one shoulder.

"Yes," I said. "Hello."

"I'm Gianni's wife, Ellie Lupo." Her smile was warm and lovely. "It's nice to meet you."

"You too," I said, shaking her hand. "Dinner was incredible. And the vineyard is so beautiful." I looked out the window again, where the setting sun had turned the sky orange and scarlet, and the vines seemed to shimmer in the light.

"Thank you." She laughed, shaking her head. "I grew up here, so I sometimes take it for granted."

Gianni approached the table and slung an arm around his wife's neck. "She takes me for granted too. I'm always telling her how lucky she is." He kissed her temple.

Dash laughed. "As someone who lived with you and your five thousand hair products, I'm gonna take her side." He rose to his feet and held out his hand to Ellie. "Hi. I'm Dashiel Buckley."

She shook his hand, her expression turning curious. "Buckley. You're not related to a Devlin Buckley, are you?"

"Yes." Dash looked surprised. "That's my brother."

Ellie's eyes popped. "What?" She thumped Gianni's chest with the back of a hand. "You didn't tell me that!"

Gianni looked unconcerned. "Who's Devlin Buckley again?"

"He's the groom at the wedding we're going to this weekend, one of the new owners of Snowberry Lodge." Ellie looked put out. "He's marrying my friend Lexi. I've told you this a hundred times."

"Oh, right." Gianni nodded, like it was all coming back to him. "I gave them some tips on the dinner menu for their new restaurant." He shrugged. "Yeah, I didn't put that together."

His wife rolled her eyes. "He never listens. And he doesn't ever give me any details—all he said was an old roommate of his named Dash was coming to see the truck."

"And that's true," Gianni pointed out. "Is it not, Dash?"

"It's true," Dash agreed.

Ellie ignored them and focused on me. "Anyway, it's so nice to meet you. Can I answer any questions about the truck?"

"I don't think so," I said hesitantly.

"The price is negotiable," Ellie said. "My dad will totally work with you."

"That's very generous." I paused. "I'm just—I'm still thinking about what I'd like to do. It's a big investment. And I need to convince my parents it's a good idea. They own the diner."

"I understand completely. I work for my parents too." She smiled like we shared a secret, and I felt a kinship with her. "Will I see you at the wedding?"

"Yes," I said. "I'll be there."

"Great! And in the meantime, please feel free to reach out if you have any questions. Let me go get you a business card." Ducking out from under Gianni's arm, she hurried toward the lobby of the inn.

"Ellie is the assistant winemaker here and runs the tasting room downstairs," said Gianni. "Do you have time to stop in there for another glass of wine before you go? It's still open."

Dash looked at me. "Do we?"

"Sure," I said, never wanting this surreal time with him to end.

"Awesome. I better get back to the kitchen, but Ellie will take care of you. Dash, good to see you." The two shook hands. "And Ari, give the truck some thought." He offered me his hand, and I took it. "I know it's a big decision, but from what Dash says about you, I bet it will be a success."

"Thank you," I said, blushing with pride and pleasure.

As we crossed the stone floor of the lobby and took the stairs down to the tasting room, Dash held my hand. At the bar, he pulled out a stool for me. When I grew a little chilly, he draped his suit coat over my shoulders. It smelled like him.

I wondered if there was anything I wouldn't do to be the woman he kept warm for the rest of my life.

• • •

We got home around eleven, and when Dash pulled up in my driveway, he put the car in park and turned to me. "Are we okay?"

I looked over at him, surprised. "Of course. Why do you ask?"

"You've been really quiet on the way home. Almost silent, in fact."

"Have I?" I thought about it and realized he was right. "Sorry. My mind is just going a mile a minute about a lot of different things."

He reached over and took my hand. "I'm probably putting too much pressure on you about the truck. I'm sorry."

"It's okay," I said. The truth was, my silence had less to do with the truck and more to do with handing my heart over to Dashiel Buckley piece by piece.

"I'm not trying to tell you how to run your life."

"I know you're not."

"I just believe in you. I want to help. And when I go back to California, I don't want you to give up on the idea that you deserve something for yourself."

"I get it. And I'm grateful to you for everything, but I can't take your money. I also need my parents to be on board. I know I'm an adult and shouldn't still worry about their approval, but this isn't just about me. And I was raised to put family first."

"You're a good girl, Sugar."

I laughed softly, heat blossoming through my chest. "Thanks."

"And I'm going to shut up about the truck now and tell you something else."

"What?"

He stroked my hand with his thumb. "I've been thinking a lot about what you said. About how being able to make people feel things is a gift."

"And you've got it," I said quietly. "You should share it."

"I want to. I'm going to work on digging a little deeper, even if it hurts. Even if it feels like exposing too much of myself. I want to do what Delphine said and take down the walls."

"Good."

"Can I stay tonight?" He always asked.

"Of course."

As we walked hand in hand to the front door, I found myself thinking about walls and wondering if I'd be wise to build some.

Chapter 17

DASH

*T*hursday morning, I got up early with Ari, kissed her goodbye, and headed home. My dad was in the kitchen having coffee and mentioned he was heading to the gym soon, and I decided to join him. On the ride there, I asked again about his trip to Tennessee and his friend who lived there, but he gave vague answers that didn't reveal much and kept trying to change the subject. Finally, I decided to be blunt.

"Dad, is the friend you went to visit a woman?"

He shifted uncomfortably in the passenger seat. "Yes."

"A single woman?"

A pause. "Yes."

"And you enjoy each other's company?"

"Yes. But we're just friends."

I had to smile. "I think that's great, Dad. Friends are the best."

"Yeah." He seemed to relax slightly. "This friend, she…she's someone I really like and admire."

"Yeah?" I drove a little slower, wanting to give my dad the time he needed to talk. "Tell me about her."

"Well, she's full of energy. She's kind. She loves to laugh." He chuckled. "She thinks I'm funny."

I grinned. "Is she pretty?"

"She's beautiful. Really beautiful." He was silent a moment. "She's nothing like your mother, though."

"That's okay, Dad. The only thing that matters is that you like her and enjoy spending time with her."

"I do. I think for a long time I just didn't see the point in spending time with anyone because I was never going to feel for anyone else the way I felt about Susan. But Julia, she…she understands that. It's okay with her."

"That's her name? Julia?"

"Yes. She's actually Kelly's mom. Xander's Kelly. Which makes it even more complicated."

"I don't think so," I said, relieved to have this out in the open. "Xander once mentioned that Kelly's dad wasn't the greatest."

"He wasn't. Isn't." My father exhaled. "But he doesn't come around much anymore." He lifted his chin. "Kelly deserved better. They both did."

I turned into the gym parking lot and found a spot. "Kelly and Xander will both be thrilled about you and Julia spending time together. I know it."

"We decided to keep it between us at the start, just because we weren't sure how it was going to go." My dad lifted his cap off his head and replaced it. "It took me by surprise, that feeling. Being attracted to someone. Wanting to know her better. Wanting to be alone with her."

I hid a smile at the color creeping up his neck. "I get it, Dad. And I don't mean to rush you. I'll keep this between us if you'd like, but I know for a fact everyone you care about will be happy for you. We've been hoping for this for years."

"I know," he said. "I just never thought I would find someone like Julia." His voice took on a reverential tone. "She's so sweet and understanding. Plus, she's spontaneous and fun. She's always up for anything."

"She sounds wonderful, Dad. I can't wait to meet her." I killed the engine. "Here's an idea. Why don't you bring her to Devlin's wedding?"

"Oh, I couldn't do that," he said quickly.

"Why not? I'm sure she could jump on a flight later today. Or early tomorrow, even. The wedding isn't until Saturday."

He rubbed his chin. "But Kelly won't even be there. Won't that be strange?"

"Actually, Dad, Kelly *is* going to be there. She's flying in today to surprise Xander. She canceled a private concert to be with him."

My dad laughed. "That's just like her! Julia is like that too. Always doing something for people she cares about."

It reminded me of what Ari had said the other night. *It's about what we'll do for the people we love.*

"I guess I could ask Julia if she'd like to come," he mused. "If you think it would be okay with everybody."

"It will be more than okay, Dad. Everybody will be thrilled." We got out of the car and walked toward the gym entrance. "Thanks for telling me about her."

"You're welcome. I have to admit, it feels good to get it out there. I didn't much like hiding what I was doing." We reached the door and I pulled it open for him. But instead of going in, he stopped and gave me a pointed look, his eyes dark and wise. "So when are you going to stop hiding what's going on with Ari?"

My jaw ticked. "Huh?"

"You heard me."

I nodded toward the open door. "Just go inside and work out."

"What, you can ask me all about my lady friend, but I can't inquire about where you've been spending your nights for the last week, sneaking in early like a cat burglar?"

"That's right."

He chuckled and patted my arm. "It's fine, son. I don't need to run inside a burning building to know it's hot. I can see the flames from here."

. . .

When we were done working out, my dad stopped to chat with a friend in the lobby while I checked my phone. I saw two new messages, one from Ari and one from Izzie.

I looked at Ari's first.

Hey, Mabel asked if I wanted
to pick her up from the airport.
I'll be back around six.

In what car?

Huh?

What car are you planning
to drive to the airport in?

My car.

I'll take you.

My car isn't THAT bad.

It is. No arguments. What
time should I pick you up?

Three. You big bully.

See you then.

Next, I tapped Izzie's text.

Hey Dash! I HAVE NEWS.
I'm heading to Bali for my yoga
retreat but there was an inquiry
about you from Katherine Carroll's
team. It came in yesterday, and
my new assistant, Beatrix, is going
to get back to them. Your luck is
changing already! You must have
cleared your cloudy energy!

Holy shit! If I hadn't been in public, I'd have pumped a fist
in the air. This was it, I could feel it. My big chance. All that
walking around naked had worked!

My cell service and internet are
going to be spotty for the next
week, so Beatrix will be in touch.
Can't wait to hear what this is
about! Cheers, darling!

I tossed my phone in my bag and stood near the door, waiting for my dad to notice I was eager to get going. I couldn't wait to tell Ari the news about my audition—at least, I assumed it was an audition. But what else could it be? I wondered when it would happen, and if I'd have to go back to L.A. sooner than I'd planned to.

My chest caved a little at the thought of leaving her behind. Even though this was a totally casual thing, saying goodbye wasn't going to be easy. I was going to miss her.

But that didn't mean I was attached, did it? Just because I didn't want to spend a night here without her and couldn't seem to go more than ten minutes without thinking of her and felt like my heart had this Ari mode it shifted into whenever she was around that made it beat extra hard and fast didn't mean strings had been created, right?

Fuck. Maybe it did. Maybe Xander had been right and even if you were careful, it just happened.

But it's not like anything could be done about it. She lived here and I lived there. She was focused on her family, and I was focused on my career. She wanted a relationship like her parents had, like Gianni and Ellie had, or Veronica and Austin. She'd told me flat out she wanted someone who'd *be there*. Be *in it*.

It just wasn't me.

Frowning, I grabbed my sunglasses from the outside pocket of my bag and slipped them on.

Once I was gone, the strings would snap.

• • •

By the time I'd gotten out of the shower, there was a voicemail and a text from an unknown L.A. number. The text appeared to be just a house address along with a day and time.

52 Beverly Park Terrace 4:00 Tuesday

I hit play on the voicemail.

"Hi Dash, this is Beatrix. I spoke with Ms. Carroll's assistant. She'd like you to be at the house at four o'clock on Tuesday. I'll text you the address. You can call me with any questions."

Tuesday. Less than a week away. That meant I'd have to change my ticket and fly back sooner than planned. I'd have to say goodbye to Ari in three days at most. My gut twinged.

Instead of dwelling on it, I called Beatrix back.

"Hello. This is Beatrix."

"Hi. This is Dash."

"Hi, Dash! You got my messages?"

"Yes, but was there any other information?" I squinted at my reflection in the mirror above the dresser. "I'd love to know more."

"She didn't exactly say. Someone else at the office took the original call from her." Beatrix sounded sorry to disappoint me. "Should I call her back and ask?"

"Could you? I just want to be prepared."

"Of course. No problem." She laughed nervously. "Sorry. I'm new at this. I'm still learning."

"No problem. Just let me know what she says."

Too restless and excited to sit around the house, I decided to go to the diner for lunch. I asked my dad if he wanted to go, but he said he had some things to do and disappeared into his bedroom with his cell phone. Smiling, I gave Fritz a scratch behind the ears and hoped my father was calling Julia to invite her to the wedding.

When I walked into the diner, I noticed Ari and a couple other Moe's employees all huddled behind the counter looking at something that might have been on someone's phone. I spied an empty stool and had just perched on it when she turned around, like she'd known I was right there.

"Dash!" Her eyes were bright, her smile wide. "It's posted! The piece Hugo Martin wrote about the diner!"

"About *her*," said Gerilyn, putting an arm around Ari's shoulders and giving her a squeeze. "I'm so happy for you, sweetie."

I set my phone on the counter and slid it toward her. "Show me," I said excitedly.

She found the article for me and handed the phone back. "Here. I have to grab some plates from the kitchen. I'll be back in a minute to get your order."

My heart raced as my eyes skimmed over the words on the screen.

In the heart of charming Cherry Tree Harbor, a family-owned eatery has been serving up tried-and-true comfort food for three generations of tourists and locals. Part homey warmth and part vintage kitsch, Moe's Diner welcomes you with hot coffee and homemade biscuits as well as a jukebox, chrome and red vinyl, and black-and-white tile floor.

Operated by the DeLuca family since it opened in 1950, Moe's recently got an infusion of fresh young energy, courtesy of Ariana DeLuca, daughter of current owners Maurizzo and Judy DeLuca, and a graduate of the Culinary Institute of America. Her passion for upscale comfort food is helping to reimagine the menu at Moe's without straying from what people love about it.

"I don't want to change Moe's completely," says Ariana, or Ari, as she's known in the small town where she grew up. "I love Moe's. The people here are family—not just the employees, but the customers too. I still want to give them delicious, filling comfort food that tastes like home. I just want to elevate it a little."

Her innovations on classic dishes were not immediately embraced. "We like a more traditional diner menu," Judy DeLuca says. "Not because we doubt her talent, but because we worry that people return to Moe's again and again because they know they'll love it. People get nervous about change."

Ari struck a deal with her parents. "Once a week I get to put two specials on the board that are a little different," she says with a laugh, "but the other two had to be Moe's stalwarts. Two for them and two for me."

As fate would have it, I stopped in on a day when she had two of her specials on the chalkboard. My opinion?

Her sophisticated twists on standard diner fare are inspired.

The Braised Short Rib Grilled Cheese is a triumph of flavors and textures. The succulent meat, braised to perfection and layered with a creamy gruyère cheese, melts in your mouth. The house-made sourdough is grilled to a golden-brown crisp, offering a satisfying crunch with every bite.

Equally impressive is the French Chicken Pot Pie. Combining traditional French ingredients like shallots, tarragon, and flaky puff pastry, DeLuca creates a pot pie that is both familiar and luxurious.

Which is exactly what the chef wants.

"I have the utmost respect for the perennial favorites," she says. "I don't want anyone to come to Moe's and feel like they won't be able to get what they came for. I just want to put my own spin on those timeless dishes. Make them more interesting, more elegant."

If my experience at Moe's was any indication, she succeeds. When asked if she'll stay at her family's restaurant or venture out on her own, DeLuca smiles. "I'm not sure what the future holds."

No doubt she has a bright future ahead of her, no matter where she ends up. In the meantime, head to Moe's Diner in Cherry Tree Harbor. Ms. DeLuca makes it worth the trip.

My chest felt like it might burst, I was so proud of her. She hustled out of the kitchen carrying two plates, and after setting them down in front of two customers, she hurried out from behind the counter. I was out of my seat already, my arms open. She flew right into them and I hugged her hard, picking her up off the ground.

"Congratulations! I'm so happy for you."

"Thank you." She was breathless with excitement as I set her down. "I still can't believe the things he said!"

"Have your parents seen it?"

She nodded. "My dad didn't come into work today, but my mom is on the phone with the local paper now. They want to do a story for our seventy-fifth anniversary this summer!"

"They must be so proud."

She lifted her shoulders and smiled shyly. "I think they are."

I grabbed her hands and gave them a squeeze. "Maybe now's a good time to bring up the *thing* again."

"Hey." She stole her hands back and clasped them against her chest. "You promised you'd stop with the pressure."

"I said I was *sorry* about the pressure. I never said I'd stop."

"You're terrible," she said, shaking her head. "But since you're here, can I feed you?"

"Always." I took a seat at the counter and watched her get back to work, trying not to think about what it would be like a week from now, when I wouldn't get to see her smile every day, or hear her voice, or make her laugh, or remind her that she shouldn't come last on her own list.

It made me want to grab her arm and pull her onto my lap and hold her close. The longing was deep and sharp, a grappling hook lodged in my heart.

This felt like more than strings.

Chapter 18

*D*ash ended up staying at Moe's until my shift was over. He sat at the counter like one of the regulars, chatting with old Gus and Larry for hours. It made me smile every time I looked over at him.

They told anyone who'd listen about the piece Hugo Martin had written about me. Between the three of them and the rest of the Moe's staff, my ego was having its best day ever. Even my mother seemed genuinely excited for me, proudly emailing the link to all her friends and even printing it out on the rickety old HP LaserJet in the office. The article—along with the accompanying photo of me—now hung on the bulletin board right by the diner's entrance.

Would it change my life? Probably not. But it was a step forward, and I'd take it.

Eventually, the diner cleared out and I locked the front door. My mother had run home to check on my dad and would come back to open for the dinner shift.

"Hey," I said, dumping out the last of the coffee from the pot. "I just have a few things to do in the office and then I want to run home and change out of my uniform before we go to the airport."

"I can wait and follow you back."

"Okay." I smiled at him. "Don't get into any trouble out here."

In the office, I removed my apron and set it aside. I'd just sat down at the desk to look at some inventory notes when I heard my phone buzzing in my purse. Reaching into my bag, I glanced at the number but didn't recognize it. It had a New York area code. Media maybe? Someone who'd seen Hugo Martin's piece?

"Hello?"

"So you still answer the phone when I call."

"Excuse me? Who is this?"

"Oh, that's right, you blocked me, like a toddler having a tantrum. But I have a new number."

I froze. "Niall?"

"Good of you to remember my voice, considering the fact that you didn't even think to mention me in your little Hugo Martin interview."

"You saw it?"

"Yeah. One of the line cooks showed it to me. Imagine my surprise when there was no mention of the mentor who hand-chose you to be his protégé and taught you everything you know."

My mouth was dry, and my gut instinct was to stay silent and take it. Or even hang up. But somehow, from somewhere, I found the moxie to talk back. "You didn't teach me anything but self-doubt. And what would you even want to take credit for? My boring ideas? My average technique? My unsophisticated palate? All you ever did was tear me down."

"That's how it's done, Chef. That's how you learn. Although you were never a very good student. It's nice your family has a tired little tourist trap that can employ you to flip burgers for people who don't know any better. God knows you wouldn't have found work in any kitchen that matters."

My stomach clenched in that horrible way it used to when he'd belittle me. "Fuck you, Niall! I don't care what you say about me, but don't ever insult my family or our restaurant. Why did you call me anyway? Was it just to ruin today for me? Is it that you can't stand to see me do well?"

"I called to congratulate you. It's *your* ingratitude that's turning this into something else."

"Don't ever call me again, Niall. I'm—" But I didn't get a chance to finish my sentence because the phone was yanked out of my hand. I looked up in surprise to see Dash standing there like an angry god, his face mottled with fury, the phone to his ear.

"Listen, motherfucker. If you ever contact Ari again, I will fucking burn your restaurant to the ground."

Too stunned to move, I watched his scowl grow more menacing.

"Yeah? Well, as far as I'm concerned, you're a fucking nobody. Stay away from her." He jabbed at the screen, ending the call, then yelled into it one more time. "Fucker!"

"Dash." I grabbed his wrist. "It's okay."

"It's not." His chest was still puffed up. "That asshole doesn't get to call you and upset you. Not on my watch."

"You don't have to watch me, Dash. I'm a big girl. I'm fine."

His shoulders slumped, and he crouched down next to the

chair. "Fuck, I'm sorry. I shouldn't have done that. When I heard his name, I just snapped. I figured he was calling because he'd seen the post about you and wanted to make it about himself."

"You were right. But I could have handled it. I'm not the same person I was last year. That said…" I smiled. "Thanks for standing up for me. That was an excellent display of emotion. Where did it come from?"

He exhaled, shaking his head. "I don't know. Just the thought of him treating you the way he used to—of *anyone* treating you badly—made me want to smash things."

I smiled and reached for the phone, blocking the number he'd called me from. "No need to smash or burn. I can't have you getting arrested before you win that Oscar."

"Might be worth it," he said.

Laughing, I rose to my feet and drew him up with me. Then I put my arms around his neck and held him close. "Niall would never be worth it. Like you said, he's a nobody. And you're my somebody."

His embrace about swallowed me whole.

Chapter 19

"The Taj Mahal!" Ari shouted.

"Yes!" Mabel pointed at her with the dry erase marker and jumped up and down. "Girls win again!"

It was the third time in a row the girls' team—Veronica, Kelly, Ari, Mabel, and Adelaide—had beaten the boys' team, consisting of Austin, Xander, me, Owen, and Dad.

"The Taj Mahal?" Xander, who'd hardly taken his arm off Kelly's shoulder all night, got off the couch and went over to the board. "What about this scribbled mess says Taj Mahal to you?"

"The onion dome at the top," Ari said. "It's obvious."

"No way. You guys cheat. I'll never believe you don't have some kind of subliminal messaging system." Xander sank down next to Kelly, who patted his leg.

"It's okay, honey. You don't have to get mad just because your team didn't recognize your blizzard."

"Maybe if he'd drawn something resembling snow and not just a bunch of dots," said Austin.

"I didn't draw just dots," Xander defended. "I drew swirling lines too. That was clearly wind, and it was obviously a blizzard."

I laughed and rose to my feet. It was weird sitting all the way across the room from Ari. I was used to being close to her. "Should we play again? Mix up the teams?"

"This is like the only time in my life I wish I could play on the girls' side," grumbled Owen, who sat on the floor petting Fritz. "Every other time, I think they're gross."

My dad leaned forward and ruffled his hair. "You'll change your mind someday."

Owen snorted. "I doubt it."

"We should probably head out." Austin rose to his feet. "We'd like to get an early start on the road to Snowberry tomorrow. The kids and I want to hike the mountain trails."

"And I want to visit the spa," said Veronica. "Lexi says the saltwater grotto is amazing."

"Ooh, let's do that too," Mabel said to Ari.

"Sounds good to me." She glanced my way and quickly tried to look as if she hadn't.

We'd been playing this game for hours now—pretending there was nothing between us. Mabel hadn't raised an eyebrow when we explained that Ari was having car trouble, so I'd volunteered to drive to the airport. Since Ari had always been around for pizza and game nights, no one thought it was out of the ordinary that she was here tonight.

But I was pretty sure everyone in the room knew what was going on except for Mabel.

"I guess I'll take off too," I said. "I still have to think about what I'm going to say during my toast."

"I bet you could wing it and be totally fine," Mabel said.

"Maybe, but I feel like I better not wing this one."

"Before you all go," my dad said. He moved to the edge of the couch and cleared his throat. "I have something to say."

"What's up, Dad?" Mabel asked.

"There's, uh, someone I'd like you all to meet this weekend."

Xander and Kelly exchanged a glance. From the corner of my eye, I saw Ari's face turn in my direction.

"There is?" Austin looked puzzled.

"Yes. You see, I've, uh, decided to bring a guest to the wedding. A friend." He sat up a little taller, squaring his shoulders. "A lady friend."

"Oh," said Veronica. "I think that's wonderful, George. I can't wait to meet her."

"Actually, you've met her." My father looked a little sheepish and turned his focus to Kelly and Xander. "It's Julia. Kelly's mom."

"*Oh*. Then I guess I have met her." Veronica laughed heartily. "And it's even more wonderful, because Julia is so sweet!" She looked over at Austin, who seemed to be frozen where he stood. "Don't you think that's wonderful, honey?"

"Yeah," he said, recovering. "That's great, Dad."

"So she's coming to the wedding?" Xander looked at Kelly. "Did you know about this?"

"I just found out this morning before I got on the plane," she said, her expression a little guilty. "But Mom made me promise not to say a word until George brought it up."

"She's flying up early tomorrow," Dad confirmed. "And I'll pick her up and drive up to Snowberry a little later in the day."

He paused. "She has her own room, of course."

"Of course," I said, suppressing a grin.

"So, Dad, have you been seeing Julia for a while?" Austin asked, trying to piece it all together.

"Just the last few months," he said. "We agreed to keep it quiet to see how things went. I hope you understand."

"Of course we do, Dad," I said. "And we're all happy for you. I can't wait to meet her."

"Me too," said Mabel.

"You'll love her." Ari grinned at Mabel. "She's really fun."

"But wait a minute—Dad, if you're waiting for Julia to arrive, does that mean Ari and I should find another ride to Snowberry?" Mabel asked.

"I can take you," I said, before anyone else could offer. "I've got a big enough car."

"Great!" My sister smiled at me. "What time will we leave?"

"Ari has to work, so maybe around three?"

Mabel looked confused. "How do you know she has to work?"

"I must have told him on the way to the airport," said Ari quickly. "But if you guys don't want to wait for me, I can drive myself."

"We can wait for you. Or Mabel, if you want to hitch a ride with Austin and get there early enough for a spa day, I can just wait for Ari."

"Do that," urged Veronica. "We've got room in our car."

Mabel looked at Ari. "Would that be okay?"

"Of course." Ari glanced at me without actually meeting my eyes. "Thanks, Dash."

"No problem."

Everyone on the couch stood and stretched, and a few people

carried their empty popcorn bowls to the kitchen.

I approached Ari and kept my voice low. "Can I give you a ride home now?"

Her cheeks reddened slightly, and she looked at my chest. "Sure. If you don't mind. I just have to put my shoes on. They're by the back door."

"No problem." I watched her leave the room.

"Dash, can I talk to you for a second?" Mabel grabbed my arm and tugged me toward the dining room.

"What about?" As if I didn't know.

She faced me, all five foot two of her, pushed her glasses up her nose and gave me a look that meant business. "I'm not going to ask what's going on with you and Ari, because it's obvious. I just want to say that I hope I'm not going to be mad at you for it."

"You won't be. Ari and I are good."

She glanced toward the kitchen and lowered her voice. "Okay. As long as you know that she's always had a lot of feelings for you."

"I know."

"And when Ari cares about someone, she cares *deeply*."

"I know that too." No one needed to explain Ari's heart to me.

"And it's all good?"

"It's all good." Except for that hook sinking into my chest.

"Okay." Mabel smiled, even as she cringed slightly. "I mean, it's weird for me, but whatever—I'll deal with it."

"As weird as Dad having a lady friend?"

Her eyes widened, and she shook her head. "Did you know?"

"Xander and I had a hunch," I confessed. "And I think it's a good thing."

"Oh, I do too," she said quickly. "It's just a surprise."

"Life's full of them," I told her. Slinging an arm around her shoulder, we walked toward the kitchen, where Ari was waiting for me to take her home.

• • •

"Mabel knows," I said as I pulled away from my dad's house.

"I didn't tell her, I swear." Ari held up her hands stick-em-up style.

"I know. You were right—she just had a sense about it."

"She didn't say anything to me. Did she seem surprised or upset?"

"Neither, really. She just sort of warned me like Austin and Xander did to be nice to you."

Ari snickered. "If they only knew how nice you are to me."

"Probably best that they don't. Mabel did seem a little squicked out."

"I will keep the details to myself," she said, making an X over her chest. "So your dad came clean about Julia—that was cool."

"Yeah." I rubbed the back of my neck. "It was. I'm happy for him."

"What's wrong?"

"Nothing's wrong." I sensed her looking at me in the dark of the front seat. She knew something was on my mind. "In fact, something might be really right. I got a text from Izzie earlier today."

She gasped. "And?"

"And apparently Katherine Carroll's assistant made an inquiry about me yesterday. She wants to meet with me next week."

"What? Dash!" She threw her hands up. "You've known this all day and you're just telling me now?"

"It's been a busy day. And I don't really know what it means."

"It means you're getting that role you want—I just know it." She squealed with joy and clapped her hands. "I'm so excited for you!"

"Thanks."

"When is it happening?"

"Tuesday," I said, pulling into her driveway.

"Tuesday?" Was she doing the math? "Wow, that's...that's soon. When will you fly back?"

"Monday." I tried to make a joke of it. "Will you be glad to be rid of me?"

She tried too. "Yes. Get lost and take all the orgasms you've been giving me with you."

"You'll miss them, huh?"

"I'll miss a lot of things, Dash." Her voice was soft, and yet it pierced my heart.

I cleared my throat. "Of course, I probably shouldn't get my hopes up. I haven't had a single audition go well all year."

"Stop." She reached over and put a hand on my leg. "You're going to get exactly what you want, Dash. I know it."

Amused, I turned to look at her, setting my forearm across the steering wheel. "You're an expert in psychic healing now, huh?"

"I don't have to be an expert to see that you put it out into the universe that you're willing to be more vulnerable in your work, and the universe answered back the very next day with this meeting. Sometimes one moment changes everything."

"Huh. Maybe you're right."

"I am." She unbuckled her seatbelt. "So if you'd like to come in and strip down to your purest self to celebrate, I know a place where our energies could meet."

I turned off the engine. "Say no more."

. . .

By the time we got inside, something was different.

I wasn't in the mood to joke or play games or even talk at all. I just wanted to get as close to her as possible. It was like I could feel the weight of the few days we had left bearing down on me. Like I could hear the ticking clock. Like I was being chased by something and only proximity to her would keep me safe.

I started kissing the back of her neck while she locked the front door. I kicked off my shoes and unbuckled my belt on the way to her bedroom. I removed every stitch of clothing from her body and mine within seconds, as if I had more than two hands. And when my head was cradled between her thighs, her hands grasping my hair, the unbearable sweetness of her on my tongue, I began to panic, wondering how many more times I would have her like this—warm and soft and whispering my name, inviting me inside.

What if I left and she moved on to someone else? What if another guy came along to watch movies with her and eat her cooking and know the sublime pleasure of her skin and her hair and her smile and her taste? What if he wasn't good for her? Who would be here to protect her?

Sliding up her body, I covered it with my own, like I could hide her away from the world. Keep her safe. Keep her warm. Keep her *mine*. I eased inside her, angling my hips the way she liked, moving with slow, steady strokes that made her arch and sigh and pull me closer. Take me deeper. Urge me with her body and her voice to fuck her harder. Faster. Make her come. As the pressure built inside me, I felt it not just in my lower body, but moving like a tidal wave into my lungs, crashing over my heart, rushing over my head. I was drowning in conflicting desires—to fight and to surrender. To confess everything and admit nothing. To attach myself to her and to sever the strings.

Then her body tightened around my driving cock and all I could do was pour myself into her with every thrust and hope somehow she knew what she meant to me.

What she'd always mean to me.

. . .

"So what are you going to say in your toast to Devlin and Lexi?" Ari lay nestled against my side, her head on my shoulder, one bare leg tossed over my hips.

"I don't know. Got any ideas for me, Miss I Read Nothing But Romance Novels?"

She laughed and continued brushing her fingertips in relaxing little circles on my chest. "Not really. Just speak from your heart. Be genuine. Say nice things about love and happily ever after."

"Hmph."

"Hmph?" She picked up her head. "Excuse me, but did you just *harrumph* at happily ever after?"

"I did not harrumph," I clarified. "I made a slightly harrumph-like noise."

She propped her head in her hand. "So do *you* believe in love and happily ever after? We've only talked about my views on the subject."

"I believe in love," I said carefully. "But I agree with you—not every love story can have a happy ending."

Her face scrunched up. "Do *not* say that at the wedding, Dash."

"I wasn't going to," I said, laughing. "But it's true, just like you said. You can love someone and end up apart. For example, one of you might not survive the sinking of an ocean liner. One of you might get on a plane to make the world safe for democracy. One of you might have to marry a real d-bag named Wessex."

"I'm so glad I made you watch all those romantic movies," she said. "You really soaked up the emotional depth."

"All I'm saying," I said, tipping her onto her back and rolling on top of her, "is that it doesn't mean you don't *love* someone just because you go your separate ways. Maybe the timing is just wrong."

"There's an iceberg ahead." She hooked her heels around my thighs and her wrists around my neck.

"Someone has to leave." I kissed her, slow and deep. Then I picked up my head and looked down at her in the dark. "But it's still real, in the moment. You can still feel it. Just because it won't last forever doesn't mean it never existed at all."

"Dash," she whispered, her palm on the side of my face.

I swallowed hard. My heart felt like a balloon inflating in my chest. "Yes?"

"If I ever get married, you are not to give any kind of toast."

By the time her words registered in my brain, she was giggling. Quickly, I turned her onto her stomach, pinning her hands behind her back. "Are you making fun of me getting in touch with my feelings?"

"I'm sorry," she said, squirming and laughing beneath me. "It just popped into my head! That was good emotional depth!

You're two for two today!"

I shimmied down her legs, clamping them together with my knees, and nipped her ass with my teeth, making her shriek. "Apologize again."

"I'm sorry!" she squealed.

I bit her again, not too hard, just enough to make a point. "Again."

"I'm sorry," she said breathlessly.

"Now tell me I can say whatever I want at your wedding." I rubbed my jaw over the spot on her skin where my teeth had been.

"What would you say?"

"I'd tell whatever clown you were marrying he doesn't deserve you."

She laughed. "How do you know he doesn't deserve me?"

"I just know." I kissed my way around the curve of one hip.

"What if he's, like, a prince or something?"

Taking her by the wrists, I placed her hands above her head and stretched out on top of her back. "He's not."

"Fine. I won't marry him."

Pushing back, I got to my knees and hitched up her hips in front of me, eyeing her perfect body with hungry delight. The soft pink of her pussy. The inviting seam from her closed thighs all the way up the crack of her ass. I licked my fingers and slid them between her legs, rubbing her slowly. Then I fisted my cock and teased her with the tip. "Good girl."

Chapter 20

Ari

"So about this weekend," Dash said on the drive to Snowberry Lodge. "How do you want to handle it?"

"You mean us?"

"Yeah." He glanced at me. "Do you want to be open about us or keep things under wraps?"

There's an us, I thought. *There's actually an us. He said so.* "What do you mean by open?" I asked, sixteen-year-old me hoping he might say something about announcing our engagement.

"I guess I mean staying together. You in my room."

I bit my lip. "I'm supposed to stay with Mabel."

"I know, but she already knows about us. I doubt she'd care."

"What if your dad or your niece and nephew realize I'm sleeping in your room and ask why?"

"I'm pretty sure my dad knows something is up between us, but there's no pressure. If it makes you uncomfortable, stay with Mabel." He reached over and took my hand. "I'm just being selfish with you, since I only have a few days left. We'll still have Sunday night."

"Right." I was trying not to think about it. Every time I imagined saying goodbye, my stomach hurt.

Which was stupid. I'd always known this had an end date. And less than twenty-four hours ago, he'd told me without actually telling me that this was not going to last.

Even if it felt like love.

The words had been on the tip of my tongue last night— actually, who was I kidding? Where Dash was concerned, they'd been on the tip of my tongue since I was twelve years old. It was a miracle I'd made it to twenty-four without blurting them out. But I chickened out at the last second and made a joke instead. I was too scared that he would think I was trying to pressure him into making promises he clearly didn't want to make.

It wasn't like I hadn't been paying attention. I understood this was just a fling. I'd accepted the fact that he'd never be mine. We'd never belong to each other. Our lives were too different. Our bodies might have been in perfect harmony, but our dreams were not.

We would always be in each other's lives, even if it was never like this again.

Just friends.

It would have to be enough.

• • •

Dash and I arrived at Snowberry Lodge just after four o'clock on Friday afternoon. It was hard not to let my fantasies run a little wild as he held the door to the lobby open for me—*if we were a real couple, this is what it would feel like to take a weekend away together.*

While Dash checked in at the desk, I texted Mabel.

YAY! We're room 304.
Come on up.

> Sounds good. Is there
> a plan for tonight?

I think tonight is sort of a girls night. We're taking Lexi out for dinner and drinks, and then maybe meeting up with the guys later.

> Okay.
> See you in a minute.

Dash approached and handed me a key card. "Here. Room three-ten. I know you want to stay with Mabel, and I am totally fine with that, but if you want to re-enact that whole sneaking into my bedroom scene, I promise not to reject you this time."

I laughed and took the card, tucking it into my purse. "Thanks."

"What room is Mabel?"

"Three-oh-four," I said.

We rode the elevator up together and walked down the hall on the third floor. At Mabel's door, I stopped and looked at him. "This is me."

"Okay." After a quick glance up and down the empty hallway,

he gave me a quick kiss. "Hopefully, I'll see you later."

I nodded and smiled, wondering if I actually had the willpower to stay out of his room tonight. "Sounds good."

He continued moving toward his room, and I knocked on Mabel's door. As she pulled it open, Dash and I exchanged one last look.

"Hi!" she said excitedly. She was already dressed in dark jeans and a black top, but her feet were bare and her hair was damp. "Come on in!"

I entered the room, which was beautifully decorated in pale woods, soft creamy colors, and cozy textures. The two queen beds were made up with thick white bedding and fuzzy camel blankets draped across the foot. The large windows overlooking the mountain let in plenty of natural light, and I went straight to the glass, dropping my bag to the floor. My breath caught at the view. "It's so beautiful," I said, taking in the grassy slopes, the budding trees, the spring flowers blooming at the base of the hill. "I'd forgotten how pretty this place is."

"Same," Mabel said. "We came to Snowberry a few times as kids, but I barely remember it. And I certainly don't remember it like this. Devlin and Lexi have made tons of changes."

I turned around and took in the relaxing decor of the room. "The place looks gorgeous. They must have spent a fortune on the renovation."

"I think they did. You should see the spa—it's incredible. The bar is cool too. I poked my head in there earlier." She perched on the edge of her bed, leaning back on her hands. "How was the drive?"

"Fine." I knelt down and unzipped my bag.

"How are things with you and Dash? I take it you forgave him for walking into the kitchen in his birthday suit?"

Laughing, I pulled out my clothes for tonight along with my makeup bag. "Yes. And things are good. Casual, you know." Maybe if I said it enough times, my heart would start to believe it.

"Cool." She slapped her hands on her thighs and stood up. "And that's all I need to hear about that."

I grinned as I stood up. "I will not subject you to any further details."

"Thank you. Oh! Let me give you a key for the room." She went over to the dresser and grabbed a little envelope. "Here. Although, if you want to sleep in Dash's room, I get it. No worries."

I took the key from her and gave her a hug. "You know what? It's girls' night, and we haven't hung out in a long time. Let's just go have fun."

. . .

There were ten of us at dinner—Lexi, her friends Winnie Matthews and Ellie Lupo, her cousin Tabitha, Veronica and Adelaide, Kelly and Julia, Mabel, and me. I sat between Mabel and Ellie, who chatted with me about her experiences in mobile catering—she did a lot of wine dinners at private homes—and patiently answered my questions about the business end of things.

At Veronica's request, Lexi told the story of how she and Devlin had met and eloped quickly to Vegas. "Probably too quickly," she said with a laugh. "There were definitely some things we had to work out after we'd already tied the knot, but I've got no regrets."

I smiled at the beautiful dark-haired woman who'd captured Devlin Buckley's heart so fast, happy for her and hoping one day something like that might happen for me.

If I could ever get out from under Dash's spell.

We met up with the guys at Snö, Snowberry Lodge's newly renovated cocktail lounge, and even though I was determined to hang with the girls and not give in to the temptation to stand by Dash's side, he came right over to me the moment I arrived.

"You look gorgeous," he said quietly. "I've never seen that top."

"Thanks." I glanced down at the black lace bodysuit. "I don't have much of a chance to wear it. I get up and put on a Moe's Diner uniform every day."

"You look gorgeous in that too. You look gorgeous in everything." He sipped his drink. "And in nothing, of course."

"Shh." My face grew hot, and I glanced around to make sure no one heard. "We're supposed to behave this weekend."

"Did I say I would behave?" His blue eyes sparkled. "If I did, it was a lie told before I saw you in that top."

I laughed softly. "You make it hard to be good."

He tipped up his glass again. "You have my key, right?"

"I have your key."

"Use it, please." He leaned closer, his knuckles brushing the tip of one breast as he whispered in my ear. "I will make it hard for you all night long."

...

I wasn't going to.

I swear to God, I was going to stay in my bed right next to Mabel's all night long. We went up to our room around one, tipsy and laughing about it, removing our heels in the elevator and walking barefoot down the hall.

"God, I'm tired," Mabel said, switching her shoes to one hand while she pulled the key from her purse. "I cannot wait to put my pajamas on and crash."

"Same."

We got ready for bed, and by the time I came out of the bathroom after brushing my teeth and taking off my makeup, Mabel was on her back beneath the covers, a satin sleep mask over her eyes. On the nightstand, her phone played soothing ocean sounds.

"Is the noise okay?" she asked, sliding her sleep mask up to peer at me.

"Of course," I said, snapping off the lamp. "Goodnight."

"Night."

After tugging off my pajama pants, I crawled between the sheets in a T-shirt. I closed my eyes, but I could still see Dash above me in the dark. I listened to the waves crashing on the shore, but I could still hear him calling me his good girl. The minty flavor of toothpaste lingered in my mouth, but I could still taste his kiss.

I lasted about fifteen minutes.

Turning back the covers, I slipped out of my bed and tiptoed over to the dresser, where I'd set my purse. Digging around, I felt my fingers close around two different key cards and pulled them both out. With one last glance at Mabel, who appeared to be sound asleep, I moved silently on bare feet over to the door and opened it as quietly as I could.

Peeking into the hallway, I made sure it was empty before stepping into it and allowing the door to shut gently behind me. The moment it clicked, I went scurrying down the hall to room 310, waved the key card in front of the sensor, and let myself in.

Dash, already in bed, sat up and switched the lamp on. He was shirtless, his hair slightly tousled.

My breath came faster at the sight of him, and I whipped off my T-shirt. "I changed my mind."

• • •

The following morning, I snuck back into Mabel's room just as the sun came up. Opening the door as quietly as I could, I left the two keys on the dresser and tiptoed back to my bed.

"You can stop sneaking," Mabel said with a laugh. "I'm not your mother."

"Sorry. Did I wake you?" I slipped back into my bed.

"I heard the door just now. But I woke up a little bit ago and saw your empty bed. Out for a morning jog?"

"Exactly." I pulled the covers up. "A little vigorous exercise to start the day. But it was more like horseback riding than running."

"Ew!" She sat up and threw a pillow at me. "I told you I didn't want any details. That is not a visual I need in my head."

"Sorry, sorry." Laughing, I flipped onto my side and snuggled in. "Do we have to get up yet?"

"No. I need at least three more hours of sleep. And then coffee."

"Perfect." I closed my eyes and inhaled, the smell of Dash still on my skin. "Wake me when you're up."

• • •

At seven o'clock that evening, Mabel and I sat side by side on two chairs in the refurbished lobby of Snowberry Lodge. The ceremony would take place right in front of the beautiful stone fireplace that dominated the high-ceilinged room. Devlin stood in front of it now, Dashiel right behind him—sexy as hell in his charcoal suit. Tonight he wore it with a white dress shirt that showed off his golden California tan and an indigo blue tie a few shades deeper than his eyes.

We chatted for a couple minutes before everyone took their seats, standing apart from the group, over by one of the large windows that looked out on the mountainside. "You look beautiful," he said quietly, maintaining a respectable distance between us. "I love that color on you."

"Thanks." I looked down at the crimson halter dress with the long flowing skirt I had on. "I like this color too."

"It's killing me that I can't touch you." His gaze traveled over my bare shoulders to the nipped waist to the V neckline.

I smiled. "Good."

"You'll come to my room again tonight, right?"

"Maybe," I teased.

Just then, Devlin approached and clapped a hand on Dash's shoulder. "Ready, brother?"

"Ready." He gave my hand a squeeze before letting it go and following Devlin to the front of the room, while I went to find Mabel and ask her where I should sit.

She leaned over to me now and whispered in my ear. "Apparently that's the Elvis impersonator who married them last fall in Vegas."

The guy took his place at the foot of the aisle, sporting the iconic white jumpsuit and some serious sideburns. Mabel and I were in the front row, with a seat open on her right for her dad.

To my left was Xander, Kelly, and Julia; in the row behind us was Austin's family.

It was an intimate wedding—less than thirty people, mostly family—but you could feel the love in the room. And as the string quartet played "It's Now or Never," which Lexi had mentioned was their Vegas wedding song, you could see the love in Devlin's eyes as he faced the staircase and watched his wife descend.

I turned to watch as well, immediately choking up. Since Lexi's parents had died when she was young, George Buckley was giving the bride away, and he looked just as proud to do the honor as if Lexi had been his own daughter.

Next to me, Mabel sniffed and took my hand. I squeezed it as my throat constricted even more, glad I'd remembered to put tissues in my purse. They passed us by, and I admired Lexi's beautiful satin dress, the veil that had been her grandmother's, and the gorgeous bouquet of white roses she carried. But it was her inner radiance that stole my breath and made my heart ache, the kind of light that only came from true happiness. I wasn't a jealous person, but I found myself envying what Lexi and Devlin had found together. I wondered if I'd ever be so lucky.

When they reached Elvis, George kissed Lexi's cheek, gave Devlin a hug, and took his place next to Mabel. She sniffed again. "I'm already a mess," she whispered. "Who knew watching one of my brothers get married would be so hard?"

Leaning over, I plucked the package of tissues from my purse, handing it to her. "Here. But save me one."

"Welcome," said Elvis. "We are gathered here today to join two hearts in everlasting love—again."

Everyone in the room laughed.

"I'll marry this woman as many times as she'll let me," said Devlin.

Mabel grabbed my hand and squeezed it again. Dash caught my eye and smiled.

I smiled too, but the room was blurry.

. . .

"If I could have everyone's attention for a moment, I'd like to say a few words." Dashiel stood at his brother's side, his drink in one hand, the other on Devlin's shoulder.

The dining room at Skadi, the restaurant at Snowberry Lodge that had been closed to the public for the occasion, grew silent.

"This is a pretty small group, but for those of you who don't know me, I'm Devlin's brother Dashiel, and I have the honor of toasting the happy couple tonight." He paused before going on. "I think I speak for everyone in the Buckley family when I say what a shock it was to hear the news that Devlin had gotten married," he began, and many in the room laughed. "Of the five Buckley siblings, Devlin was the least likely to get hitched first. He'd never once expressed any interest in tying the knot, and while he was serious about many things growing up—his stellar grades, his insanely fast one-mile run time, his Verlander rookie card that I definitely did not take to school to impress friends without his knowledge—dating wasn't one of them."

"Good," said Lexi with a satisfied smile as everyone around the table chuckled.

Dash waited for the laughter to fade, then went on. "A couple weeks ago, when I got into town, I even said to our brother Austin, 'I can't believe he got married so fast.' And Austin said something like, 'When you meet Lexi, you'll get it.'" He looked down at his sister-in-law. "And he was right. I do."

Lexi touched her heart and smiled up at him.

"Sometimes one moment changes everything," he said, sending a little shiver up my spine. "You place the right bet. Take the right chance. Meet someone who makes you a better version of yourself. And if you're smart, you realize that no matter what path you're on or goals you've set or dreams you're chasing, none of it matters as much as being with that person." He looked at Devlin. "And my brother has always been the smartest guy I know. There's no doubt in my mind their dreams are better together."

Devlin tapped Dash's hand on his shoulder.

"The Buckleys have always been close. We've been there for each other through good times and bad"—his voice caught slightly, and I sucked in my breath—"and we were raised to believe there is nothing more important than family. So now, please raise a glass and help me welcome Lexi to the bunch, even though the girls did not need another player on their Pictionary team." He lifted his drink. "To Devlin and Lexi, the not-quite-newlyweds, may you enjoy a lifetime of health, happiness, and family game nights. Cheers!"

The wedding guests all raised their glasses and some shouted "Hear, hear!" After taking a sip of my sparkling wine, I caught Dash's eye as he walked back to his chair and sat down again, right next to me.

"Well?" he asked over the din of forks clanking on glasses. "How did I do?"

I smiled. "You were brilliant. Very heartfelt. I was all choked up, and then you made me laugh."

"Good." He mocked wiping sweat off his forehead. "I'm glad that's done."

I rubbed his shoulder. "You dug deep."

"I tried."

"Your heart energy came through loud and clear. Delphine would be so proud of you."

He laughed. "Thanks." Then he shocked me by putting his arm along the back of my chair, leaning over, and planting a kiss on my temple. "But it was you I wanted to impress."

My heart was galloping wildly. "We are not being very discreet right now."

"Do you care?"

I shook my head. "Do you?"

"Nope. Have I told you how beautiful you look in that dress?"

"A few times," I said, laughing as I tucked my hair behind my ear. "But you can say it as much as you want."

"You look beautiful in that dress." He put his lips at my ear. "Please tell me I'll get to take it off you later."

"Your chances are good," I murmured, running a hand along his thigh.

"Is it too early to leave?"

I burst out laughing. "We haven't eaten yet, Dash."

"The only meal I care about is under that red dress."

My skin burned with desire. "Be patient. We've got all night."

But I was just as anxious as he was to be alone.

We only had two nights left.

• • •

We managed to make it through dinner, through cake and dancing, through late-night cocktails and snacks in the bar. But eventually, Dash came up behind me and whispered in my ear once more. "You have a choice."

"Oh?"

"We can either walk out of here together or I can throw you over my shoulder and carry you out. But one way or another, we are going up to my room in five seconds."

I looked over my shoulder at him. "Either way makes it pretty obvious what we're doing."

"Four."

"Xander is looking at us right now."

"Three."

"I should let Mabel know."

"Two."

"Okay, okay," I said, laughing. "Don't do anything crazy. How about you walk out, I'll tell Mabel what's up and meet you in the lobby."

"Fine. But if you're not out there by the time I count to ten, I'm coming back in to do something crazy."

"I'll be out there before you can count to ten, I promise."

He dropped a kiss on my shoulder. "Good girl."

• • •

Up in his room, Dash didn't even bother taking the dress all the way off. He set me on the edge of his bed and knelt at my feet, his head disappearing beneath the flowing red material. Only after he'd pulled my skimpy underwear off and made me come with his tongue did he stand up, shrug off his suit coat and yank his tie loose, toeing off his shoes at the same time. I jumped to my feet, eager to help, desperate to be skin to skin.

I slipped the tie from his collar. I tugged the belt from the loops. My fingers trembled as I made my way down the column of buttons on his dress shirt. With every piece of clothing I removed, my heart tripped harder, its drumbeat accelerating in my ear. T-shirt. Pants. Boxer briefs. Finally, he was naked in front of me.

Crushing my lips to his, I ran my hands all over his skin— chest and arms and shoulders. I slid my fingers into his hair. I raked my nails down his back. I grabbed his ass and squeezed.

"Dress. Off," he growled into my mouth.

I spun around. "Buttons at the back of my neck. Zipper down the side."

He cursed as his big hands fumbled with the tiny buttons, eventually working them free from the loops. Finding the zipper pull at my ribcage, he dragged it down, and the dress fell like rose petals to my feet. Turning to face him, I threw my arms around him as our mouths came together. Wrapped in his solid embrace, I luxuriated in the heat of his chest against mine, the taste of his kiss, the hard length of his cock pressing against my belly.

He picked me up and dropped me onto the bed, stretching out above me. I could tell by the way he moved this would not be playful or patient. Within a minute, he was filling me up, driving inside me with deep, powerful strokes. I didn't care—I wanted him that way, fast and hard and *right there, yes, yes, yes…* I pulled him closer, begged him not to be gentle, not to hold back. I said his name again and again, just to feel it on my lips, like someone might take it away from me. I bucked my hips beneath his, matching his fevered rhythm, his frantic pace. Our skin grew damp, our muscles straining, and then we couldn't hold back anymore, our bodies releasing the tension in glorious bursts of shared bliss.

When it was over, I didn't want to let him go. I clung to him with my arms and legs, desperately hoping I wouldn't embarrass myself by crying, but my throat was tight and my eyes were teary and I was having a hard time controlling my breath.

One sob escaped, and then another.

Dash, still breathing hard, picked up his head. "Hey. You okay?"

"I'm fine." I started to laugh, even as the tears kept coming. "I have no idea why I'm crying. I'm sorry."

"It's okay," he said, his voice soft. He smoothed my hair. "That was kind of intense. Maybe I was too rough."

"No, no." I closed my eyes, willing the damn waterworks to stop. "It's not that. I'm just being overly emotional. Don't pay any attention to me."

"There must be something," he said, his voice warm and soft. "Talk to me."

"I think… I think it's just hitting me that you're leaving in a few days."

"Yeah. It hit me tonight too." He continued to play with my hair, winding curls around his fingers. "I wish I didn't have to go back so soon."

"It doesn't really matter when, Dash. You were never here to stay." I managed a shaky smile as tears leaked from the corners of my eyes. "I know that. I know what this was. I guess I just didn't realize it would hurt so much when you left."

He kissed my forehead, letting his lips rest there. "I didn't realize it either. Fucking Xander was right, wasn't he?"

Despite everything, I laughed. "We can never tell him that."

"Ever."

"God, Dash." I put my hands on either side of his face. "Why couldn't you have been a disappointment? Why did you have to be wonderful?"

He grinned. "Sorry?"

"You should be. How is anyone supposed to compare?"

"I feel the same. I look at you, and I wish…" He closed his eyes for a moment, and I held my breath. "I wish things were different, Ari. I wish I could make you happy."

Fresh tears spilled. "You're making this worse."

"I'm sorry. I don't know the right words to say."

"Say you'll thank me in your Oscar acceptance speech."

He smiled. "Of course I will. I made a deal."

We lay side by side for a while, saying nothing, just listening to one another's heartbeats. But soon, hands started to wander and mouths went searching, our bodies frantically seeking closeness once more, knowing our time was running out. Afterward, we fell asleep with limbs tangled, the sweat still drying on our skin.

The next thing I knew, someone was pounding on his hotel room door. "Dash? Ari? It's Mabel! Are you in there?"

Dash sat up and ran a hand through his hair. "What the fuck? What time is it?"

Glancing at the bedside clock, I pulled the sheet up to my chest. "Barely eight. Do you think something is wrong?"

"I don't know." Grumbling, he got out of bed and pulled his suit pants on. "Just a second!" he yelled, zipping them up on the way to the door. He pulled it open. "What's going on?"

"Is Ari in there?"

"Yes."

"I need to talk to her."

"Mabel, can this—"

"I'm serious, Dash. It's about her dad."

Chapter 21

*f*ear and worry gripped my heart. Behind me, I heard Ari make a startled noise and within seconds, she appeared at the door, wrapped in the thick knit blanket from the bed.

"What happened?"

Mabel's scared expression did little to ease anyone's panic. "Your mom called me," she said to Ari. "She said she's been trying to get ahold of you but you weren't answering your phone." Her eyes grew shiny. "Your dad was rushed to the hospital in the middle of the night. He had a heart attack."

Ari gasped and leaned against me. "Is he okay?"

"He's in stable condition." Mabel, who'd thrown a sweatshirt on over her pajamas, lifted her shoulders. "That's as much as I know."

"I've got to get out of here. I've got to talk to my mom. I need to see my dad." Ari started to cry, huge tears rolling down her cheeks, her shoulders shaking. "But I can't seem to move."

"Oh, honey, he'll be okay. He's got to be." Mabel looked at me. "What can we do?"

"I'll get her back home," I said firmly. "You tell Dev and Lexi and everyone else what happened. Say we're sorry we had to leave without saying goodbye, but it was an emergency."

She nodded. "They'll understand. I'm going to get dressed and help her pack."

"Good idea. Hey, can you grab something real quick she can wear right now so she doesn't have to put her dress on again?"

"Yes. Be right back." Mabel hurried down the hall.

When I closed the door, Ari turned to me with tear tracks running down her cheeks, her mascara smudged beneath her eyes. "Dash, you can't leave! Your family is all having brunch today. You need to be with them."

I took her by the shoulders. "Ari DeLuca, how many times are you going to make me explain that you are family to me? Now we don't have time to stand around and argue, and my mind is made up. You call your mom. I'm going to get dressed and throw my shit in my bag. When Mabel gets back with clothes, put them on and then we'll go collect your things and hit the road. I'll have you back in Cherry Tree Harbor in one hour. Where's your phone?"

"In my clutch." She moved toward the bed, searching the floor. "Which I probably dropped right...there!" She scooped up her purse and fumbled through it. Locating her phone, she wailed pitifully when she saw the screen. "I had it turned off! I missed sixteen texts and eighteen calls!"

"You didn't know," I said gently. "Call her now."

She tapped the screen and brought the phone to her ear.

"Mom? How is he?"

I stood opposite her, watching her fight panic. Our eyes met, and she kept looking at me while she listened. Every few seconds, she interrupted with a question.

"Stable? What does that mean? Is he talking? They're keeping him, right? What kind of tests? Bypass? When would that happen if they decide to do it?"

Gradually, the hysteria left her voice, and I could see her gain control of her breathing. When Mabel knocked on the door, I answered it, taking the joggers and sweatshirt from her hands. "Thanks."

"Any word?"

"She's talking to her mom now. I think he's okay, from what I can tell. He might need a bypass."

She nodded. "I remember when Dad had his heart attack. So scary."

"But he's good now," I pointed out. "Better than ever."

"Definitely." She peeked around my shoulder. "Okay, I'll go back to my room and start putting her stuff in her bag."

"Thanks. See you in a few."

After I closed the door, I tossed the clothing for Ari on the bed, got dressed, and quickly packed up my stuff. By the time I was done, she was off the phone. "He's okay right now," she said, her brow furrowed with worry. "I guess he can talk and he's out of immediate danger for the moment. But they're probably going to do a bypass. He should have been treated for heart problems long before now."

"Dads are stubborn," I said. "Mabel brought you some clothes. Want to throw them on and we'll go grab your bag and head out?"

"Yes." But instead of reaching for the sweats, she reached for me, and I took her in my arms, blanket and all, pulling her close. She started weeping again, and I just held her and let her get it out, the way she'd done for me in her kitchen last week. "Sorry," she sobbed into my chest. "I'm getting your shirt all messy with snot and tears and last night's eye makeup."

"I don't care." I kissed the top of her head and stroked her back.

After a couple minutes, she was calmer, her breath still coming in irregular hitches, but her tears slowing. "Okay," she said, wiping her eyes. "Okay. I need to get myself together and get home."

"Ready when you are." Gently, I took the blanket from her and then held up the sweatshirt for her to slip her arms and head into. I tugged it down to her hips and handed her the joggers.

"Thank you." She stepped into them, tugging them up to her waist. "This means everything to me, Dash. I don't know what I'd do without you."

"You don't have to know that." I gathered up her dress, heels, underwear, and purse. "Come on. Let's go."

• • •

I took her straight to the hospital and waited for her in the family lounge area. She'd told me to go, that she could find another way home and wouldn't be leaving for a while anyway, but I didn't feel right leaving her there. I told her I'd hang out for a little while and use the time to catch up on my texts and emails.

After a couple hours, she appeared in the lounge holding two cardboard cups. "Hey," she said, looking weary but better. "I brought you some coffee."

"Thanks." I took one cup from her, and she sat down next to me. "How's your dad?"

"He's okay. I mean, he looks terrible—pale and haggard and hooked up to tons of machines—but he's breathing and not in pain. He's sleeping a lot, but he did wake up and talk to me." She smiled wryly. "He asked who was managing the diner."

I chuckled. "Of course he did."

"My aunt filled in for my mom this morning, but I told him I'd close up later."

"Need help?"

She shook her head, placing a hand on my leg. "No. You've done enough for me. You don't need to spend your last night in town working at Moe's Diner."

I took a sip of my coffee and tried not to think about tonight being my last. "My dad called. He sends his best wishes for a fast recovery and says he has lots of tips for getting healthier."

"Oh, good. He looked so great yesterday. And how cute were he and Julia on the dance floor together?"

"He seemed happy," I agreed. Julia was exactly as everyone had described—lively, beautiful, kind, and best of all, she truly appeared to adore my father. She lit up whenever he looked her way, and he was obviously just as enamored, eagerly opening doors for her, pulling out her chair, offering his arm when they walked side by side. I'd never seen that side of him. It made me feel good to know he would not be lonely.

"He really did. And it was adorable that he stood in for Lexi's dad." Sighing, she tipped her head onto my shoulder. "It was a beautiful wedding. I'm sorry we had to leave early."

"Don't be. Devlin texted and said he and Lexi are thinking of your family, and they were glad you were there."

"That's sweet." She straightened up and yawned. "Can I ask

you for one last favor?"

"Of course."

"Can you run me home so I can clean up and get my car? Then I'll come back and give my mom a chance to go grab a shower. When she gets back, I'll head to the diner."

"Is that all you need? A ride?"

"Yes." She paused. "What time is your flight tomorrow?"

"Eight a.m."

She looked down at her coffee cup, flicking the edge of the plastic lid with her thumb. "Your dad will want to see you tonight."

"We're all getting together for dinner at his house at six." I put a hand on her leg. "Can I see you afterward?"

"I won't be home from the diner until after ten."

"I don't mind."

"You have to get up so early, Dash. It's an hour and a half drive to the airport."

"I know."

"Won't everyone think it's weird that you're leaving to go somewhere on your last night home?"

"I think they all know what's going on by now. And if they ask, I'll tell them the truth. I want to see you before I go." I met her eyes. "Is it okay?"

Her eyes filled, and she nodded. "It's okay. I can't promise I won't be a little emotional."

"Lucky for you, I'm an expert at emotions now." I put my arm around her, kissed her temple. "Don't worry about a thing."

• • •

Outside, the skies had turned gray, and raindrops were just starting to fall. After dropping her off, I went home and crashed for a couple hours, lulled to sleep by the gentle roll of thunder and the steady hum of rain showers on the roof. When I woke up, I did some laundry, including my sheets, and packed up most of my things. I was hoping to spend the night at Ari's house. Then I called Beatrix, who didn't answer, so I left a message.

"Hey, this is Dashiel Buckley. I'm just wondering if you heard anything more from Katherine Carroll's team about Tuesday. Let me know, thanks."

I sent a quick text to Ari checking in, and she said she was back at the hospital. There were no changes in her dad's condition, but she was pretty sure he'd have a bypass within the next few days.

My dad and Julia arrived home in the early afternoon, and the rest of my family came for dinner around six, even Devlin and Lexi. Since everyone was exhausted from the weekend, it was a fairly early night, Austin heading out with Veronica and the twins by eight, followed fairly quickly by Xander and Kelly, then Devlin and Lexi. Mabel, who was staying at the house, trailed me upstairs, leaving just Dad and Julia in the living room.

"Have you heard from Ari?" she asked, following me into my room.

"No. I was hoping you had."

"Nope." She flopped across the foot of my bed, head propped in her hand. "I feel so bad for her. She's so close to her dad."

"I think he'll be okay." I started placing the last of my clean laundry into my suitcase.

"Ari said you guys spent a lot of time together while you were home."

"I guess."

"She said you were really good to her. Helped her out a lot. Even took her to see some kind of food truck."

I shrugged, moving some things around in my bag. "I just want to encourage her to believe in herself. Her parents are a little stuck in their ways, and some dickhead ex of hers made her doubt her talent."

"I know. She was a wreck after that. But she sounds so much better now. Whatever you said to her really did sink in. She told me she wanted to talk to her parents about the truck—of course, that was before everything with her dad."

"I offered to buy it as an investment in her, but she won't let me." I closed my suitcase and zipped it up.

"She mentioned that. It's really sweet, Dash." She paused. "You must care about her."

"It's Ari," I said, trying to sound offhand. "Of course I do. Everyone does. She's like one of the family."

"That's not what I meant. Why can't you admit you have feelings for her?"

I finally stopped moving around and met her eyes. "Because there's no point. She's here and I'm there."

"So you're just going to forget about her?"

"No, but we both went into this knowing we were just friends that were going to *stay* just friends."

"Okay," she said. "If you say so. I've just never heard either one of you talk about another person or look at another person or act around another person the way you guys are with each other. It's actually kind of nauseating."

"It was just a couple weeks of hanging out," I said, grabbing my jacket from the back of my door. "No big deal."

"And where are you off to now?" she asked, her tone laced with phony innocence.

"I don't really think that's your business, Mabel."

She burst out laughing and hopped off my bed. "Whatever. You know, for a good actor, you're doing a shitty job pretending not to be in love with her."

"I'm not in love with her," I scoffed, although my heart thundered hard in my chest.

"Okay." She patted my cheek. "Then I'll just give you a hug and tell you to have Ari call me when she can." Throwing her arms around me, she gave me a squeeze. "It was good to see you."

"You too." I hugged her back. "Come visit me in California sometime."

"I'd love that. Safe travels. And good luck at your audition—keep us posted."

"Thanks. I will."

She let me go and wandered down the hall into her old bedroom, and I tossed my coat over my arm and took my bag down the stairs. Julia and my father looked over at me.

"Heading out, son?"

"Yeah, I'm going to run over to the diner and see if Ari needs anything. She's not answering my texts, and I just want to make sure everything is okay."

"She's working tonight?" he asked, rising to his feet.

"Yeah, you know Moe. His first concern was for the diner."

My father chuckled. "He needs to retire."

"Hopefully, he'll slow down after this." I went around the couch to give him a hug. "I might not be back tonight."

"I understand." He thumped my back a few times. "You tell her we love her and we're here."

Julia jumped up and threw her arms around me as well. "Have a safe trip back home."

"I will. Very nice to meet you."

"You too." She laughed brightly as she stepped back. "It's funny, I've heard so much about you, I forgot that we hadn't already met! I feel like I know all George's kids personally, he talks about you all so much."

"I can't help it." My dad shrugged. "I'm so proud of them."

"As you should be." Julia slipped her arm through his. "You've raised wonderful people with big hearts, but that's no surprise."

He smiled at her, and I felt like a third wheel. "Well, I'm out. I'll check in with you tomorrow, Dad. Take care, okay?"

"Will do, son. And good luck at that audition. Knock 'em dead."

"Thanks, I'll try." I gave a final wave, scratched behind Fritz's ears, and headed out.

I tried calling Ari again, but she didn't answer, so I decided to just show up at the diner. If she was already gone, I'd head to her house and then try the hospital.

Since it was late on a Sunday—and still pouring rain—I found a parking spot on Main without any trouble, right in front of Moe's. Between the swish of the windshield wipers, I could see the diner's lights were still on. Jumping out of my car, I hurried through the rain toward the door. Through the front windows I could see the place was empty except for Ari, who stood with her back to me, wiping down a table inside a booth. The jukebox must have been on, because I heard music playing. As I raised my fist to knock on the glass, I was reminded of the first time I'd done this just a couple weeks ago—the morning after she'd sliced her hand.

It was incredible how much had happened since then. How much had changed.

My sister's voice echoed in my brain. *For a good actor, you're doing a shitty job pretending not to be in love with her.*

But that was ridiculous. I wasn't in love with her. You didn't fall for someone in less than a month. Surely that took a lot more time and effort. Of course, my parents had always maintained they fell in love at first sight. The story was that my dad told my mom on their first date he was going to marry her—and six months later, he did. Was that just family lore?

Maybe it was just these damn strings. Maybe it was just that we'd had such a good time together and now it was over. Maybe this hole opening up in my chest was just sadness that we had to say goodbye—a perfect reminder of why I didn't enjoy *feelings* related to loss. Missing someone was the fucking worst.

At least I'd have this emotion to dig for if ever I needed to convey the heartbreak of leaving someone I cared about behind.

Because I had to leave. That wasn't a question. Everything I wanted, the life I'd always dreamed about, was out in L.A. I'd worked my ass off, and I was only halfway there. I was only twenty-seven. I couldn't give up now, not when such a huge opportunity was on the horizon. But for one insane moment, I thought about running in there and begging her to come with me—leave her family and Moe's Diner and this town behind, and just make a new life for herself out in Hollywood.

No, that was wrong. Not only would she think I was insane to suggest something so drastic, but her life and dreams were here—she wanted to take over Moe's and make it her own. She owned a house she loved. She told me that night we'd sat out on the dock that she wanted to stay in Cherry Tree Harbor, that she was a small-town girl at heart. I couldn't ask her to uproot herself and throw all that away for me.

But standing there with rain dripping off my hair, watching her turn and look at me like she'd known I was there, I honestly wished I could.

She rushed to the door, unlocked it and pulled it open. "Oh

my God, come in. How long have you been out there? I'm so sorry, I didn't hear you knock. I had the jukebox on."

"I hadn't knocked yet." I ran a hand through my hair, sending water droplets spraying. "But now I'm getting your floor all wet."

"I don't care about that." She looked up at me, and I saw her red, swollen eyes.

My arms came around her immediately. "What's wrong? Is it your dad?"

"No, he's a little better, actually. I'm just emotional, I guess. I can't seem to stop crying." Tucking her head beneath my chin, she wrapped her arms around my waist. "It's been a long day."

"I know. What can I do to help? And don't say nothing, because I'm already here and I'm yours for the rest of the night. I said goodbye to everyone else already."

"You did?" She sounded surprised.

"Yes." I loosened my hold on her slightly and leaned back at the waist, tipping up her chin. Her eyes were puffy, and her nose was red, and her cheeks were wet with tears, but she was still so beautiful it hurt. "There's no one else I'd rather be with."

A new song came on the jukebox, and I recognized the opening lines. "*Now I've had the time of my life…*" I cocked my head. "Hey. Is this the song from the movie?"

She smiled sheepishly. "Yeah. I know it's goofy, but it's one of my good mood songs. And I needed a lift."

I bent down and grabbed her around the thighs, and when I straightened up, she rose into the air.

"Hey!" Laughing, she thumped my shoulders. "It was just a metaphor! I didn't mean an actual lift, I meant a mood lift!"

"It worked, didn't it?"

She grinned down at me. "I guess it did."

Loosening my grip, I let her slide down my body until her

feet touched the floor. "Feel better?"

"Yes."

I kissed her. "Good. Now let's get this place closed so I can take you home for some horizontal mambo."

. . .

Back at Ari's house, we turned off the lights, locked the doors, and went into her bedroom together. We undressed each other slowly. We put our hands and mouths all over each other's bodies. We breathed one another in. Although we both had to be up early—me to catch a flight and Ari to open the diner—we stayed awake long into the night. No promises were made and nothing was said about tomorrow. She fell asleep in my arms, and I wondered if I'd ever have what we'd shared with anyone else. It seemed impossible.

There was only one Ari.

. . .

"I have to go." Dressed and ready, I sank down on the edge of the bed where she was still lying on her side, her head resting on her arm.

"Okay."

I leaned over and pressed my lips to her shoulder, her cheek, her forehead, and finally her lips. "Thanks for everything."

"I didn't do anything."

I brushed her hair away from her face. "You did lots of things. You listened to me. You inspired me. You created a masterclass in emotional depth with nothing but your television and your taste in incredibly sappy movies."

"If I'm being honest, that might have been an excuse to spend time in the dark with you."

"If I'm being honest, you didn't need an excuse." Her smile tightened the vise around my heart, and I tugged one of her curls. "Am I finally forgiven for kicking you out of my bed?"

"Yes."

"Thank God." More quietly, I said, "I had such a good time with you. The time of my life."

She laughed a little, even though her eyes were sad. "Our song."

"Always." I smiled, rubbing her bottom lip with my thumb. "Are we good, Sugar?"

She swallowed before answering. "We're good."

"I'll call you when I get home." I rose to my feet.

"Dash?"

At her bedroom doorway, I turned around. "Yes?"

"Will you do something for me?"

"Anything."

She smiled, but her breath hitched, and she wiped her eyes. "Don't call me right away, okay? I just need—a little—time." She struggled to get the words out. "To get past this."

That vise cinched hard. "I understand."

"Thank you." She clutched the blankets to her bare skin, and it took every ounce of strength I had not to rush back into the room and take her in my arms.

Fifteen seconds later, I was walking down her driveway toward my car, wondering how long this unbearable tightness in my chest was going to last.

I was finding it hard to breathe.

Chapter 22

DASH

When I landed in L.A., I discovered I had a voicemail from Beatrix.

"Hey, Dash. Great news! I spoke with Katherine Carroll's assistant, and she said this isn't an audition—you already have the part!" She laughed gleefully. "She said all you have to do is show up at the house at four. I already texted you the address, so good luck, and let me know how it goes. Bye!"

Still sitting in my seat in first class, I stared out the window slack-jawed as we taxied to the gate.

What the fuck? Had I heard that right? I already had the part without even having to audition? It seemed too good to be true—could the universe be *that* impressed with my newfound willingness to be more vulnerable? I was almost afraid to listen to it a second time.

But I did, and the message was the same. I had the part.

My first instinct was to call Ari, and I nearly tapped her name in my phone before I remembered I'd promised not to contact her for a little while. Frowning at my phone, I realized there was no one else I really wanted to talk to at that moment, no one else who'd really understand how fucking *monumental* this was.

On the drive home from the airport, I called Izzie, who didn't answer, and then tried Beatrix.

"Hello?"

"Hey, this is Dashiel Buckley."

"Dash! Did you get my message?"

"I did, but I just want to make sure I understand. I already have the part?"

"That's what she said. Amazing, right?"

"Yeah, but…it's just so crazy. I've never even met Katherine Carroll."

"She must have done her research on you after Izzie reached out. Something she saw impressed her!"

"I guess." What the hell could she have seen that was so impressive? *Malibu Splash*? That guest arc on *Law & Order*? The ad campaign for Hot Bod Sunscreen?

"Face it, Dash. You've got charisma. She saw through the character of Bulge to your raw talent."

I scrubbed a hand over my jaw. Checked my reflection in the rearview. "Maybe."

"Wait until we tell Izzie," she bubbled. "She's gonna flip."

"Is she still off the grid?"

"She must be. I haven't heard from her in a day or so. Listen, you know what they say—don't look a gift horse in the mouth, right? The assistant definitely said you had the part in question, and all you had to do was show up Tuesday at four."

"I can handle that," I said, my confidence growing.

"Let me know how it goes, okay? I'd say good luck, but you don't even need it!"

"Thanks, anyway. I'll be in touch." Ending the call, I debated breaking my promise to Ari. Then I thought about those tears in her eyes and the catch in her voice when she asked me to give her time.

I couldn't be so selfish.

...

That evening, I had dinner delivered and ate it alone in front of the television. It wasn't nearly as good as anything Ari made, and I missed her company, her laugh, even her sappy taste in movies. In fact, as I flipped through channels, I came across a romantic comedy I'd never seen before that looked right up her alley. I watched for a few minutes and reached for my phone.

Then I flopped back, frustrated and scowling. How long was this going to go on?

I lasted a few more minutes and gave in. If she wanted to ignore me, she could, but on the off chance she was willing to talk, I needed to check in with her.

> Hey. Has it been long enough?

Long enough?

> For me to reach out. I know I'm
> supposed to give you time.
> It's harder than I thought.
> You're on my mind constantly.

You're on mine too.

                                            How is your dad?

He's improving. I'm at the hospital
right now. He says hello.

                                            Say hi for me.

Did you make it back home?

                         Yes. I'm sitting here eating dinner
                         (not as good as your cooking) and
                         watching a romantic movie. What
                                        have you done to me?

Haha. What's the movie?

                         I don't know the name but it
                reminds me of something you'd like.

Who's in it? What are they doing?

                         Sandra Bullock is pretending to
                         be the fiancée of someone in
                         a coma but she's spending a
                         suspicious amount of time
                                        with his brother.

OMG I LOVE THAT
MOVIE SO MUCH

I smiled, because I could hear her saying that and I knew just
what expression was on her face as she typed. I wished she was
on the couch next to me so badly.

My thumbs hovered over the screen, wondering what to do

with the things I was feeling. I had no experience with this. I missed my walls.

> Guess what?

What?

> My agency says my meeting
> tomorrow isn't an audition.
> Apparently I already have the role.

WHAT?!

Gray dots faded in and out, then disappeared. Five seconds later, she was calling me.

"Hello?"

"Dash! Hang on, I'm going in the hall. Be right back, Dad!" A couple seconds later, she was back. "What the heck? You've got the role in *All We've Lost*? The one you wanted?"

God, I loved the sound of her voice. "That's what the message said. I'll know more tomorrow."

"I can't believe it!"

"Me neither."

"But also, I *can* believe it. You're that good, Dash. Never doubt yourself."

"Thanks. Tell me what's new with your dad." As she filled me in, I wandered aimlessly around my house. I bought the one-story Spanish style home with white stucco walls and terra-cotta roof last year. It had two bedrooms and baths, plus a beautiful kitchen I couldn't help picturing Ari in as I crossed through it. I'd have given anything to have her there right now and not on the phone.

At the back of the house, I opened up the sliding glass door and stepped out onto the patio. Today had been hot and sunny, and the red clay tiles were still warm beneath my bare feet. I sat on the couch, propped my heels on the fire pit, and let the sound of her voice fill my head, trying not to think about the hollow ache in my chest.

"That's great," I said after she'd finished telling me about her dad's progress. "So he can have the bypass by the end of the week?"

"Hopefully. The doctors think so."

"I'm glad."

Silence.

I opened my mouth to say a hundred different things—*I miss you, I wish you were here, I think I might be in love with you*—but nothing came out. I was too afraid I'd make things worse, not better.

"I should go," she said after a minute.

"Not yet," I blurted. "Don't go yet."

"Dash."

"I'm sorry." My eyes closed. "I'm just not used to missing someone like I miss you. And I just fucking saw you this morning."

"It will get better. It has to."

"Come see me," I said impulsively. "I'll fly you out here."

"I can't leave the diner."

"I hate this, Ari."

She made a hiccupy noise that made me think she was crying.

"Fuck, I shouldn't have called."

"I called you, remember?"

Placing my feet on the ground, I leaned forward, elbows on my knees. "I'm sorry. I'm fucking this up. I just want to know when I'll see you again."

"I'm going to be honest—I don't think visits here and there are going to work, Dash. I'll start hoping for things that are never going to happen. I'll want more."

"You deserve more." And she did. Someone who'd be there for her every day. To help her with the house and rub her feet and hold her when she was overwhelmed or sad or scared. To take her to carnivals and eat fried pickles and ride the Ferris wheel and taste her salty kiss as it descended. To remind her not to put herself last.

"And you deserve the chance to follow your dreams," she said. "I would never stand in the way of that."

I closed my eyes, swallowing hard. "I know."

"Let's just give it some time, okay?" She was openly weeping now, and it broke my heart to think of her alone in that hospital hallway. "It will let up."

"What if it doesn't?"

"Then you find a picture of me and draw horns and a pencil-thin mustache on my face."

I smiled, despite the open wound in my chest. "Okay."

"But Dash?"

"Yeah?"

"I have to let you go."

I wasn't sure if she meant on the phone or in life, but I supposed it didn't really matter.

Not every love story could have a happy ending.

• • •

That night, to distract myself as much as to prepare for tomorrow, I spent hours poring over the script I had for *All We've Lost*. Closing my eyes, I imagined what it would feel like to be Johnny, this character who'd lived nearly a hundred years ago. Despite the century between his experiences and mine, I needed to put myself in his place. What would it have been like to leave everything I knew and loved behind? To be willing to sacrifice my life for a cause greater than myself? To take a bullet and be left in enemy hands? To fall in love with a woman behind enemy lines who nursed me back to health? To allow her to risk her life for me, and then to love her so much I'd return to save her?

The story felt different to me now. I felt like I understood something I hadn't when I read it the first time. Then, I'd pictured myself playing the role as if I was watching the film on a screen—I was on the outside of my performance. Now, I felt the character take root deep within my body. In my mind. My heart. My gut. I made up memories for him. People he'd left behind. Things he'd said. Dreams he'd had.

The following morning, I did my best to shake off the restless night and channel some good energy by taking a long run, lifting some weights, meditating, and even walking around my house naked for a while. But being naked reminded me of Ari, and my energy felt as cloudy as the sky, which was completely overcast.

Relax, I told myself. *You already have the role.*

But I still wanted to prove I was worthy of it. That I had the emotional depth necessary to make the story come alive. To make people feel.

A few minutes before four, I rang the doorbell of the house at 52 Beverly Park Terrace. It was a huge home in an exclusive neighborhood on a gated street, and as I stood on the doorstep I felt out of place—like I should be there delivering a pizza instead.

I heard Ari's voice in my head. *Never doubt yourself.*

The door opened, and a woman who was not Katherine Carroll—she was a lot younger, maybe in her twenties—appeared. "Hello!" She smiled brightly. "You must be Dash."

"Yes."

"I recognize you from *Malibu Splash*! Although you're wearing a lot more clothing." She gestured to my dark jeans and button-up shirt.

I laughed politely. "I thought it might be best to show up in something other than a bathing suit."

"I hope you brought it," she said with a wink. Then she held out her hand. "By the way, I'm Olivia, Katherine's assistant. Thanks so much for coming."

"Of course." I shook her hand and stepped into the two-story entry. "I couldn't believe it when I got the message. This is such a thrill."

She laughed. "Well, I'm sure you're used to this kind of thing."

"Not really."

"Follow me," she said, walking down a hallway on the right. "The girls are out in the back, but we don't want them to see you yet. It's so cloudy and chilly today, isn't it? Not the best day for a pool party, but not much we can do about the weather. You can change in here." She opened up a door to a powder room.

Girls? Pool party? Something wasn't right.

"Sorry," I said. "I'm a little confused. What am I changing into?"

"Your costume," she said, like I should have known.

"What costume? Something for *All We've Lost*?"

"*All We've Lost*?" She shook her head. "What do you mean?"

The walls of the hallway pressed closer. "I think there might be some, uh, confusion about what I'm doing here today," I said slowly.

"You're here because you were hired to play Bulge at a *Malibu Splash* themed birthday party." Her head fell to one side.

"Is that not what you were told?"

"Birthday party?" I almost put a hand on the wall to steady myself.

"Yes. For Katherine's niece, Pinky. She's turning thirteen today, and she's a huge fan of yours, so I contacted your agency to see if you were available to 'play lifeguard' at the party." She put air quotes around the word. "It was Pinky's one big request."

"Oh my God." I closed my eyes. Inhaled and exhaled.

"Is everything okay? You can still do it, right?" Her voice was worried. "Is something wrong?"

"Yes. Something is wrong." I opened my eyes. "I was under the impression that today was a meeting related to being cast as Johnny in *All We've Lost*."

"Oh." She blinked. "Wow, something really got lost in translation there."

"It really did." I wanted to die. Not only did I not get the role of my dreams, I was a fucking birthday party clown.

"I'm so sorry. I did talk to several different people at the agency, but I thought I was clear about what the job was. Oh, dear." She glanced toward the back of the house and looked at me again, her eyes tearing up. "Katherine will be so upset with me if I messed this up. Her niece is so important to her."

"It's okay. I can do it. I just—thought this was something else."

"Thank you!" Olivia threw her arms around me. "Thank you so much! The girls are just going to be so happy. And so will Katherine."

"Is she here?"

"Not yet. But she will be." Olivia checked her phone. "Okay, it's just about time. Do you have your suit?"

"I'm afraid I don't."

"Oh shoot!"

Olivia looked so distraught, I held up a hand. "You know what? I have some clean red shorts in my gym bag that look kind of like the suits Bulge wore. I can put them on."

"God, you're the best, Dash. I don't know how to thank you."

I thought about asking to meet Katherine, then realized I'd have to do it dressed in nothing but my red gym shorts. That wasn't the impression I wanted to make. "It's fine. I'm glad to help out."

As I headed back outside to where my car was parked in the drive, I considered just jumping in it and speeding away from this house, this town, this industry, the dream I'd had since I was small.

But then I thought about what Ari would say if she were here. *You never know what opportunity is around the next corner. One moment can change everything.*

I grabbed my gym bag and headed back inside the house.

. . .

Twenty minutes later, barefoot, bare-chested, and barely hanging on to the last remaining shred of my dignity, I walked out onto Katherine Carroll's pool deck, where a bunch of adolescent girls were lounging around in bikinis. The decibel level when they spotted me was like the whine Ari's car made when you turned right, times one billion. I wasn't sure my ears would ever recover.

After the screaming subsided, the girls all introduced themselves—they had names like Plum and Eddie and Scribble—and wanted a million pictures. After the photo shoot was over, I was sort of hoping to leave, but the girls begged me to show off the backflip Bulge always did off the swimming dock on the show. They'd written it in because I could actually do it, but eventually the showrunners had gotten too nervous about injuries.

"That was mostly a stunt double," I explained.

"So you can't do a backflip off the diving board?" Scribble challenged me with a look.

"I can do one," I said, eyeballing the diving board. It had been a while, but this day had already delivered several punches to my ego. I couldn't take another one.

"Show us!" shouted a tall, skinny girl holding her phone. Her name was a state, but not one you'd expect like Montana or Dakota. Maine? Oregon?

"I guess I could," I said, heading for the deep end of the pool. The girls cheered as I stepped onto the board and walked out on it. When I reached the edge, I turned around and let my heels hang off the back. I bounced a few times, saying a quick prayer that I could actually still execute this trick. "Here goes," I muttered under my breath.

With one final bounce, I jumped into the air, tucked my knees into my chest, and launched myself back over the water. My feet went in first, and I let myself sink to the bottom, pushing off and rising to break the surface while my audience cheered.

"Did you get it on video, Alaska?" Eddie shouted.

"Got it!"

"Do it again!"

"Can you do a front flip?"

"Do a cannonball!"

"Throw me in the pool!"

"Me first, it's my birthday!"

Giving in to the reality of the afternoon, I hauled myself out of the water and got back on the diving board. Then I spent the next hour performing flips and cannonballs, letting them rate my splashes, throwing them into the water, and having tea parties at the bottom of the pool.

Eventually, the girls started shivering, and Olivia came out and said there was bubble tea and warm clothing waiting in the pool house. Everyone dried off, and I figured that was the perfect time for me to make an escape, but that's when Pinky came over and took me by the hand. "You can't leave yet," she said. "The party's not over."

I allowed myself to be dragged into the pool house, where the girls were all stepping into what looked like big blue fleece bags, and pulling hoods over their heads that had eyes and jagged white edges.

It took me a second to realize what they were—shark onesies.

"We have one for you too, Dash," Pinky said excitedly.

And just when I thought the day couldn't get worse, I found myself pulling on a shark onesie, which was so narrow around my ankles I had to waddle over to the couch, where I sat with ten seventh graders, sipping bubble tea and answering questions about my life.

"Where did you live when you were our age?"

"How many brothers and sisters do you have?"

"Do you have any pets?"

"What's your favorite color?"

"Who's your favorite music artist?"

"Do you have a girlfriend?"

The pool house definitely got quieter after that one.

"No," I said, sipping my bubble tea.

"Do you like anybody?"

I hesitated.

"He likes somebody," Eddie said confidently.

"Who is it? Do we know her? Is she an actress? Is it the girl who played Selena on *Malibu Splash*?"

"No, no," I said. "It's—it's someone from back home in Cherry Tree Harbor."

They all scooted closer. "What's her name?"

"Ari."

"What does she look like?"

"She has curly brown hair and brown eyes."

"Just like me," someone whispered.

"Is she an actress?"

"No. She's a waitress—her family owns a diner. But she went to culinary school, and she's an amazing chef."

"Do you have a picture of her?"

I had some pictures on my phone, which I'd set down over on the bar where we'd gotten the bubble tea. A few women were sitting there now—I hadn't even seen them come in—and I realized with dismay that one of them was Katherine Carroll. Was this how I was finally going to meet her? After shuffling over to the bar in a fucking shark onesie? At this point, did I even care?

"Hang on," I said. "Let me go get my phone." After standing up, I gave the girls a big laugh as I Charlie-Chaplin-walked over to where I'd left my phone. The women were seated farther down the bar, and I was hoping to escape without talking to them, but Olivia called my name.

"Dash," she said from where she stood behind the bar. "Let me introduce you to Katherine."

Reluctantly, I turned around and waddled closer to them. "Hi," I said. "I'm Dashiel Buckley." I pushed my shark hood off and held out a fin.

Katherine, who was seated closest to me, shook my hand and

smiled. Possibly she was in her forties, although it was hard to tell someone's *actual* age in L.A. Her long blond hair was gathered in a ponytail, and her skin was fair and smooth. "So nice to meet you. Thank you very much for being here today. My niece was just ecstatic when I told her."

"Best birthday gift ever," said the woman seated on the other side of her, leaning forward to flash me a grin. "I'm Pinky's mom, Nicole."

I nodded, wishing I was wearing something—*anything*—else. "Glad to meet you both."

"You're so good with them," Nicole said. "Do you have kids? Sisters?"

"No kids. One little sister."

"Well, you're a natural. And such a good sport." Katherine laughed. "I can't believe they made you wear the shark onesie."

"Dash! Come on, where's the pic?" Pinky called from the couch.

"Better get back to your adoring fans," said Olivia. "And thanks again for coming." She clasped her hands at her chest and gave me a look that said *you saved my ass.*

"Sure." Leaving the women at the bar, I shuffled back to the couch and sank down between Pinky and Plum. The rest of the girls huddled around us. After opening up my photos, I found some recent ones I'd taken of Ari—mostly her in the kitchen, but I also snapped a couple the night I'd taken her to Etoile, and there were some from Devlin's wedding too. "That's her," I said, scrolling through them one at a time.

"Ooooh, I love her hair!"

"She's so pretty!"

"I love that red dress!"

"Aww, you're so cute together!"

"So, wait. How come she's not your girlfriend?" Alaska wanted to know.

"Because she lives in Michigan and I live in California."

"Why can't she just move here?"

"Because she loves where she lives. Her family is there. Family is very important to her."

"Is it important to you?" Plum asked.

"Yes."

"Where's *your* family?"

"They're in Cherry Tree Harbor too."

"So why don't you move there?"

"Because my work as an actor is also important to me. And my work is here."

"Do you love her?" Pinky demanded from my left.

"I—" I tugged at the neck of my onesie. Suddenly I was sweating. "That's kind of a hard question."

"No, it isn't," she said. "Do you think about her a lot?"

"I can't *stop* thinking about her," I confessed.

"Really?" The girls all leaned in.

"Really. She's the best, sweetest, most generous person I know. She makes me laugh, and when I make her laugh, it feels like someone just handed me a million bucks. When I'm with her, I'm always happy. I can be my real self and not have to hide anything. And she's so beautiful—sometimes I just look at her, and I think my chest might explode."

A chorus of sighs surrounded me.

"Have you kissed her?"

"Um. Yeah."

"French kissed her? Like, you touched tongues?"

"Yes," I said, squirming a bit.

"And you liked it?"

I shook my head. "This is weird, you guys."

"Dash." Pinky put a fin on my arm. "You're so in love with her."

"Definitely," said Alaska.

"It's so obvious," said Plum. "Haven't you ever been in love before?"

"No," I told them. "I've never said those words about anyone. I've never even thought them. But then, I've never felt this way either."

"That makes sense," said Pinky. "You need words you've never used to describe the feeling you've never felt."

Alaska sighed. "I've been in love like ten times."

"Same," said Plum.

"So you never told her you love her?" asked Seven from where she was perched on the back of the couch.

"No."

"Why?"

"Because I—I didn't want it to be true."

"Just because you don't say a thing out loud doesn't make it not true," Scribble said.

"I realize that," I said. "But the situation is complicated, okay?"

"No, it isn't," said Pinky. She snatched my phone. "What's her number? Let's call her. I vote you tell her now."

"I second."

"Thirdsy."

"The matter is not up for a vote, you guys." I grabbed my phone back. "We are not calling her."

"Give us one good reason why not."

"Because she asked me not to."

Plum narrowed her eyes. "What did you do?"

"Nothing! It's just that even if I did love her—"

"You do," said Scribble. "We've already established that."

"And she loves you too." Alaska pointed at the photo open on my phone, a selfie I'd snapped of us at the wedding. I was grinning at the camera but she was looking up at me, her expression one of pure adoration that even now made my chest tighten. "You can tell just by that picture."

"Okay, but not every love story has a happy ending." I felt triumphant delivering the final zinger.

Every single one of them looked at me like I was nuts.

"What's that supposed to mean?" asked Eddie.

"In the movies," I mansplained, "not every love story has a happy ending."

Collective eye roll beneath shark hoods.

"Movies aren't *real*, Dash," said Alaska, flicking my shoulder. "They're written by people like my mother."

"And produced by people like my aunt."

"You're an actor. You should know that."

"We're not talking about a fake love story in a movie," insisted Scribble. "We're talking about a real love story. *Yours*."

"You get to write it. Start to finish."

"And produce it."

"You can even star in it!"

"Give her one that's better than any movie, Dash," said Pinky. "Make her dreams come true."

"What does she want?" asked Eddie.

"I don't know." Agitated, I ran a hand through my hair. "You guys are moving too fast."

"You know her," said Pinky with quiet intensity. "Think about it. What does she really want more than anything?"

I thought back to things she'd said. "She wants to take care of the people she loves. She wants to make people happy."

"What does she *need*?" asked Plum.

"I don't know."

"Yes, you do. Don't be a jerk."

I stared at her and realized I *did* have the answer. "She needs someone to put her first."

"See?" Alaska flicked my shoulder again.

"So just tell her you love her and figure out how to be the one that puts her first," said Pinky, with an air of finality and a regal wave of her fin in the air. "Problem solved. Who wants cake?"

Chapter 23

ARI

On Thursday evening, I let Veronica talk me into meeting her for a glass of wine at Lush. She was already at the bar when I arrived, and she slid off her stool to hug me. "Hey. How *are* you?"

"I'm okay." I hugged her back and sat on the stool next to hers. "Sorry I missed dance class this week. Monday was Mabel's last night in town, and we had dinner together."

She waved a hand. "Oh, goodness. Don't worry about that. How's your dad?"

"He's okay. He had the bypass yesterday and he's recovering nicely. I think he'll be able to go home in about a week."

"I'm so glad to hear it."

The bartender came over and I ordered my usual pinot noir. When it arrived, I took a big sip.

Veronica rubbed my back. "You're holding up so well. It must have been hard saying goodbye to Dash on top of everything with your dad."

I nodded, feeling sadness grip my throat again. I couldn't seem to get off the verge of tears this week. "It was awful."

"You guys looked so happy together at the wedding."

"We were." I set my glass down and slumped over. "God, Veronica. Why did I think I could keep my feelings for him casual?"

"I don't know, sweetie."

"I should have known better. I've loved him for too long. There was too much history."

"That's probably part of what makes your connection so good."

"He has this way of being protective like a big brother, but also *not* like a brother at all. Did I tell you about the phone call?"

"What phone call?" Veronica sipped her wine.

"My asshole ex—the chef in Manhattan—called my cell the day the Hugo Martin post came out, just to make sure I wouldn't enjoy it too much. He spewed a bunch of bullshit about how he taught me everything and how dare I neglect to mention him, blah blah, but that didn't even bother me. That's just the usual narcissism."

"I can't believe you hadn't blocked him already."

"I had. He must have gotten a new number. But anyway, he didn't really piss me off until he insulted Moe's—then I kind of lost my cool and yelled at him. I was in the office at the diner, and Dash was there waiting for me—he heard me raise my voice and realized who I was talking to."

"Uh oh."

"He stormed in there and grabbed the phone. Threatened to burn down Niall's restaurant if he ever contacted me again."

Veronica's eyes widened. "Holy shit! Were you mad?"

"No! I mean, maybe I should have been—I can fight my own battles—but I appreciated that he wanted to stand up for me. I've talked about Niall and the ways he made me doubt myself, so Dash already had something against him." I sighed. "He apologized for going off. He said the thought of someone treating me badly made him want to smash things."

"Aww. It's sort of cute, Dash behaving like a hotheaded caveman—only in *that* situation, of course."

"I know. He was just trying to show me he's in my corner. And he's so beautiful and fun and sweet and sexy," I moaned. "Why won't he just let me love him until the end of time? Is that too much to ask?"

Veronica laughed. "I don't think so. How did you guys leave it?"

"The same way we found it. We're just friends."

"Are you going to at least visit each other?"

"What's the point, Roni?" I despaired all over again. "He offered to fly me out there, but then what? I just go running off to L.A. every couple months, if that? Pine away for him the rest of my life? His career is about to blow up, I just know it. He doesn't need a hometown honey."

"Maybe that's exactly what he needs," countered Veronica. "Someone who knew him when. Someone he can be himself with. Someone who will always be honest and real. He probably meets a lot of fake people or people who just want things from him. Being with you is probably such a relief for him."

I shook my head. "It doesn't matter. His life and dreams are in one place, mine are in another, and for a little while they overlapped, but that's all. I'm not harboring any delusions that we have a future."

Veronica sighed. "It doesn't seem right that you guys are so good together, but you won't give it a chance."

"It's not about what's right. It's about what's real," I insisted. "Maybe in the movies, the Hollywood celebrity falls for the small-town diner waitress, but this is real life. My life. And it's not happening. The sooner I accept it, the better."

"Have you talked to him?"

"Not since Monday night. I asked him not to call me for a while. I told him I needed some time." I closed my eyes. "I should be over him in a hundred years or so. Maybe more."

"Oh, honey." Veronica tipped her head onto my shoulder.

"I'm serious. I can't remember a time in my life when I didn't love him, and right now, I can't imagine a time when I won't. It's like those years I spent trying to hate him were all for nothing. He's just got this *hold* over me." I picked up a cocktail napkin and dabbed at my eyes. "Every night, I lie in bed and dream that he comes back and says, 'I was wrong. I can't stay away from you. Let's make this work.' It's so stupid! I'm sixteen all over again!"

"It's not stupid. You love him."

"I wish I didn't."

"You need something to take your mind off him. Something fun and exciting. Want to take a girls' trip or something?"

"I can't right now. Maybe after my dad is back on his feet." Setting down the napkin, I took another sip of wine. "There is one thing that might excite me—although I can't say it won't remind me of him, since it was his idea."

"What?"

"A Moe's food truck. A little catering business that I'd run

on my own with a menu I'd create. Something a little more me."
Just talking about it lifted my spirits.

Veronica gasped. "That's a great idea!"

"Dash and I went to see one while he was home. Abelard
Vineyards is selling their current truck, and his friend Gianni is
the chef there. It's not a bad deal, but it's still crazy expensive."

"Can you get a loan?"

"Maybe. I could try."

"I'm sure a bank would approve you! With the Moe's Diner
name behind you, plus your training? And they're so popular
now! Who doesn't love a food truck?"

"Uh, my parents?"

Her face fell. "Really?"

"They're just so old-school. I mentioned it to my mom a
couple weeks ago, and she didn't really get it, or she pretended
not to." I shrugged. "But in her defense, she was really distracted
by my dad's health. She could tell something was off that day—
we both could."

"So maybe the timing was just wrong." Veronica perked up.
"Once your dad gets through this, can you try talking to them
again? Maybe in the meantime, you do a little research on getting
that loan."

I nodded. "That's a good idea."

"I'm here if you need me, Ari. We all are."

· · ·

Later that night, I lay in bed, staring into the dark and trying
not to think about the empty space next to me. I'd changed the
sheets, hoping it might take the scent of him from the room, but I

could still smell him. Still hear him calling me his good girl. Still feel the warmth of his skin against mine.

I flopped onto my side, facing away from the place he used to fall asleep with his arm around me.

I missed it all.

Chapter 24

DASH

*F*or three days, I lay around my house in sweatpants and bare feet, unshaven, unmotivated, and unwilling to show my face in the world.

I turned down invitations to see friends, ignored my inbox and social media, and avoided responding to any of my family's texts asking how the meeting had gone. I didn't have the energy to work out, I couldn't bring myself to care what I looked like, and I certainly didn't feel like walking around naked.

I kept hoping Ari might reach out, but she never did. I kept hoping the days would get easier without hearing her voice, but they dragged. Every night, I crawled into bed alone, hoping I'd fall asleep without longing for her, but it never happened.

And if my personal life was a train wreck, my professional life was a dumpster fire on the side of the tracks.

The humiliation from Tuesday refused to let up. Was it a sign? Should I just call it quits? Host a game show? Was Milk still interested? I saw the announcement that the role of Johnny in *All We've Lost* had been cast—damn that Tom Holland—and I mourned the loss like it had actually once been mine.

I finally spoke with Izzie, who apologized profusely for the miscommunication and told me not to give up. "At least you're on Katherine Carroll's radar now," she said brightly.

"Izzie, I'm on her radar wearing a shark onesie," I grumbled, stretched out on my couch in sweats and an old Two Buckleys T-shirt. "That's not the impression I wanted to make."

"Well, maybe it just wasn't meant to be. Beatrix feels terrible, by the way. She asked if I was going to fire her."

"No, don't fire her." I frowned at the ceiling fan. "I'll just feel worse."

"Well, cheer up. Something good is bound to come your way."

We hung up, and I stared at my phone, longing to call Ari and confess the entire debacle. She'd probably find a way to make me laugh about it. See the humor in the miscommunication. Reassure me my time was still coming, I had a gift, I shouldn't give up.

She was simply the best, just like the song said.

But I couldn't tell her I loved her. The thought of it paralyzed the muscles in my throat.

And a bunch of adolescent girls were not qualified to give me relationship advice. They didn't know me, they didn't know Ari, and they certainly didn't know how hard a relationship could be—especially if you lived on opposite sides of the country. They were just kids. They thought you could write your own life like a script and give it the ending you wanted.

If only it were that easy.

But I had to admit, they'd said some things that made me think.

I knew what she wanted in a relationship—she'd said it right out loud. *I just want someone to be there. Be in it with me.*

But how was I supposed to *be there* when I *lived here*? There was no getting around it. So what the fuck was the point of all these fucking feelings that had come surging forth once my heart energy was unclogged? They weren't making my life any better or lighter or easier.

I scowled at my phone. This was some real bullshit. The universe wasn't handing over any breaks. I hadn't gotten the big role. I'd done everything Delphine had said to do and I was right back where I started, alone with my shit.

No, I was worse off, because now I was potentially in love with a girl who lived a million miles away, and we couldn't be together.

This was all Delphine's fault.

Jumping off the couch, I threw a baseball cap on my head, shoved my feet into some slides, and grabbed my keys. I was going to drive to her shop and tell her so.

. . .

The same sandwich board advertising the same psychic bullshit was out on the sidewalk, and I felt like kicking it over as I marched past. I stormed into the shop, a chime going off above my head. Inside, I stood there in a huff, feet spread, chest puffed up, chin jutting.

"Can I help you?" asked a tall, skinny guy with long hair

behind the register.

"I'm looking for Delphine." My eyes scanned the shop, but all I saw was the back of a woman with a long blond ponytail examining some crystals.

"She's in the—"

"Dash." Delphine had appeared from behind the beaded curtain. The resemblance to Ari seemed less strong to me now, but it was still enough to ratchet my anger up another level. "How are things going?"

"Terrible." I scowled and pointed at her. "And it's all your fault."

She didn't even look surprised—further proof of her guilt. "Would you like to come back and talk about it?"

"Yes, I would," I said, storming past her and throwing the beaded curtain aside. The room looked the same—black walls, stained glass lamp with beaded fringe shade, table holding crystals, cards, and hand sanitizer.

"Take a seat," said Delphine, following me inside.

"No, thanks. I'll stand." But what I did was pace.

Delphine lowered herself into her chair. "You seem upset."

"I am upset. You lied to me." I knew I was being loud and obnoxious, but I couldn't help it. She wanted feelings? I'd give her feelings!

"I did?"

"Yes. You told me that if I walked around naked and got more comfortable being vulnerable, I'd get what I wanted."

Delphine hesitated. "I'm not sure that's *exactly* what I—"

"Yes, it is! You said all I had to do was strip down to my purest self and knock down the walls around my heart. You said what I sought was within. Well, I did all that and unless I was seeking misery and humiliation, it didn't work!"

"I see. Could I convince you to sit down and just breathe with me for a moment?"

I eyeballed her suspiciously. "Why? So you can feed me more nonsense about my constipated heart energy and then charge me for it? Right now all I want is to plug it up again!"

"No. I won't charge you for this. I'm only curious. I want to listen." She gestured to the chair opposite her. "Please. Sit."

After a moment's pause, I reluctantly slumped onto the chair. Folded my arms over my chest.

"Thank you." She gave the sanitizer a few pumps, rubbed her hands together and placed them face up on the table between us. "Give me your hands."

Again, I hesitated. Again, she waited patiently. Finally, I sat up and laid my palms on top of hers.

"Oh," she said after a moment. "Interesting."

I rolled my eyes. "What?"

"Your heart energy *is* unblocked. It is lighter and flowing freely and powerfully." She paused. "Your ego is still strong, but your heart has more room now. I can see that you've taken down some walls."

"But it didn't work," I said. "I didn't get the part I wanted. The universe made me think I had the part and then yanked the rug out."

"Dash, these things aren't 'if you do this, then that happens.' You can't cause something to happen at a particular moment if it's not supposed to happen right then. You can only open yourself up to the possibility. You can be ready to receive it. You can even act as if it's already happened, but the universe is not a vending machine. You can't put the money in and expect the reward to pop out."

"That's not what you said before," I snapped.

"Yes, it is," she said calmly. "I told you to stop hiding from your emotions. I told you not to be afraid of them. I told you that tearing down those walls would allow you to access the deepest reaches of your heart. Are you telling me now that you haven't felt something deep and meaningful since you were here before? Because your energy is saying something different."

"It's probably saying I'm in love," I grumbled. "And that's all your fault too."

She barely hid her smile. "Tell me about it."

I went through the entire story, from the moment I strolled around the corner in my dad's kitchen naked to the moment I said goodbye and walked away from her house—edited for content, of course.

"Wow," she said. "It sounds like you two have a special connection. One that goes back a lot of years with many layers to it. Possibly even a past life."

"Okay, but the problem is that in *this life*, I can't be with her."

"Yes, you can. You're just scared."

"I'm not—" I stopped. "Okay, fuck it. Yes. I'm scared."

"Keep going," she urged.

"I just feel like…" I closed my eyes and swallowed. "Like I've got this proof, you know? That life is suddenly cruel. That the things and the people you thought would always be there can be taken away from you. And it will fucking hurt."

"That's true, Dash."

"So you have to do what you can to shield yourself from the bad stuff."

She shook her head. "You end up shielding yourself from *everything*. Even the good stuff. And the good stuff is *really* good—it's family and friends. It's that role you want. That house you live in. That dream you have. It's love, Dashiel. Don't hide from it. Let it in. Let her in."

"But not every love story can have a happy ending." It felt like less of a zinger today.

"Maybe not," Delphine agreed. "But yours can. Picture it. Right now. Just imagine it. What does it look like? Sound like? Taste like? Smell like? How do you feel inside that future?"

I stared at her in silence, imagining it. A life with Ari in it. Then I closed my eyes and felt chills sweep over my skin. I saw her in a dozen different places—lying on the couch with her head in my lap, cooking in our kitchen, dancing at a wedding surrounded by family, sitting on the couch at family game night. I heard her laughing at something I said, sighing my name as I covered her body with mine, moaning with pleasure as she fell apart beneath me. I tasted everything—a sweet and salty kiss, tarragon and puff pastry, a gas station hot dog, fried pickles at a carnival, braised short ribs on homemade sourdough bread. I smelled that bread in the oven. I smelled the lake rippling in front of us with the moon shining on its surface. I smelled the scent of her warm, soft skin. I felt my fingers running through her hair, my bare chest pressed against hers, the velvet texture of her tongue all over my body.

Her hand in mine. Her head on my chest. Her kiss, her kiss, her kiss.

But I felt other things too, things that weren't physical. I felt the urge to protect her. To help her. To watch her succeed at her dream. To play whatever role I could in her happiness.

Just like that, I could see it stretching out in front of me. A life side by side. Not without bumps, not a straight line, not without peaks and valleys, but a road taken together. Dreams shared. Love. Loyalty. Family. My entire body warmed like I'd just stepped from the shadow into the sun.

I stood up. "Oh my God."

"You see it," Delphine said, sitting back.

"I see it. I fucking see it." I shook my head in disbelief.

"Because you're open to it. It's not a prediction, it's just a possibility."

"Doesn't matter. If it's possible, I'll do what it takes to make it reality."

She smiled. "You really fell hard for this girl. What is it about her?"

"God, I could name a thousand things—her sense of humor, her kindness, her devotion to her family. Her work ethic, her honesty, her generosity. Her cooking—her fucking *cooking* could make me cry. She's beautiful and sweet and she makes me feel so good. She's like a soft place to land, you know? When things are hard, she just makes them better. She makes *me* better."

Delphine nodded slowly. "Go get her, Dash. The future is all in your control."

I raced through the curtain before remembering my manners. Parting the beads with my hands, I stuck my head back into the room. "Thank you, Delphine. I'm sorry I barged in here like that. It wasn't nice. I hope the universe won't hold it against me."

She laughed. "You're welcome, and it's okay. The universe is forgiving, and so am I."

Grinning, I rushed out of the shop and jumped in my car. On the drive back to my house, I made a phone call I hoped would set everything in motion.

And give her a moment that would change everything.

Chapter 25

Ari

"Hi, Dad." I smiled at him as I entered his hospital room Saturday afternoon. "How are you feeling today?"

"Like I'm ready to go home," he said, scowling at the nurse checking his vitals.

She laughed. "Another few days or so, Moe. You're almost there."

I stayed out of the way as she finished up and smiled at her as she left the room. "I saw Mom at the diner as I was leaving. She said she'll be up later."

My dad sighed. "I don't know why. It's so boring here, I'm gonna lose my marbles. Come sit by me and tell me something exciting."

I kissed his cheek and took the chair by his bedside. "I don't have anything very exciting to tell you."

"How's the diner?"

"It's fine, Dad. Same as always."

"You sneak any new specials on the menu this week?"

I shook my head. "Just the old favorites."

"Cook anything new at home lately?"

"No." I studied my hands, clasped in my lap. "I haven't felt like cooking much."

He studied my forlorn face. "What's wrong, angel?"

"Nothing, Dad." Forcing a smile, I said, "Just get better, okay? When you get out of here, we're going to start taking some walks together. And I'm going to share some recipes with you that have more heart-healthy ingredients."

"I'd like that. You can make anything taste good, even kale." He adjusted one of the pillows behind him and settled more comfortably. "But why don't you tell me what's going on with you? We haven't had a good talk in a while."

"Nothing is going on with me. I wish there was something, but there's nothing. Same old, same old." I looked out the window. The rain had finally let up after a few days, but the sky was still overcast.

"Maybe that's the problem."

"There's no problem, Dad." *I'm just in love with a guy who doesn't want to be in a relationship with me. It's fine. I'll get over it someday.*

He was silent for a moment. Then he exhaled. "Trattoria DeLuca."

I shifted my focus from the window to him. "What?"

"Da Maurizio. That's what I was going to call my place."

"What place?"

"The place I wanted to open instead of running Moe's Diner."

"I never knew you wanted to open your own place."

"I did. I had a space all picked out and a menu planned. I had a vision."

"What happened?"

"My father got sick. And my mother needed me to run Moe's. My sister had just gotten married and had a baby on the way—she couldn't handle it. My mother said if I didn't take it over, she'd sell it. She refused to hire anyone outside the family to run things, and we couldn't really afford it anyway because of all the medical expenses. So my choice was Moe's Diner or Da Maurizio."

"And you chose the diner."

"I had to, didn't I? It had been in my family for decades. It was beloved in the community. It had been my grandfather's dream."

"So you set your own dream aside."

"I did. And I don't regret it."

I looked out the window again. "That's good, Dad."

"But I always wondered what if, you know?"

I swallowed. "Sure."

He was silent for a minute. "Your mom mentioned something about a food truck."

Frowning, I shook my head. "She wasn't supposed to say anything about that. It was just a silly idea I had, but it's—"

"It's not silly. I like it."

My jaw fell. "You do?"

"Yeah. Want to tell me more?"

"Uh, sure. But Mom said you guys had always avoided getting into any kind of catering."

"This doesn't sound exactly like catering though. The people would come to you, right?"

"Well, they'd hire me. And I'd bring the truck there and sell or serve right out of the window. Like at a carnival, but at a street fair. Or someone's wedding. Or a graduation party."

He smiled. "That sounds like fun."

"I think so too. And I could experiment a little with the menu. That way, I wouldn't be messing with anyone's old favorites at Moe's, but I could be creative."

"Sure," he said, nodding. "Like those dishes you served that Hugo Martin. I've been showing all my nurses his article about you."

I laughed. "You don't have to do that."

"I'm proud of you, Ari. You're too talented for Moe's, I know that."

"Not at all, Dad." I put my hand on the blanket and leaned forward. "That's the thing. Comfort food doesn't have to be cheap or unsophisticated or unhealthy or unimaginative. It just has to taste great and make people feel good. Maybe remind them of something they've had before but presented in a new way."

"I like that," he said. "Let's go for it. Where do we buy a truck? How much do they cost?"

"Well, I've only looked at one, and the sale price is about forty thousand dollars. And that's before the exterior paint job."

He pursed his lips. "Forty K, huh?"

"Yeah, I know it's a lot. So maybe this isn't the right time to—"

"We can do it."

"I just think maybe we ought to wait and see—"

"I don't want to wait."

"But Dad, you're going to have a massive hospital bill, and more medical expenses as you recover, and Mom thinks—"

"I know what Mom thinks," he said. "In fact, I know what Mom thinks before she even thinks it. And it's not that she's wrong, she's just worried about us and wants to protect us. So she's thinking from a place of fear."

"But there is a lot of risk," I pointed out. "We should be scared."

"Well, I'm not." He lifted his chin. "How many good years do I have left? I want to do exciting things, take chances, watch you go after something you want and succeed. I want you to have the chance I never did."

I smiled, my throat growing tight. "There's no guarantee I'll succeed, Dad. I could fail in a big way."

"Chi non fa, non falla, angel," he said. "My grandmother used to tell me that when I was learning to cook. It means 'he who makes no mistakes makes nothing.'"

"I like that." My eyes filled. "I've made plenty of mistakes, and I'm sure I'll make more. But I want to make you proud."

"That's a given, angel." He reached for me, and I came into his arms and gave him a hug. "You go see if that truck is still for sale. I'll talk to your mom and the bank. If we have to take out a loan against the house, we'll do it."

"You're the best, Dad," I said, tears falling freely. "I don't know how to thank you."

"Get me out of this place."

Laughing, I let him go and wiped my eyes. "I'll give it my best effort."

He gave me a tired smile. "You always do."

• • •

I didn't waste any time. As soon as I got behind the wheel of my car—which ran much better these days—I pulled Ellie Lupo's card from my purse and called her.

"Hello?"

"Hi, is this Ellie?"

"Yes, it is."

"Hi, this is Ari DeLuca. We met—"

"Ari, hi! How are you?"

"I'm good."

"How's your dad? We heard what happened while we were up at Snowberry. That's so scary."

"He's improving. He had bypass surgery Wednesday and he's on the mend. He's going to be fine."

"What a relief. I'm *so* glad to hear it."

"Thanks. Listen, I'm calling because I finally had a chance to talk with my parents about the truck, and I'm interested in buying it."

"Oh." She paused. "Oh, shoot."

My heart stuttered. "What's wrong?"

"It's sold. Someone just bought it yesterday."

"Oh." My spirits deflated. "That's—that's too bad."

"I'm so sorry, Ari. I didn't realize it would happen so quickly. I feel awful."

"No, no—it's fine. It's totally not your fault. I dragged my feet."

"Maybe you can find another one for sale."

"I'm sure I can." I tried to sound optimistic. "Now that I have an idea of what I want, I know what to look for."

"Reach out if you need anything, please."

"I will. Thank you."

"Good to hear from you. Take care."

After we hung up, I tossed my phone onto the passenger seat and gripped the wheel with both hands. It was fine. It was just one truck. It didn't mean this wasn't meant to be. I could find another one.

And maybe it would even be better to find one that didn't remind me so much of Dash, of the time we went to see it, of the conversations we had, of the nights we spent, of the way he always kept me warm.

Those memories were vivid enough.

Swallowing back the tears, I turned on my car and drove home.

Chapter 26

Dash

I t took me less than twenty-four hours to get everything in place. On my way to the airport, I called Xander.

"Hello?"

"Hey." I could hear the noise of the pub in the background.

"You're alive. We've been wondering."

"Sorry. I'm alive." I smiled. "It's just been a crazy week."

"How did the audition go?"

"Shitty."

"So you didn't get the part?"

"Not even close."

"Sorry, dude."

"Don't be." I realized I didn't even care anymore. The only role in life I wanted right now was the guy who got to call Ari his own. "Everything is great. But I need a favor. You busy tomorrow morning?"

"No. What do you need?"

"A ride."

"A ride where? Are you in town again?"

"I will be. I'm flying in on the red eye. I have something I need to do tomorrow and I can't drive myself."

"What is it?"

I explained what I was doing, and he started to laugh.

"So will you help me out?" I asked while he continued to guffaw in my ear.

"I'll help you out," he said. "But first you have to admit I was right about the strings."

I grimaced. "You're such an asshole."

"Say it, or I'm not driving you."

"I could ask Dad."

"Dad's in Tennessee. Not getting back until tomorrow afternoon."

"I'll ask Austin."

"He's delivering a table to Chicago tomorrow."

"Fine. You were right about the strings," I said through my clenched teeth.

"Thank you." He paused. "So you're sure about this?"

"I'm sure. You know, you said something a few weeks ago while we were standing outside the diner that I keep thinking about."

"I'm a thought-provoker, it's true. But what was the thing?"

"You said something like, 'Anything I can do to make her dreams come true, I'll do it.'"

"Yep."

"And you said something about the distance being hard, but that you couldn't imagine your life without her. That's how I feel about Ari right now. Like I know it's not going to be easy, but whatever it takes, I'll do it. If she says no, she says no, but I have to try."

"She's not going to say no," Xander said.

"She might. Nothing is certain."

"Wrong. Some things are certain, and one of them is that I have eyes. And those eyes can see. And what those eyes saw while you were here is that she's in love with you, and what those eyes have seen since you left is that she's fucking miserable. She doesn't even look like the same Ari."

My gut clenched. "You've seen her?"

"She worked last night. I gave her tonight off because she looks like she hasn't been sleeping. She's messed up, dude. You gotta fix this—but *only* if you're going to do right by her."

I punched the accelerator a little harder. "I'm on my way."

• • •

At the airline gate, I pulled my hat down low and sat in a corner, facing the wall. While I waited for my boarding zone to be called, I checked my messages. There was a text from Mabel, who I'd confided in; one from Veronica, whose help I would need tomorrow; and a voicemail from a number I didn't recognize. I hit play and put the phone to my ear.

"Hello, this is Katherine Carroll. I'm sorry to call out of the blue like this, but my assistant Olivia confessed the mix-up at the party and gave me your number. You were so good with the girls, and I appreciated it even more once I learned the truth about why you thought you'd been invited. In fact, I really could not get you off my mind, and usually when that happens, it's my intuition talking to me. And then I happened to be at Delphine's shop for a reading that day you came in. I apologize for eavesdropping, but I heard your conversation, and I was even more convinced that I needed to reach out. I was in the process of doing a little research on you when my office called with the news that Tom Holland has a scheduling conflict and can no longer shoot *All We've Lost*. I wondered if you might still like to read for the role of Johnny? No promises, of course, but I think you have the right look, and I like the fact that you haven't done any major films before. Feel free to have your agent reach out to my office, and we'll get a meeting scheduled. Have a great day."

I stared at my phone. I looked around, expecting someone to jump out and say it was a setup. I listened to the message again, trying to decide if it was actually Katherine Carroll's voice or one of my friends playing a joke.

Could this be real? Was the universe just fucking with me now?

I dialed my agent.

"Hello?"

"Izzie. You're not gonna believe this." Too agitated to sit still, I popped out of my chair and paced back and forth while I told her about the message. "Do you think it was really her?"

"I know it was, because I'm the one who gave Olivia your number yesterday," she said excitedly. "I was dying to tell you, but she asked me not to say anything because she wasn't entirely sure what Katherine was going to do with it, but Dash! This is amazing!"

"I don't even know what to do with myself." I put a hand on my head. "I'm about to get on a plane to go back to Michigan and tell this girl I love her. I was ready to give up on Hollywood."

Izzie squealed. "Get on that plane, Dashiel Buckley! Hollywood will be here when you get back, and we'll figure it out."

I heard my zone being called. "I gotta go change my life, Izzie. I'll call you later."

• • •

After I picked up my rental car at the airport, I drove straight to Xander's house. It took every ounce of willpower I had not to go directly to Ari's, but I stuck to the plan. We hit the road in his SUV before eight, both of us chugging coffee in groggy morning silence.

When we turned into the drive at Abelard, I texted Gianni.

Hey, just pulling in.

Great! I pulled the truck into the
Etoile lot, so just head there.

See you in a few.

I directed Xander where to go, and then I saw Gianni standing next to the truck, talking to Ellie as two kids jumped in and out of the driver's seat. They looked a little younger than Owen and Adelaide, maybe not quite school-age yet.

We parked a safe distance away and approached the truck. "Morning," I said, shaking Gianni's hand. "Thanks for doing this so early on a Sunday."

"Are you kidding? We've got two kids under six. We're up early every day." He turned to Xander and offered a hand. "Xander, right? We met at the wedding."

They exchanged a handshake while Ellie corralled the kids and brought them over. "Morning, guys. This is Claudia and Benny."

I smiled at the carbon copies of their parents. Benny especially looked just like I imagined Gianni did at that age—floppy dark hair, dimpled smile, and a look of complete recklessness in his eyes, like there was no dare he wouldn't take. The girl was pretty like her mom, with big blue eyes and long brown hair. "Nice to meet you."

They mumbled hello, and Gianni put an arm around his wife. As I looked at their family, I felt something that might have been envy tug at my insides. They made it look so easy. So nice.

"This is so exciting," said Ellie. "I cannot tell you how horrible I felt when Ari called yesterday."

"Sorry about that," I said. "I had no idea that would happen."

"I was so flustered! Thank God Gianni had told me the entire thing was a surprise."

"See? I do listen sometimes." Gianni looked smug.

We chatted for a few minutes before Xander took off and Ellie shepherded the kids into the inn, where they were going to see their grandparents. Gianni handed me a file folder containing service records for the truck as well as manuals for the kitchen equipment. There would still be paperwork to complete and insurance issues to deal with, but Ari would have the keys in her hands in just a couple of hours.

"Thanks for everything, man." I shook Gianni's hand once more and opened the driver's side door. "Fuck, I hope I can drive this thing."

Gianni laughed. "You'll be fine. Take it slow."

"I will. Hey, can I ask you something?"

"Sure." He stood with his feet spread, arms folded across

his chest.

"How did you know it would be like this—what you have?" I gestured in the direction his wife and kids had gone.

"I didn't. I had no fucking clue."

"Really?"

"Yeah. Ellie got pregnant after we were stranded in a snowstorm at a motel for a couple days."

"Shut the fuck up," I said. "Really?"

"She couldn't stand me," he said, laughing. "I was the last guy on earth she thought she'd end up with. And I had no interest in being a husband or a father at the time. But the universe is funny like that. Sometimes it just hands you a plate. And you can be like, 'Excuse me, I didn't order this,' and the universe is like, 'Just eat. You're gonna love it.'"

I laughed. "And you did?"

"And I did." He paused. "Are you thinking that way about Ari? I know you said you weren't dating, but then I saw you at the wedding."

"Yeah. We were trying to keep things quiet, but it didn't really work." I readjusted the cap on my head. "I'm not really thinking that far ahead with Ari—I've got things I want to do and so does she—but for the first time in my life, the idea of having a family doesn't seem so out there."

He shrugged. "You don't have to rush it. Although a ring might have been less expensive than a food truck."

Laughing again, I climbed in. "Ari is that girl who'd rather have a food truck than a diamond. Although maybe someday, she'll have both from me."

"I have a feeling," Gianni said.

I pulled the door shut and rolled down the window. "Thanks for everything."

"My pleasure. Let me know how it goes."

I turned the key and headed back to Cherry Tree Harbor, my excitement growing with every mile that brought me closer to home.

Closer to her.

Chapter 27

Ari

"More coffee, Gus?"

"Sure, Ari." The old-timer pushed his half-empty cup toward me, and I refilled it. "Thanks."

"You're welcome. Larry?"

He nodded, and I poured more for him too, giving both of them a smile I didn't feel. I could do it—the muscles in my face worked, my mouth would stretch, my lips would curve up—but it might as well have been a mask. I hadn't smiled for real in days.

After my conversation with Ellie, I had idly hunted around on the internet for another truck, but my heart wasn't in it. Veronica, who'd come up to Buckley's Pub with Austin last night, had given me a hug and told me not to worry. "Food trucks aren't one-of-a-kind," she pointed out. "Another one will come along."

"I know," I said. But it wasn't the one-of-a-kind truck I was mourning the loss of, and Veronica knew it.

She was sitting at a table now with Owen and Adelaide, since Austin had left early this morning on a business trip. In fact, the twins were approaching the counter now with mischievous grins on their faces.

"Hey, guys." I tried my best for a real smile. "What's up?"

"We have something for you," said Owen.

"It's a note."

As if they'd argued over who'd actually get to hand me the note and decided they'd do it together, each of them held a corner of a folded piece of paper as they laid it on the counter.

"What's this?" I glanced at it as I set my coffee pot down.

"Read it," Adelaide urged.

"It's from—" Owen's sentence was cut off by his sister's hand over his mouth.

"Owen. It's a sur*prise*."

I picked up the note and unfolded it, my breath catching as my eyes skimmed the words scribbled in cursive.

Make it count. Meet me in the kitchen.

Immediately I looked over at where Veronica was sitting. She smiled.

"What does it say?" Adelaide asked eagerly.

"It says I'm supposed to go into the kitchen." My heart had taken off running like a racehorse out of the stall. What was going on?

"Do it." Owen clapped his hands.

Gerilyn appeared at my side, her expression sly. "Go on, honey. I'll cover you."

Tucking the note in my apron pocket, I wandered to the kitchen door and swung through it.

Then I gasped, my hand flying to my mouth.

Standing not six feet away from me was Dash, wearing a grin so joyful and familiar I could have wept. "Oh my God!" Forgetting that I'd said I didn't want any visits, I went running into his arms and felt myself swept right off my feet. "What are you doing here?"

"I came to surprise you."

"It worked." I inhaled his scent, burying my face in his neck—God, I'd missed him. What did it mean that he was here?

"I brought you a present."

"You did?"

"Yes." He set me on my feet. "Close your eyes."

I closed them and he took my hands.

"Walk forward, okay? I've got you." He led me out the back door, which someone must have opened for him. "Keep them closed."

"They're closed." I heard the door shut behind me, felt the breeze on my skin. "Can I open yet?"

"No." He let go of my hands, took me by the shoulders, and gently spun me around so I faced the back of the diner. "I want to say something first."

"Okay." Barely able to breathe, I felt him press up close behind me. His hands covered my eyes.

"I was worried you wouldn't trust me," he said.

"I've always trusted you."

"That's good. Because trust is going to be important."

"For what?"

"For the future. For what I hope we can have."

Hope was shooting through my veins like dynamite. "You hope we can have a future?"

"Yes. I know it will take work, but I'm willing if you are."

"I'm willing," I said breathlessly.

"Good. Because I'm definitely going to need your help with something." He took his hands from my eyes, grabbed my shoulders, and turned me around. "Open your eyes."

I opened them, and my jaw dropped. The Abelard Vineyards food truck was parked right in front of me, except that someone had written Moe's on the Go in a fat black marker on the side. "Dashiel Buckley! What have you done?"

"I bought a food truck. That's what I need help with."

"*You* bought this truck?"

"I did." He wrapped his arms around me. "I had this idea, see, about elevated comfort food, and I was wondering if anyone at Moe's Diner would like to partner with me."

I started to laugh. "Just anyone?"

"Well, I did have a particular someone in mind." He slipped out from behind me and took my hands so that we stood face to face. The sun lit him from behind, making him look otherworldly handsome, as if he needed the assistance. "It's yours, Ari. I got it for you. And I didn't even break any promises because you said you wouldn't borrow money from me, but you never said you wouldn't accept a gift."

"Oh my God." I shook my head. "You are impossible to argue with. You twist everything around. I don't even know what to say!"

"Say you'll accept this. Say you want to be with me, even though it will be hard. Say you feel what I feel, and you want to be in this with me."

I cradled his face in my palms. "I want to be in this with you. I feel what you feel."

His arms slid around my back, and he rested his forehead on mine. "Then say you love me."

I smiled, and I felt it with my whole heart. "I love you."

He kissed me, and my entire body radiated with happiness. "I noticed you didn't say anything about accepting the food truck."

Laughing, I let my head fall back. "I accept. And I will work my tail off for you, partner."

"God, I missed the sound of your laugh."

"I missed everything about you. And we were only apart for six days."

"I know. The separations won't be easy. But when I'm not on set, I'll be here with you. And even though we'll be apart sometimes, we'll know what we have. Say we can do this."

"We can do this, Dash. I've waited so long for you. We can make this work."

"I think so too." He kissed me again, then wrapped me in his arms, speaking low in my ear. "I know not every love story can have a happy ending. But this one does."

I had to choke back a happy sob to reply. "This one does."

• • •

After I finished my shift, Dash accompanied me to the hospital, where we visited with my parents and told them about the truck. My father offered to pay Dash back right away, but he wouldn't hear of it.

"I want to be business partners," he insisted. "It's an investment."

"Moe's Diner doesn't have partners," my father said. "We're family." He opened his arms, and Dash gave him a hug.

My mother leaned over to me and whispered in my ear. "He's very handsome, isn't he?"

"Yes," I said, laughing. "But he's a lot more than that."

Chapter 28

Dash

f inally, we were alone.

As if we'd been apart for six years and not just six days, we lost control the moment Ari's front door was shut behind us. Our mouths sealed together, we tore at each other's clothing, bumping into walls as we made our way to her bedroom. In mere minutes, I was moving inside her, my hips driving hard, her hands pulling me deeper.

"Sorry," I said after the shared climax had shuddered through us both, "that was way too fast."

"It was perfect." She was still panting. "I didn't want to go slow. I missed you too much."

I rolled to the side, taking her with me, our bodies still joined. Pushing her hair off her face, I rubbed her lower lip with my thumb. "I feel like I have so many things to tell you. Like I've been gone for months, not days."

She smiled. "Tell me everything."

I filled her in on all that had happened, starting with the birthday party mix-up. She listened with wide eyes—until I got to the part about sitting around with the girls wearing the shark onesie, which made her laugh so hard she cried.

"You should have heard them giving me advice on my love life," I said. "They were so sure they had it all figured out."

"Just like me and Mabel at that age."

"You guys were never that bossy. They were like, 'Just call her, just tell her you love her, just turn your life upside down in an instant. Don't be a jerk.'"

"You weren't a jerk," she assured me, stroking my hair. "I never thought that. It would have been easier if you were."

"I was so fucking miserable the next few days."

"Me too," she said. "I went to work, I visited my dad, I even saw Veronica, but I just felt hollowed out."

"I'm sorry." I kissed her lips. "I was being stubborn. I was hanging on to something that wouldn't let me see the mistake I was making."

"What was the something?"

"Just, like...an old fear that anything can be taken away from you at any time. So it's better not to care about anything or anyone too deeply."

"What made you realize it?"

I smiled. "You're gonna laugh."

"Is it funnier than the shark onesie?"

"It's close. I went back to Delphine."

Her eyes went wide. "Did you really?"

"Yes. I started to get pissed that I'd done all the things she said, and not only was there no big movie role, but now I had all these *feelings*. I wanted my walls back."

Ari laughed. "What did she say?"

"She told me the universe isn't a vending machine. You don't put the money in, punch the number, and get the prize. But she could sense that I'd done the work. She said my heart energy was flowing freely, but I was still closing myself off out of fear."

"So how did she get you to conquer it?"

"Somehow she opened my mind to the possibility of us. She made me picture it. She made me feel it—I'm telling you, it was some voodoo shit. But it just felt so fucking right. So *good*. I knew right then I'd do anything to have it, even risk the hurt."

She laid her hand on my cheek. "If it were up to me, you'd never hurt again."

"I think it's probably unrealistic to imagine life without any pain, and there will be bad days, but knowing you're there at the end of them will make all the difference."

"I'll be there," she whispered.

"So will I." I circled her wrist and lifted her hand from my face, kissing her palm. "I want to be in this with you, just like you said. I want to take care of you. Lift you up. Give you everything."

"I want to work for it." She smiled seductively. "But I will let you spoil me. You're very good at it."

"It will be my pleasure." I kissed the inside of her wrist. "There's something else."

"What else could there be?"

I rubbed my lips back and forth against the soft skin of her inner arm. "I have an audition for *All We've Lost*. A real one this time."

"What?" She placed her hand on my chest. "Tell me!"

I told her about the message I'd gotten from Katherine Carroll and how Izzie had confirmed it was real.

"I can't believe you've known this the whole time, and you're just getting around to telling me about it."

"Well, I had other things to focus on. More important things. Like getting you back."

She kissed me. "You never lost me, Dash. You've always had my heart."

"You had mine too. I just didn't know it."

Her lips curved into a smile. "Can I keep it?"

"For as long as you want."

The look in her eyes told me how long she'd been waiting to hear that. "How about forever?"

"You know I love a happy ending."

She laughed. "The diner waitress gets the movie star. I love this story."

"I love you."

Her laughter faded and she kissed me again. "I love you too."

Epilogue

ARI

TWO YEARS LATER

"*A*nd the Oscar goes to…" The beautiful actress in the long sequined gown opened the envelope. I held my breath. "Dashiel Buckley for *All We've Lost*."

The music swelled along with my heart and my tears and my pride in Dash, who squeezed my hand and drew me to my feet. After placing a hard kiss on my lips, he turned to the row behind us and hugged his two co-stars and finally, Katherine Carroll, whose eyes were glossy.

With one last look at me, he made his way to the stage, shaking a couple hands on the way, and accepted the statue from the actress. After kissing her cheek, he looked in disbelief at the award and took his place at the podium.

"Oh my God," he said. "I hardly know where to start."

My eyes were so blurry. I had to fan my face to get them to clear up a little. I had so much makeup on—applied by a glam squad in my hotel suite earlier this afternoon—and I didn't want to ruin it. I knew the cameras were on me. Cameras were often aimed at me these days. I'd gotten used to seeing myself on the internet or in magazines, and I'd given up trying to always look perfect. Dash had made it clear he loved me for me and didn't want me to look like a Hollywood starlet.

But tonight was different. Tonight, I wore the red satin gown, the Cartier jewels, the updo, the lashes, the siren lip. When Dash saw me, he kissed the back of my hand and told me I took his breath away.

"My dad, my siblings, my entire family—I love you so much. Thank you for always believing in me. And being in my corner. My mom hasn't been with us for a long time, and yet she's with me every day, and I know none of this would be possible without her love shining down on me." He glanced up. "Thank you, Mom."

I dabbed at the corners of my eyes and felt Katherine pat my shoulder.

"So many people had a hand in getting me to this incredible moment. Ms. Walsh, my first-grade teacher, who made me love acting. All the directors and producers and fellow actors I've worked with over the years—I've learned from every single one of you. To the Academy, for this unbelievable recognition. I don't feel worthy of it, but I will do my best to live up to the honor you're giving me tonight. To Katherine Carroll." He smiled, maybe remembering the shark onesie. "Thank you so much for seeing something in me. For taking a chance on an unknown, whose box office draw was unproven and whose talent was raw at best. You set this in motion with your intuition and generosity, and you put me up here with your vision and artistry and skill. I am forever in your debt."

I glanced at Katherine over my shoulder, unsurprised to see her dabbing at her eyes as well. Earlier, she'd told us her niece and all the birthday party attendees were watching, eager to see their favorite actor win the big award. Dash went on to thank a few more people involved with the production, and the entire cast and crew for making him better. Finally, he looked at me.

"And to Ari, who owns my heart." He placed a hand on his chest. "Thank you for encouraging me to open it up to the world. It's because of you that I understood what a man is willing to do for someone he loves. Our story is still being written." The music began to play, indicating it was time for him to wrap up, and he nodded. "Thank you all, and have a great night."

Everyone applauded as he walked off, and I gave up trying to hold it together, bawling my eyes out into a tissue. If the world saw me cry, so be it. My heart was full.

. . .

Dash and I celebrated all night, hitting all the big parties, fielding all the usual questions from reporters, and posing for a thousand photos. We didn't make it back to our hotel suite until four in the morning, our cheeks numb from smiling, our feet sore from standing, our stomachs growling with hunger. We ordered room service and went out on the balcony, where I sat on his lap under the stars.

I looked up and saw one go shooting across the sky. It didn't surprise me at all—this entire night was full of magic. I made a wish, the same one I'd been making nearly all my life.

"Tired?" Dash asked, tightening his arms around me.

"I will be tomorrow."

"It is tomorrow."

"Hush. I'm still enjoying this night."

"It has been pretty unforgettable."

Sighing, I kicked off my heels and held his head close to my chest. "It feels like a dream. Is this a dream?"

"Maybe."

I closed my eyes. The last two years had been surreal. After getting the role of Johnny, Dash had given his all to the production, which involved grueling shoots in mud and rain and freezing temperatures halfway across the world. There had been delays and rewrites and reshoots. I learned more about the movie business than I'd ever wanted to. But Dash had remained grateful and dedicated, and his hard work had paid off. Critics had praised his sensitive, nuanced portrayal of a man torn between love and survival—many mentioned his emotional depth. Audiences had swooned at his romantic charisma. And the box office returns had been fantastic. The studio was thrilled.

And casting directors had taken notice—Dash had plenty of offers to choose from now, and we often looked at scripts together and talked about what kind of project he should do next to stretch his creative muscles. I wanted him to do a rom-com, of course. Dash wanted to play a villain. "They have all the fun lines," he insisted.

When he wasn't on set, Dash was in Cherry Tree Harbor with me. He hadn't sold his house in Los Feliz, since he sometimes needed to be in L.A. for work, but other than when he was shooting, we were together. The separations weren't easy, but so far, we hadn't gone more than three weeks without seeing each other, and the time apart made our time together that much sweeter.

I was busier than ever at the diner. Thanks to Hugo Martin's post and the local news stories about our anniversary, Moe's was thriving. Our last two summers had been our best ever. Moe's on the Go was a huge hit, and the extra income was helping to pay down the loan my parents had taken out for new kitchen equipment. I was enjoying more creative freedom with the menu, and best of all, my dad's health was much better. He still hadn't retired completely, but he exercised more, ate better, and took more time off. We hired another manager to give my mom some relief and gave longtime employees a nice raise. In the back of my mind, I had an idea for a cookbook, and Dash had encouraged me to see it through.

Our lives and schedules and jobs and family obligations had been so hectic, in fact—Austin and Veronica had gotten married, Xander and Kelly were engaged, Julia had moved into George's house in Cherry Tree Harbor, and Mabel had earned her master's degree and been accepted to a PhD program—we never really discussed our own future.

"My dad called," Dash said. "He and Julia watched the show together."

I smiled. "Mabel, Kelly, and Veronica have been texting me all night wanting to know about the parties and who was there."

"My brothers reached out too. And your parents."

"Everyone is proud of you." I kissed his head.

He took my left hand in his right, palm to palm, interlocking our fingers. "It means everything that you were with me tonight."

"Where else would I have been, silly?"

"Nowhere. You're always there for me. I want you to know I don't take it for granted."

"I know you don't," I said softly. "And I could not have been more proud to be the one by your side tonight. Thank you for choosing me."

"I want you by my side for more than tonight, Ari." He reached into his tux's inside pocket and took out a small box. "I want you forever."

I'd gone completely still. "Dash," I whispered. "What is this?"

He opened the box, and a diamond glittered in the dark. "It's something I've been thinking about for a while now."

I was afraid to move. Speak. Or even breathe. What if I broke the spell?

"Before you came along, I never thought about love or marriage or starting a family. It always seemed too monumental, too drastic, too permanent. Something that older people did once they had all their other shit figured out or ran out of fun ideas." He smiled. "And then suddenly there was you, and I realized that love makes you *want* to do drastic, monumental, permanent things. And I can't think of anything more fun than building a life and a family with you." Taking the ring from its black velvet cushion, he slid it onto my finger. "Will you marry me?"

I watched the ring glide past my knuckle and sparkle brilliantly in the starlight. "Dash," I whispered. "You just made all my wishes come true."

"Is that a yes? You'll be my wife?"

"Yes." I laughed, taking his head in my hands once more, kissing his lips. "Yes!"

He kissed me back, wrapping me in his arms. "All I want is to make you happy, Sugar."

"Will you stop calling me Sugar?"

"Never."

I laughed as my small-town heart rocketed up among the stars. "Good."

BONUS

CONTENT

ARI

"Dashiel Buckley, for heaven's sake!" I shook my head in disbelief as he sauntered into the kitchen stark naked.

"What?" He pulled open a cupboard door and took down a mug. "It's not like anyone is here. And we never have the house to ourselves, Sugar. We should take advantage of it."

Our kids had slept over at Xander and Kelly's house the night before. Their daughter Serena was ten—the same age as our daughter, Wren—and their daughter Dakota was seven, just like our son, Truman.

"We did take advantage of it," I reminded him, stirring a little cream into my coffee. "Twice already."

"A man should feel free to walk around his private home unencumbered by the starched vestments of his public life," Dash pronounced grandly as he poured himself a cup of coffee. Then he glanced at his ass. "Besides, don't you still like the view?"

Leaning back against the counter, I laughed as my gaze traveled over his body, still incredibly toned at age forty-one. "I still like the view."

"Good." He gave me a kiss before lifting his mug to his lips. "I still like my view, too."

"Thank you."

"I'd like it even better if you were naked."

I rolled my eyes. "You just saw me naked in the shower."

"Did I? I can't recall." He tugged the belt on my robe, and it fell open. "Oh yes, this does seem familiar."

I laughed again as he set his coffee on the counter behind me, slipped his hands inside my robe, and buried his face in my neck. "Dash. We don't have time."

"I'm fast. I have experience."

"We have to be at Xander and Kelly's in an hour, and my hair is still wet."

"I like all of you wet." He moved his lips to my ear. "But only for me."

"You're impossible. And you're going to make us late." But he knew exactly how to touch me, how to make my skin tingle and my insides tighten and my body come alive with desire for him.

"Please, Sugar," he whispered, one hand stealing between my thighs, one finger stroking me softly. "I missed you so much while I was gone. You can't blame me for wanting you all to myself for a little while longer."

I moaned as his mouth moved down my throat, blindly setting my coffee mug on the counter behind me. Resisting Dash hadn't gotten any easier in the nearly twelve years we'd been married, especially since he was often gone for weeks at a time on a film shoot. When the kids were tiny, we'd often accompany him on location, but once they started elementary school—the same one we'd both attended, the same one we'd once visited for Show and Tell—we'd agreed that stability was best. The absences were hard, but our devotion to each other never wavered. Family meant everything to us. Not just the four of us, but our extended family, too.

And boy, had it extended.

Austin and Veronica had gotten married at Christmastime the year Dashiel and I had first gotten together. Veronica had been eight months pregnant with a son by the following summer, when Xander and Kelly tied the knot. Luke was now thirteen, and his sister Vivian was eleven. The twins had been thrilled to become a big sister and brother. They were twenty-two now—Owen was studying marine biology at U.C. San Diego, and Adelaide was majoring in musical theater at the University of Michigan.

Xander and Kelly had built a huge home in the woods about half an hour outside of Cherry Tree Harbor and proceeded to fill it with five children: four girls ranging in age from twelve to five, and then a boy named George, after his grandpa, who was now three.

Speaking of grandpa, George was turning eighty this summer, and we were all gathering at Xander and Kelly's for a family photo and celebration today. He'd wed Julia Sullivan in a quiet ceremony at Cherry Tree Harbor's town hall the same year Xander and Kelly got married, but with much less fanfare. We'd all walked the two blocks from the town hall down to the Pier Inn for a wedding dinner, the twins scuffling through the crunchy autumn leaves, Austin pushing newborn Luke in the stroller, the air crisp and cool. As Dash had slipped his hand through mine, I remembered hoping my wedding day would be filled with just as much laughter and love and light.

And it had been. My father had walked me down the aisle in Cherry Tree Harbor's Chapel by the Sea on a late summer afternoon. Everyone who mattered to us was there, and the whole place had erupted in cheers when the officiant pronounced us Mr. and Mrs. Dashiel Buckley. We kissed, danced back down the aisle to "I've Had the Time of My Life," burst out into the sunshine, and kissed again. The best part was, we were still just as much in love now as we had been on that day.

Sometimes I still couldn't believe I married my best friend's older brother. That I was Ariana Buckley now. Mabel and I sometimes joked that we'd shared everything two best friends could share—even a last name. Of course, hers had changed since she'd gotten married, but she and her husband didn't live too far from Cherry Tree Harbor. Funny thing, she married a guy named Joe Lupo, who was the younger brother of Gianni Lupo, whose father-in-law sold us the original Moe's food truck years ago.

But that's a story for another time.

Although Dash and I hadn't been in a rush to start a family, Wren had come along by surprise—which we were delighted about. Truman arrived and completed our family three years later.

Devlin and Lexi had sworn up and down they weren't in a hurry to start a family, either, but they'd barely been married for a year when Lexi announced her pregnancy. Then she promptly jumped up from the Thanksgiving table and ran to the bathroom because the smell of turkey made her sick. We'd teased her about it every holiday since. Their kids—also a boy and a girl—were roughly the same age as Austin and Veronica's. The entire Buckley clan always spent the days between Christmas and New Year's at Snowberry Lodge, and rang in the new year at the resort together.

Dashiel and I had sold my little house and purchased a larger one with a little more privacy on the edge of town. While the kids were young, I hadn't worked at the diner too often, and my cousin ran Moe's on the Go. We had two trucks now, and business was great. Now that Wren and Tru were a little older, I could often be found behind the counter at Moe's, and sometimes behind the wheel of the food truck. My parents had retired and spent the cold months in Florida, but they still returned to Michigan during the summers. They told me often how proud they were to see both of their beloved children—me and Moe's diner—thriving.

I was happier than I ever thought possible. I missed Dash when he was gone, but I knew what made our dreams work so well together was that we understood they took sacrifice. Was life perfect? Of course not.

But it was close, I thought as my husband swept me up in his arms and carried me back to our bed.

It was pretty damn close.

He tossed me onto the mattress, and I landed on top of the covers that were still twisted and wrinkled from this morning's romp. Sprawling above me, he settled between my thighs, my knees bracketing his hips. "You know," he said, brushing a damp lock of curly hair from my face, "sometimes I still can't believe you're mine."

"Seriously?" I laughed. "Even after all this time?"

"Especially after all this time." He lowered his lips to mine, kissing me softly, sweetly. "I want you to know I don't take you or this family or anything about what we've built for granted. I feel lucky every single day."

My heart tried to break its way out of my chest, like it might jump into his. "I do, too. Sometimes I think about the nights I used to spend dreaming about holding your hand in the hallway at school, or imagine what it would be like to go on a date with you. I'd kiss my pillow and pretend it was you on my front porch."

He smiled, making my belly flutter, just like he'd done back then if he so much as looked my way. "That's cute."

"I was waiting for you to look my way and realize I was meant for you," I said dramatically, cradling his face in my hands.

"Sorry I made you wait so long."

"Don't be." I lifted my head off the pillow and kissed his lips. "Your timing was perfect."

He started to laugh. "I will never forget that day when I walked into the kitchen naked at my dad's house and saw you standing by the door. The look on your face."

"My eyes went straight for your crotch." Squeezing my eyes shut, I groaned. "I was so embarrassed."

"But did you like what you saw?" He nipped at my chin.

"Too much. That's how I cut my finger that night—I was distracted by the memory of your naked body."

"That's right! I forgot about that—I had to take you to the emergency room." He turned his face into my palm and kissed my fingers. "You were nervous because you hated needles."

"You stayed with me the whole time."

"Of course I did. You were stuck with me by then. You just didn't know it yet."

I grinned. "You took very good care of me. You still do."

"Well, you're my favorite person. It only makes sense." Reaching down between us, he stroked me gently with his fingers. "And I love taking care of you."

My eyes drifted closed as he eased inside me, burying himself deep within, filling me completely. It felt so good, for a moment I was scared to open my eyes again. "Dash," I whispered. "If I dreamed this life, don't wake me."

"Don't worry, Sugar," he said as he began to move. "This dream is ours forever."

Acknowledgments

As always, my appreciation and gratitude go to the following people for their talent, support, wisdom, friendship, and encouragement...

Melissa Gaston, Kristie Carnevale, Brandi Zelenka, Jenn Watson, Hang Le, Corinne Michaels, Anthony Colletti, Rebecca Friedman, Flavia Viotti & Meire Dias at Bookcase Literary, Nancy Smay at Evident Ink, Julia Griffis at The Romance Bibliophile, Katy Cuthbertson, One Night Stand Studios, the Shop Talkers, the Sisterhood, the Harlots and the Harlot ARC Team, Club Harlow, and my amazing readers!

And once again, to my family, for putting up with me while I disappeared every day into a fictional small town...I love you.

*Don't miss the exciting new books
Entangled has to offer.*

Follow us!

 @EntangledPublishing

 @Entangled_Publishing

 @EntangledPub

AMARA
an imprint of Entangled Publishing LLC